William G. R. Hamilton was born in Glasgow in February 1960. After leaving his homeland when his father passed away in January 1980 he has covered the length and breadth of England looking to find his fortune. William has been married to his wife Lisa for the past 23 years and has two children, Graeme and Eva. He has worked in various roles from a barman to a General Manager in his career and has enjoyed every minute of it.

The idea to write a novel came totally out of the blue and has sparked his imagination into overdrive. This is where he hopes that his readers are impressed and share the same enthusiasm and adventurous concepts as himself.

He really enjoys writing after starting less than 12 months ago. Since completing this thriller, Hamilton has almost completed the sequel to *What a Wicked Web We Weave*, as well as finishing two children's books under the pen name George Rosling.

He hopes to keep the readers on the edge of their seats with Tony Lodge and company for at least five novels and who knows, maybe many more.

William hopes you enjoy reading *What a Wicked Web We Weave* as much as he enjoyed writing it…

William G. R. Hamilton

WHAT A WICKED
WEB WE WEAVE

AUSTIN MACAULEY PUBLISHERS™

LONDON • CAMBRIDGE • NEW YORK • SHARJAH

A CIP catalogue record for this title is available from the British Library.

ISBN 9781528900621 (Paperback)
ISBN 9781528900638 (Hardback)
ISBN 9781528900645 (E-Book)

www.austinmacauley.com

First Published (2018)
Austin Macauley Publishers Ltd™
25 Canada Square
Canary Wharf
London
E14 5LQ

My Favourite Mother-in-Law...

This book is dedicated to someone that I loved, admired and respected for over 25 years. She unfortunately lost her battle against cancer just before Christmas 2017 after fighting the disease for almost 18 months. She was one of the most loving, thoughtful and family-oriented people that I have had the pleasure to meet and will be sadly missed. She would always ask how my book was going every time I saw her, she was the inspiration for me to keep going.

So Christina Margaret Chatfield (nee Gregory) this is for you and your loving family, we all miss you so very much.

Chapter One

"Wakey, wakey, rise and shine Mr Lodge," Becky said, prodding Tony in the side, "it's your big day so get ready to surprise the world," she told him with a smile.

Tony couldn't believe it had been almost 12 months since she moved in with him. They met at a mutual friend's birthday party two years before and hit it off instantly. They started as friends, and then dated for 12 months before making the commitment to move in together. Becky was reluctant at first when she found out Tony had not long split up from his partner of 10 years, Lucy Palmer, and had a two-and-a-half year-old daughter.

Rebecca Doyle – his friends told him was single, but a hard nut to crack. Many had tried, but she was having none of it. An Irish girl originally from County Antrim, and as stubborn as a mule.

Tony put his arms around her and pulled Becky towards him. His lips were puckered ready for a nice soft kiss. "SHOWER….NOW!" she said in a raised voice pushing him away. "There will be none of that this morning Tony Lodge."

She was making a special breakfast to prepare him for the first day in his new job.

"Quick shower then we eat," Becky said pointing towards the bathroom.

Becky was so different from his ex-girlfriend. Becky had long straight dark hair, Lucy had short blonde. Becky was tall with nice long legs; Lucy was short with chunky legs. Becky always looked and dressed sexy; Lucy looked frumpy and dressed like a woman older than her age. Becky was 25 and Lucy

28. Becky took pride in her appearance; Lucy took pride in bringing up her daughter Mellissa.

Tony always thought that maybe he saw one as being the "love" and one as being the "lust" but he hadn't decided which was which, being a 34 year old man with high testosterone.

When he arrived downstairs there was a fantastic breakfast on the dining room table, bacon, sausages, eggs, hash browns, mushrooms, beans, tomatoes and toast. There was a pot of tea waiting to wash this feast down if or when he managed to eat it.

"Wow," he gasped, "how do you expect me to concentrate on my work after eating all this, it will take me all day to digest it!" but still managed to eat the lot apart from a hash brown and a few beans.

It had arrived, Tony's first day on the "fraud squad" as it was known. After two really difficult interviews where he was put through the mill, he was offered the job. He had worked for the department of work and pensions for 10 years in different roles in different offices, working his way from admin clerk into a supervisory role. This was the one he had been waiting for, the elite part of the department that always worked behind closed doors, now he was in. He would be working out of the main office based in Edinburgh and couldn't wait.

He had attended an induction course three days earlier on the Friday and was given a folder containing three live cases to look at over the weekend. They consisted of the following:

Case One

A single parent claiming benefits is reported to having a long-term partner living with them. The partner is allegedly in full-time employment and they have two children together. The partner has been living at the address for over five years and the claimant started on benefits over 12 months previous.

Case Two

A male claimant receiving incapacity benefit has been reported to be working on a local building site climbing ladders and carrying materials around the site. The informant suggests that they are also being paid cash in hand by the contractor.

Case Three

A claimant receiving housing benefit is allegedly sub-letting the property on a contractual basis to a tenant whilst working in a hotel as a live-in kitchen assistant.

"If you had the choice, which one of the three would you opt for?" Becky asked.

"If it was up to me I would choose case number three," he replied. "I think there could be more to investigate in that one."

"Me too," she said with a smile.

After 10 years working for the department he hadn't been as excited as he was today. Tony was told to be at the Edinburgh office no later than 8:30 on Monday morning, but he arrived before 8 o'clock to settle himself in and miss the traffic.

The three other members of the fraud team, who he had met briefly on Friday, were already there. Iain Logan, Julie Moore and his ex-girlfriend's brother Lance Palmer. Lance was two years older than his sister, which made him 30, and the other two looked to be in their early thirties according to Tony. Lance was always pleasant and friendly when they met but Tony put that down to Lance being his daughter Mellissa's uncle and godfather.

They were all led into a room at the end of a long corridor by site security. It reminded him of an old classroom at school. It had rows of tables and chairs in fours and a blackboard at the back of the room with chalk and a duster. The walls were littered with posters with statistics all related to fraud over the past 5 years, he was very impressed.

The fraud department manager Heather Mooney walked into the room. She was closely followed by two men dressed like they had just walked out of The X Files. They wore black suits, bright white shirts, black ties and black shoes and socks. All that was missing was the sun glasses, but they were indoors so it would have looked out of place, not that they didn't already. One of them was carrying a briefcase, black of course.

Heather had been with the DWP since leaving school, if you wanted to know anything about anything she was your girl. Strict but fair was the rumour in camp, but don't get on the wrong side of her they said.

"Okay let's get started," she said, tapping the desk with her keys, "I would like to welcome Tony Lodge; he's been working in the department in a number of various roles for the last 10 years. I'm sure his experience and expertise in certain areas will bring added benefit to the fraud team."

"Thank you Heather," Tony acknowledged nodding his head.

"I hope you studied the cases over the weekend," she said looking around the room, "it's important to be prepared."

They all mumbled and raised their eyes, which Heather took to be a yes.

"Iain you're on case one, Julie case two and Lance you're on case number three. Collect your things guys and let's get this show on the road," Heather said escorting them to the door. "Let's go."

When the last one left Heather closed the door and turned the key in the lock.

"Tony, meet Chris Higgins and Samuel Wong from the Special Investigations Department, SID for short," Heather said sitting down at the desk. "I bet you're wondering why you're still here and not on one of those cases."

"Slightly yes, but I'm sure you will enlighten me," Tony smiled.

"We received a phone call on the fraud office answering machine early on Friday evening," Chris told him, "a message was left by an anonymous caller asking the fraud department to investigate one of our top senior managers."

"Luckily someone was still in the office when the caller left the message and they contacted me straight away," Heather confirmed. "I contacted SID and asked for their advice. Chris and Sam were sent to meet me at the office on Saturday morning. After listening to the message several times we had to decide if we needed to take further action."

"I presume that's the reason we're here?" Tony asked.

"Yes Tony," Sam replied, "as Heather said we had to make a decision on our next step."

"And?" Tony asked curiously.

"Instead of going in with all guns blazing and putting our top officers on the case," Heather explained, "we decided to go with caution and take it slowly to start with."

"That's where you come in Tony," Chris told him, "you're the new kid on the block so it won't arouse suspicion if you're floating around asking questions."

"Under what proviso?" Tony asked.

"We've extracted a copy of the conversation," Heather told him, "let's listen to the tape and see what you think first."

Sam clicked open the briefcase and took out a CD player and CD. He plugged it into the wall and Heather leant over and switched it on.

"This is a message for your National Fraud Manager. Investigate Raymond Hessler, especially his past and family members. It's too risky for me to identify myself at the moment, it's important that this is resolved as soon as possible. Don't ignore this call it's NOT a hoax."

The caller then hung up.

"What do you think?" Heather asked.

"First impressions I would say the caller was serious, but I would have to listen to it a few more times," Tony said.

"Have you heard of Raymond Hessler?" Chris asked.

"Of course, he's one of our chiefs in the Carlisle branch. Been with the department for 20 years or so."

"24 to be exact," Sam told them, "it will be 25 years in January 2018."

"Even I didn't know that," Heather chuckled. "I thought I was the only one that spent her life at DWP."

"What do you think then Mr Lodge?" Chris asked him.

"I'm game," he replied, "not bad for my first assignment in the fraud department," he smiled.

"What do you need to get started?" Heather asked him.

"I've got transport so maybe a quiet office somewhere that has a link with all the DWP databases?" Tony asked. "As well as a printer, telephone, administration tools and hopefully a coffee machine to keep me awake."

"Okay, I will see what I can organise," Heather said.

"Just to let you know," Sam added, "the hierarchy think this is a hoax and would prefer it to be dealt with as a matter of urgency."

"No pressure then," Tony joked.

"Take the CD with you and spend the rest of the day at home formulating a plan," Heather told him, "it's easier to concentrate somewhere comfortable and quiet, so I'm sure you would be more comfortable working from home."

"Just one more thing," Sam told him, "this is classified as top secret so you're not allowed to discuss it with anyone apart from the four of us in this office."

Heather passed him a folder.

"You will find a copy of the CD, a bogus case to study in case anyone asks what you are doing and my direct office and home number in case you need to discuss anything."

"Mine and Samuel's numbers are in there as well," Chris said.

"Happy days," Tony replied with a nervous grin.

The journey from the Edinburgh office to his house would normally take him around 25 minutes, but he couldn't remember any of it. The case was going over in his mind the whole time: "senior management fraud", "formalise a plan", "top secret, don't tell anyone, not even Becky".

It was just before 10am when he walked through his front door. Who would have thought he would have been given a case like this as his first assignment and be at home before 10 o'clock in the morning, definitely not him that's for sure.

He placed the CD in the main sound system in his lounge and played it over and over again until he could almost recite it word for word. The caller was a middle-aged woman with what sounded like an exaggerated "scouse" accent. The caller was definitely not from Liverpool Tony thought; you can't mistake one of these girls when they talk to you. "Nice try but you can't fool me," he smirked.

Tony was on his way to the kitchen to make himself a sandwich when his mobile rang, it was Becky.

"Can you talk?"

"Yeah, I'm just on my break," Tony lied, "just about to have a sandwich," he couldn't tell her he was at home, it would raise too many questions.

"Which one of the cases did you get?"

"None of them sweetheart, I'm getting mine this afternoon after lunch."

It had been two years since they got together and during all this time Tony had never lied to her, he didn't feel comfortable. Becky worked as a personal assistant for a well-known solicitors firm; he could trust her with his life. He would have to talk to Heather when the time was right, Becky wouldn't tell a soul.

"See you later Mr Lodge, love you lots," Becky said, blowing him a kiss over the phone.

"Love you too Miss Doyle, you spoil me," he said, blowing her a kiss back.

His phone rang again 10 minutes later; it was his ex-Lucy Palmer.

"Hello handsome," she said.

"Hi Lucy, what's wrong?" Tony asked.

"Nothing, I was just checking it was still okay for you to have Mellissa on Friday as arranged?"

"Of course it is. I wouldn't let my baby down"

"How's the new job going?"

"Crikey, give me a chance," he snapped, "it's only lunchtime on my first day."

"I hear you weren't given a case this morning," she commented, "and you were left in the room with your boss and two bouncer lookalikes."

"Lance doesn't waste much time," Tony said, annoyed.

"I was just checking everything was okay."

"Yes Lucy it's fine," Tony said, "tell your brother the two bouncers as he called them are also new recruits from a different department and Heather has been asked to show them the ropes."

"Oh, okay."

"And also tell him I will have my case this afternoon if he's interested and I will let him know what it is the next time I see him."

I think this must have frightened her off as she said her farewells and told him that she would see him at 6 o'clock on Friday.

Tony enjoyed spending time with his daughter, Mellissa and Becky got on really well too. Becky treats her like her own and she loves it, lots of affection and more presents on special occasions.

Lance shouldn't be discussing his or Tony's work with his sister, even though it was their father that got Tony the job in the first place 10 years ago. Lance followed him into DWP five years later, but he went straight into the fraud department without any previous experience, lucky Lance.

The next call was from Heather, she had found him an office in Gretna Green, approximately 20 miles from Carlisle. It was last used 12 months previously when they were training staff after the benefits were amalgamated into one when Universal Credits were introduced. It was ideal; it was in a quiet area with ample parking for up to 20 vehicles and could accommodate at least 15 staff inside.

Heather told him the key would be sent via courier the following morning arriving no later than 10am. She had also taken the liberty of booking him into a private hotel in Gretna until Friday. It saved him travelling between offices and made more sense on this occasion due to time restraints. The big boys upstairs wanted this episode sorted, and quick.

Tony pressed the play button again this time he was armed with a pen and paper and wrote the conversation down in sections so he could analyse it when he got to his make shift office in Gretna in the morning.

"This is a message for your National Fraud Manager"
"Investigate Raymond Hessler, especially his past and family members"
"It's too risky for me to identify myself at the moment"

14

"It's important that this is resolved as soon as possible"
"Don't ignore this call it's NOT a hoax"

"All ready to rock," Tony thought.

They had lived together now for 12 months and hadn't spent even one night apart, now he had to break the news that he was going away for at least three, he wasn't looking forward to it. Becky had made him a special breakfast, now he had the time on his hands to make her a special dinner – her favourite.

Spaghetti Bolognese with lots of mushrooms and just one garlic clove. Her nan had given her the recipe when she was a teenager and showed her how to cook it from scratch. *Cook the mince* she told her *until all the excess fat was removed etc., etc.* Becky had shown Tony many times over the past 2 years, but more frequently since they moved in together. His spaghetti Bolognese was almost as good as her nan used to make, she told him. Tony never told her but he used to add at least half a glass of Chianti to the sauce when it was cooking; it gave the flavour an extra bite.

He was really out to impress this time, out came the linen table cloth and place mats, table mats, the silver cutlery and condiment set, the expensive wine glasses.

Becky almost had a heart attack when she came home from work, "What the…" she didn't have time to finish her sentence before Tony had removed her coat and shoes and sat her at the table.

"Dinner is served madam," he said with a massive grin on his face.

Dinner was excellent as usual and was complimented with a couple of glasses of red wine. Becky was full to the brim and couldn't eat anymore even though Tony had prepared her favourite pudding, apple strudel with custard. This could be eaten hot or cold on another day they decided as Tony went upstairs and ran her a hot bath. While she soaked, Tony finished off the washing up so she could relax when she came downstairs. He had washed, dried and put everything away in their rightful places by the time Becky walked back into the lounge.

"Okay Mr Lodge what's going on?" she asked.

Tony explained that he had to go away until Friday with his work. He told her that the Carlisle office had the best record of solved fraud cases for the past five years, and new starters were sent there to train with what they deemed to be the best. It all sounded good but as Tony knew it was a load of baloney.

"That's not a problem," Becky told him, "it will give me chance to visit my parents for a few days."

Becky's parents moved over from Northern Ireland when she was a baby because of her dad's work commitments. He was a hydraulic engineer with a company in Dundee and had now worked his way into the managing director's role. They lived in a beautiful cottage in Bridge of Earn that they bought as a retirement home a few years earlier.

"It will give me chance to play catch up with my mum," she said, "I haven't seen her for a couple of months."

"Good, at least I know you won't be on your own," Tony said relieved.

"Is this stopping away lark going to become a habit?"

"I shouldn't think so my dear, it's only a training exercise," Tony said crossing his fingers.

"Let's hope so," she said giving him a stare.

"Feet," Tony gestured, "give them here."

Becky loved to have her feet massaged, it was so relaxing. After 10 minutes she was snoring her head off like a pig. Tony managed to sneak past her as she slept and get a couple of things ready for the morning.

She was still fast asleep when he came back downstairs so he picked her up and carried her upstairs like a baby, she was only petite. Just as he laid her down on the bed she woke up.

"Make love to me Tony Lodge," she said.

So he did, for over an hour, it was just like the time when they first made love almost two years ago.

Tony remembered the first time he made love to Lucy. She was only 17 and a virgin, they learned how to please each other day by day, week by week and month by month. Sex was excellent and frequent he remembered, until Mellissa was born then it all changed.

Now Becky was his lover and she knew what he liked and vice versa, it was wonderful. He rolled off and gave her a hug and a kiss on the top of the head. Becky was no pushover, it took him a couple of months to get her into his bed, she had only had two serious relationships before him. She had to be sure this time, it had to be right.

She had her first boyfriend when she was 18 at senior school.

Most of her friends had been caught and were mothers before their 18th birthday, so she swore she would wait until she was married.

However curiosity got the better of her and she eventually gave in. She split up with him not long after due to him losing interest as he got what he wanted and Becky wondering what all the fuss was about, she wasn't impressed.

Her second relationship was a bad one; she ended up in an abusive relationship when she was 19.

She lived with Robert Cowie for 12 months and he used to keep her locked in the house, only letting her out to visit her family.

He wouldn't let her go to work in case she talked to someone from the opposite sex. When they went shopping and he thought she had looked in someone's direction he used to beat her when they got back home.

It was her mum that finally reported him to the police and got him arrested.

When she moved back with her parents she found out she was pregnant. After many discussions and buckets of tears she decided to have a termination.

Maybe one day they would have a child of their own. Tony loved this girl so much; nobody was ever going to hurt her again especially when he was around.

Tony woke up in the morning just as Becky was coming out of the bathroom after a shower.

"What a beautiful sight," he thought, "you're one lucky guy."

"Good morning sleepy head," Becky said.

"Morning beautiful."

"You must have been tired last night, you never even moved."

"Excited I think, about my new job."

"Don't forget to call me, you're not on holiday," she said laughing.

"I won't don't worry," he assured her, "I don't have to leave here until about 10 o'clock."

"Lucky you. Have a wonderful day," Becky said kissing him on the lips as she walked out the door to work.

The doorbell rang at 09:32 exactly. Tony was looking at the Pulsar watch his daughter had bought him for Father's Day.

The postman greeted him with a smile, a package and a clipboard to sign. Inside the package were the key, and a map with directions to the office in Gretna Green.

It took him an hour and twenty minutes from door to door and he arrived with the key in hand.

The door was already open.

"Hello," he shouted, "is there anybody in here?"

"In the back office," a young female voice responded.

Tony walked through and found a young girl at a desk with cables everywhere.

"Hi," he said, "I'm Tony Lodge."

"Monica," she replied, "Monica Lawrence from the I.T. department in Carlisle."

"Hopefully you were expecting me," Tony said.

"I was, but they said you were due about 3 o'clock."

"I'm a keen bird, I'm eager to get started."

"Well it won't be for at least half an hour or so," she told him, "but they asked me to fit the coffee machine in the front office and that was my first job. So help yourself and I will give you a shout when I'm finished."

"Lovely," Tony said, "would you like a drink?"

"Not unless you want it all over your computer and keyboard," she smirked. "I will have one when I've finished."

Tony had a coffee then unloaded his car.

He put the main bulk of his things in the office where Monica was working and decided to use the front office with the coffee machine for his quiet room.

He put the CD player he borrowed from his house along with the CD and notepad etc. in the quiet room.

"Ready when you are," Monica said.

He sat down and she went through the procedures on accessing the databases without having to log out of one into the other, this would save time.

He had a master code that would allow him to access any of the databases 24 hours a day.

"Even I haven't got that level of access," Monica said, "you must be important."

"Not really," he said, "just a man on a mission."

Monica left her emergency number, "Just in case," she told him, but she assured him he wouldn't have to use it.

He was impressed by her confidence, and hoped she was right.

He had a quick look around the office to familiarise himself with where everything was.

Front entrance and lobby, three offices on the right hand side of the building, toilet and bath/shower room on left hand side next to the rather large kitchen and dining area.

Very cosy and smart, he thought.

He then sat at his desk in the back office, logged into the system, poured himself a cup of coffee and prepared to start his first assignment as fraud officer for the Department of Work and Pensions.

Chapter Two

John and Angela Palmer settled down in the study with a glass of sherry and looked each other in the eye.

"I wonder how long it will take them to start the inquest after your phone call dear," John said to his wife.

"I only pray we've done the right thing after all these years" she replied.

"I just want all this mess cleared up before my time runs out," he said, "I don't want you or the kids in trouble when I've gone. I just want it over and done with," he said wiping his eyes.

It took them both almost two weeks to digest the news this time.

He had beaten cancer before, but the stress and strain had taken its toll.

They couldn't go through it all again, this time was different.

The consultant told them the cancer had spread and there was no cure. He could prolong his life through chemo or radiotherapy, but even then the consultant wouldn't expect him to last longer than six months.

The news was devastating and over the past two weeks they had debated whether or not to tell the kids, but decided against it, for now.

Angela made the call late on Friday afternoon, she didn't want anyone to answer, so she left it late enough to leave a message on the answer phone.

It was awkward as both her daughter and granddaughter lived in the same house, so she had to wait until they were playing in the garden at the rear of their country mansion in Wetheral Pastures in Cumbria.

Lucy and Mellissa loved it there, they had their own rooms and plenty of space to play when the weather was nice.

They moved in after she split up from Tony over two years ago.

They had sold their family home, paid off all the bills including the mortgage, so Lucy could make a fresh start.

She received the equity from the sale by mutual agreement as Lucy had sole custody of their daughter.

Tony saw Mellissa every other weekend and would stop with him for one or two nights depending on their engagements.

Tony and Becky had a weekend apartment in Scotby near Carlisle; it was left to Becky by her nan but was too far away from both their workplaces to stay there permanently.

It was perfect when Tony's daughter stayed as it wasn't far from her grandparents' house so she could either be dropped off or picked up.

Angela had disguised her voice but wasn't very good at impersonating accents. It took her 3 attempts before she finally had the confidence to leave a message.

"This is a message for your National Fraud Manager (pause) Investigate Raymond Hessler, especially his past and family members (pause) It's too risky for me to identify myself at the moment (pause) It's important that this is resolved as soon as possible (pause) Don't ignore this call it's NOT a hoax."

She hung up quickly and gave a massive sigh of relief.

She hoped it would do the trick and someone would take notice when they heard the message.

It definitely did the trick and yes, they were taking notice.

At first they were going to make the call in 2014 when John was originally diagnosed with cancer, but decided to delay it until they had a better idea on how the treatment was going.

The family went through a rough time during his illness starting with the separation, then split of Lucy and Tony.

Lance also decided to come out of the closet and introduce his family to his long-term boyfriend Geoffrey Cropper.

Geoffrey had been his dad's accountant for the last 10 years and was six years older than Lance.

John had no idea Geoffrey was gay, never mind his son.

John and Angela welcomed him into their family with open arms, which was a relief to everyone.

John was having terrible mood swings and was getting more and more depressed as time went on.

The doctor prescribed medication but the family didn't think it was working.

Fortunately Angela was the rock in the family, holding everything and everyone together over the worst two years of their lives.

If she hadn't been so strong the family would have fallen apart.

Then out of the blue a miracle happened.

After several tests and checks the cancer had gone.

John was given the all clear, the treatment the consultant had recommended had worked, someone liked him after all, he thought.

The family started to gel again as one, and even had two weeks' holiday in a villa in Spain to bond together again. The Palmers were back.

They didn't want a return to those bad days again, that was why Angela talked her husband into keeping it away from the children.

This time John had accepted his fate and wanted to put everything right for his family before his time was up.

"I wonder who they will use to investigate the case?" John asked.

"Hopefully not Lance," Angela said, "I don't think he would be able to cope once it got further into the investigation."

"You're probably right dear," he agreed, "we will find out I'm sure. You never know, they might give it to Tony. Now, wouldn't that be a surprise?"

"It would," Angela said, "but not the sort of case to give somebody on their first day I wouldn't have thought."

"I've seen some stranger things in the DWP over the years, so watch this space. I can imagine the delight on his face if he found out the truth."

"I don't think so Jonathan, you never did like that lad and I don't know why, he was wonderful for Lucy," she said sighing, "Lucy was always happy when they were together, and when Mellissa was born I thought they were the perfect little family. I wished then they would have got married but for some reason he never asked her."

"That's in the past, leave it there dear," John snapped.

Angela always had her suspicions that her husband was behind their breakup, but she couldn't find out how or why.

Throughout Tony's relationship with Lucy John and Tony never got on, as far as John was concerned he wasn't good enough for his daughter. He was a college dropout dating his baby girl, unfortunately for John; Lucy was madly in love with this man.

So he was finally persuaded to get Tony a job working for the DWP, he started in November 2007.

Tony worked hard and managed to secure promotions over the years. Unknown to him these were influenced and organised by John Palmer.

John was always more excited about the progress and career of his son Lance. He was an A+ student at school then passed two degrees in economics and science at university. Lance was looking to start his own accountancy business as soon as he finished university, now it clicked why after his announcement about Geoffrey Cropper.

Then suddenly his priorities changed and he wanted his dad to get him a job with the DWP in the fraud section. It cost John a lot of favours but Lance started in June 2012 working for Heather Mooney.

Tony accessed the database on the system that opened the information on employees and typed in the name Raymond Hessler:

Date: 06-01-93 *Office*: Glasgow *Position*: Admin Clerk
Date: 09-02-95 *Office*: Glasgow *Position*: Senior Clerk

Date: 14-02-99 *Office*: Glasgow *Position*: Senior Finance Clerk
Date: 01-08-02 *Office*: Glasgow *Position*: Assistant Finance Manager
Date: 05-11-06 *Office*: Carlisle *Position*: Finance Manager

An impeccable work history with the DWP since starting in January 1993.

Promotions all the way, until transferring to Carlisle as Finance Manager on 5th November 2006.

His personnel file showed him as married, but nothing else.

Tony concentrated on Hessler's employment in the Glasgow office before he went to Carlisle. He wanted more information on his personal life.

He contacted his previous manager in the finance department, who was extremely complimentary telling him that his promotion to Finance Manager in Carlisle was well deserved.

He also told him that Ray was a very private person that kept himself to himself.

He was married and had 2 children.

In the seven years he had worked with him in the finance department he had only met his wife, Jenny, twice.

She didn't often attend Christmas parties or work functions, but neither did Ray.

They had a son and a daughter, Adam, who would now be 24, and was in the armed forces, and Amy, 22, who was a veterinary surgeon.

He had only met his children once at a Christmas party the year after Ray was promoted to assistant manager.

This was in 2003 when Adam would have been 10, and Amy 8, his wife was also there and they looked like a very happy family.

He also spoke to a couple of Ray's co-workers in Glasgow who confirmed that he was a very hard working and committed member of the team.

Tony had told them the reason for the call was to track down friends and family to attend a surprise presentation in January 2018 on his 25th anniversary with the DWP.

As far as he could see, this seemed to work a treat as people were only too happy to give him information.

"Investigate Raymond Hessler, especially his past and family members," the caller had said.

Nothing stood out apart from how good a worker and colleague he had been for 13 years in the Glasgow office.

His next step was to contact Hessler's current boss in Carlisle.

As far as Tony was aware nobody else knew about the call to the fraud department, but he had to tread carefully.

Charlie Grant had taken over the Senior Manager's position in the Carlisle office after the previous manager had retired in April 2007.

Charlie told him that the previous manager, Archie McPhee was given the task of setting up the new branch and putting the management team in place before he retired.

Although Raymond Hessler was one of his current senior managers he had always kept him and his colleagues at arm's length, so he didn't really know anything about him personally.

He suggested Tony contacted Archie McPhee as he was the one that hired him in the first place.

Tony wasn't impressed by Charlie Grant, he was arrogant and it felt like he had a chip on his shoulder.

He then looked at the management structure set up by Archie when the new office opened in November 2006.

Raymond Hessler – Finance Manager
Fiona Jacklin – Administration Manager
John Palmer – Benefits Manager
James Cooper – Social Funds Manager
Louise Tausney – Housing Benefits Manager

The official transfer date from their previous roles was 05/11/2006.

***

Angela Palmer was preparing dinner for the family. This was the first time for over a month they had invited Lance and Geoffrey. Lucy and Mellissa would also be there as a matter of course and it was a nice family atmosphere.

"Did you see Tony yesterday, Lance?" his father asked him. "It was his first day working with the fraud department wasn't it?"

"Can we leave work conversations till after dinner please?" Angela piped up.

"That's okay Mum I don't mind," Lance said, "I've almost finished anyway. Yes Dad I saw him briefly as we were given our assignments and more or less thrown out of the office."

"And Tony was left in the room with his boss and two bouncer lookalikes according to Lance," Lucy butted in.

"Yes and Lucy asked Tony who they were, and he said they were new recruits that Heather had to show the ropes too," Lance sniped.

"Okay you two calm down," John said, "so the two guys were dressed like bouncers?"

"They were Dad, overdressed or what?"

John looked across the table at his wife and they both nodded to each other. "Special Investigations Department," they both thought at the same time.

***

Tony logged back into the employee database and looked for a contact number for Archie McPhee, he found two.

Archie was still on the existing database, but highlighted in blue to show he was no longer in active employment with the DWP.

He arranged to meet him at 7 o'clock in his local pub in a little village called Moffatt which was 31 miles from Gretna Green.

Archie had bought him and his wife a retirement home. "A bungalow," she told him, "I hate those bloody stairs," so a bungalow it was. They moved in not long after he retired in 2007 and was within walking distance of the village centre.

"The Coachman," Archie told him, "it's on the High Street, you can't miss it."

The village clock was on the third strike when Tony walked into the bar.

Archie was sitting in the corner next to a glowing fire.

He knew it was him as he waved his hand when he walked in, and had a folder in front of him with the old DWP logo all over it.

His glass was almost empty with what looked like Guinness in front of him.

"Would you like a pint Archie?" Tony asked.

"Guinness please Tony I'm allowed one more according to the wife," he laughed, "only have two pints she tells me, you've got to watch your blood pressure."

"Pint of Guinness and a fresh orange juice with ice please," Tony asked the barman.

"Come and sit down," Archie signalled, "Jack will bring them over. Put them on my tab Jack and get a drink for yourself."

Jack nodded and pointed for Tony to sit at the table, so he turned round, walked towards Archie and sat himself down.

"How can I help you then matey?" he asked. "What's this all about? You didn't really tell me much over the phone."

"It's Raymond Hessler's 25th anniversary of starting with the DWP in January," he told him, "so we are trying to get friends and family together and organise a surprise party, it's better to do it away from the office so he doesn't catch wind of it."

"What do you need to know?"

The barman brought the drinks to the table.

Tony's orange juice looked like a cocktail with slices of orange and cherries darted through a multi coloured umbrella.

He wasn't sure if Jack was trying to impress him, or if he was having a laugh.

He would have preferred the Guinness; it looked like a proper pint.

Jack obviously looked after his beer and the place looked immaculately clean.

The smell of food was wafting from the kitchen and if he hadn't had fish and chips before he left Gretna he might have been tempted to try the food as well.

"I'm just after what you can tell me about him and any of his family, something juicy preferably," Tony smiled.

"Okay Tony," Archie said. "Let me give you a little bit of background information from before and after Ray started at Carlisle. I was the general manager working in our office in Belfast and had been there from when I joined the DWP in May 1976."

"Crikey, 30 years in Belfast during the troubles, it must have been horrendous."

"It wasn't much fun at times, but everyone rallied together and we coped with it," he continued. "I got a call from head office in London asking me to go to an urgent meeting. When I got there they showed me the plans of a new office that was in the final stages of being built in Carlisle," he explained, "they hadn't found a permanent manager yet, and they knew I was retiring in April 2007 and was looking to move back to Scotland with my wife. They wanted me to use the rest of my days before retirement setting everything up and putting a management team in place. They had already started the selection process and had shortlisted two applicants for each position. They said that should make things easier for me but it actually made it harder as I could have chosen any of the two candidates for each spot, but they left it up to me to make my choice." He opened up the folder with the DWP logos. "I probably shouldn't have, but I kept my family tree of managers I selected for each post as well as all the information on each of them that helped me make my choices," he said proudly "I hope you're not working for one of the departments where I could get into trouble for keeping this information?" Archie said looking closely at Tony.

"No, I'm just little old Tony Lodge on a mission," he said biting his gums.

He wouldn't have to mention this to anyone when he had finished his enquiries.

Archie started getting the information out of his folder one by one laying them separately on the table.

Fiona Jacklin, Raymond Hessler, John Palmer, James Cooper and then Louise Tausney.

He then passed Tony the information he had collected on Raymond Hessler.

He flicked through the information quickly. Wife, two kids, been with the DWP since January 1993, started as input clerk to assistant finance manager in nine years. Various awards in lecturing, hobbies were golf, football, rugby, a sporty person it seemed.

"Apart from his wife and kids do you know if he had any other family?" Tony asked.

"He had a sister, her name was Helen, and her married name was Helen McCabe. I think her husband was called Jim, or Jack, something like that," Archie said.

"Any other family you know about? It will help me to get in touch and invite them to the presentation."

"He never mentioned anyone else, not even his parents. I'm sure his sister and her husband were killed in a car accident shortly after I retired," Archie shrugged.

"McCabe you said?" Tony asked to confirm.

"Yeah, Helen and Jim McCabe I'm sure it was," he confirmed.

Tony flicked through the next two files...

Fiona Jacklin, married, one child, been with DWP since May 1993.

John Palmer, married, two children, been with DWP since January 1993.

The folder for Louise Tausney and James Cooper had two parallel lines marked from corner to corner with 'DECEASED' written in between the lines.

"What happened to those two?" Tony asked.

"Louise Tausney died on 10th October 2015. Suicide, she lost both her parents earlier in the year and her husband left her in July. She had nobody to fall back on as her son had emigrated with his wife and kids in 2011. They put it down to depression built up over the year. She took an overdose of tablets washed down with a bottle of brandy. She then went to bed and goodnight Vienna," he said sadly, "she was a very attractive looking woman, an eye catcher to say the least, always was. Why do people like that kill themselves? It's such a waste."

"And James Cooper?"

"James died on Christmas Eve 2015. He was out celebrating Christmas in Glasgow, got completely slaughtered out of his mind. Went to catch the last underground in Govan and was so drunk he couldn't keep his balance and fell in front of the train," Archie said, "there was a police enquiry which lasted about two weeks. It was then deemed as accidental death due to the alcohol levels found in his blood stream. He was more than three times over the normal amount, I'm not surprised he fell over or passed out."

"Were they both still working for the DWP at the time of their deaths?"

"Yes, both of them were doing well as far as I'm aware, that's why I'm surprised about Louise," Archie said, "I used to enjoy our monthly meetings when we first started, everyone was out to help each other and they would all raise issues that were affecting them. If she had a problem we would have solved it before it came to suicide, I'm sure of it."

"It's nice to have a good team," Tony said.

"It was, they all went out for a drink after the meetings, I'm sure they put the world to rights. I went once or twice but I felt like an old fossil so I eventually left them to it," he said smiling, "unfortunately when Charlie Grant took over, he had a different management style. They employed him from outside the DWP so all the old timers weren't keen on him, especially my five managers. He stopped the monthly meetings so they used to hold their own get together each month and even spent weekends away every two or three months," he told him.

"How do you know all this?"

"They all kept in touch with me for a long time after I retired, we got on so well, especially John Palmer," he smiled, "he was a good bloke, he always told me he wanted my job, it used to make us smile."

"Did you know he had cancer?"

"Yes, I heard he was diagnosed in 2014, I haven't heard anything since," he said sadly, "his wife Angela was a lovely girl, they went together like two peas in a pod. I heard their daughter Lucy had a baby, a girl I think. The last time I spoke to John he told me she had met a great guy and he was hoping at some time they would get married," he said smiling.

Tony thought the old goat didn't like him; maybe this was just a smokescreen to hide the truth.

"I can't understand why Charlie Grant would change something that worked," Tony said.

"As far as I'm aware Charlie Grant was all for Charlie Grant. All he wanted was for someone to recognise his achievements by making sure everyone around him reached their monthly targets. It looks like it worked as he's still there," he laughed.

"He was so far up his own ass he wouldn't see what was going on around him, that's why my five always stuck together and played him at his own game," Archie said with pride.

"Just to let you know Archie, John Palmer got the all-clear in April 2016, the cancer has gone," Tony told him.

"That's fantastic news," he said, "I hope we can see each other again soon, it would be nice to reminisce."

"I'm sure he would like that Archie," Tony said. He didn't think it would happen anytime soon, but who knows.

Tony said goodbye to Archie McPhee and the barman at the coachman; you never know he could be back for a Guinness and a hot meal sometime in the future.

Chapter Three

The Palmers had just finished their meal; Lance and Geoffrey were getting into their car and heading home.

Lucy disappeared upstairs to bath Mellissa and get her ready for bed; John and Angela were alone at last.

"So the Special Investigations Department are involved already," John said.

"It sounds like it with Lance's description of the two guys," Angela agreed. "Tony could also be on the case if he was kept behind."

"Let's not jump to conclusions my dear; at least we know they're doing something about your call, that's the main thing."

"If Tony is involved in the case I'm sure it will be sorted in plenty of time so we can relax and enjoy the rest of your remaining days."

"Let's hope so my dear, let's hope so."

***

Tony made the 40 minute trip back to his hotel in Gretna, It had been a long day and he needed a shower then some sleep. So far nothing had been achieved, but questions had been raised and there were a couple of things that he thought would need further investigation. This could take a while, three days might not be enough, Friday might come a little too soon.

It was just before 10pm when he got back to his room and he hadn't called Becky, *oops*. It was a bit late but what the hell, it only rang twice before she picked up the phone.

"Hiya sweetheart," he said, "I'm sorry it's so late I just got back from the office, a gruelling day today, sorry Becks."

"I've been waiting for you to call Mr Lodge," she said in a strop, "I thought you had forgotten about me already."

"I would never forget the love of my life, never in a million years," he said in a baby voice.

It worked.

"I should think not, how was your first day in Carlisle?"

"Stressful," he said, "I met loads of people and was given lots of projects to do, I will tell you all about it when I get back Friday."

"I look forward to it," she said genuinely.

"I miss you Rebecca Doyle, wish I was there now."

"I don't think so Mr Lodge, my mother is sitting beside me asking why it's taken you so long to call," she laughed.

"Give your mum a big kiss from me and wish her a good night's sleep," he said grovelling.

"She said same to you. Call me tomorrow but not so late please. I've got to get up early for work remember, it takes a bit longer from my mother's house."

"I will darling, sweet dreams."

"Goodnight. Sweet dreams to you too," she said hanging up the phone.

Tony jumped in the shower then lay in bed thinking about his day. The next thing he knew the alarm was going off at 7am. After hitting the snooze button a couple of times he eventually got out of bed at 8 o'clock.

He hadn't had the luxury of a lie in for a long time so he was taking advantage of it. After all the office was only a five minute drive from the hotel and he was working on his own.

He decided to eat breakfast at the hotel as it was included in the price. Not quite the feast he had the morning before, but scrambled egg on toast with sausages on the side was more than enough.

He arrived at the Gretna office at 8:45, opened the door with his key, plugged in his computer consul and switched it on.

He was heading towards the front office to have a coffee when as if by magic two figures appeared in front of him.

"Good morning Tony," Chris Higgins said, getting himself a cup, "we've been here since 8 o'clock."

"You should have called me last night," Tony told him, "I didn't get back until 10."

"We thought we would surprise you," Samuel Wong said.

"I thought Cilla did surprise, surprise," Tony said sarcastically.

"Do you want the good news or do you want the good news?" Chris asked.

"Well obviously it's got to be the good news," Tony said watching the coffee machine make his latte.

"We've both been sent to be your lap dogs until the case is solved," Chris said jokingly. "We are under specific instructions to work closely with you in the background but not to show our faces within the department."

"They still want it to be a soft approach and see what we can come up with," Sam told him.

"I wondered why you were dressed so casual," Tony commented. "You both look smart; I thought it was your day off."

"Casual but smart, that's the one," Sam said laughing.

"Where are you up to?" Chris asked.

After they had worked out how to operate the coffee machine and get the right drink, they sat down at the table in the back room.

Tony updated them on his progress from the day before, including his calls to the Glasgow office and his visit to see Archie McPhee.

"I made some notes," Tony said, "this was my action plan for today before you guys turned up."

Tony had written down to check on the deaths of the two managers that started in Carlisle the same time as Hessler and to dig a bit deeper into Hessler's background.

"What can we do to help?" Chris asked.

"If you guys don't mind could you focus on the two deaths? It just looks a bit weird that Hessler is accused of fraud and two of his colleagues are dead within a few months of each other in 2015."

"Sounds good," Sam said, "let's head for the library monsieur Higgins."

"The library?" Chris asked.

"The tabloids," Sam said shaking his head. "If you want to find anything out, it should be in the local paper."

"Good thinking Mr Wong," Chris said tapping him on the shoulder.

"I will stay here and checkout Raymond Hessler," Tony said, "see you guys when you get back."

Chris and Sam had shared transport since they became a partnership with SID three years ago.

A C4 Picasso was a small people carrier, ideal for their job. If they had to pick up individuals or groups it fitted the purpose.

Chris loved to drive so he was always behind the wheel. He switched on his reliable satnav and typed "Carlisle library" into the unit. Steady traffic was predicted and approximately 35 minutes to their destination.

Chris had been with the department for seven years after being transferred across from Manchester. He was of mixed race, his father originally from Jamaica and his mother from Kensington in London.

Sam joined the SID department three years ago and was paired up with Chris from day one. Sam on the other hand was born in Taiwan and came to the UK to study English at Edinburgh University, and decided to stay.

They had a few disagreements at times, but worked well together and nearly always got results.

Chris felt undermined when he was asked to tag along with a novice on this case, but at least it was something different from the normal mundane and boring stuff they were used to.

The Special Investigations Department normally got the cases that were in between the fraud department and the criminal investigation team at the local police station. They eventually had to make the decision whether it was worthy of prosecution or not.

Most of the time it was not, otherwise it would have been passed straight to the police.

Tony logged back onto the DWP database, this time looking for links between Hessler's family and the benefits department.

Maybe that's what the caller meant when they said:

"Especially his past and family members"

If it was fraud then his family he presumed would be involved, so he proceeded to look at each one individually.

Jennifer Hessler – only child maintenance.
Adam Hessler – never claimed benefit
Amy Hessler – never claimed benefit
Helen McCabe – only child maintenance
James McCabe – not found on any database
Jim McCabe – not found on any database
Jack McCabe – not found on any database

The system couldn't locate the sister's husband. It was definitely McCabe as it found his sisters details, he tried different combinations but came back with the same result – nothing.

***

Chris and Sam decided to investigate one of the deceased managers each.

Chris had James Cooper and Sam, Louise Tausney.

They arrived at the library at 11am and found two computers available next to each other.

Chris checked his notes: Louise Tausney (53) born 01.05.62 address 24 Low Road, Keswick. Husband – Ralph, son Jake (married emigrated to New Zealand 2011).

Keswick was only 37 miles away from the office in Carlisle, so a bit to travel for work. Died 10/10/15.

He typed "Keswick local papers" into the computer and it gave him the option of three. The main tabloid was the Keswick Chronicle so he searched for news items via the chronicle under her name and between 09th and 16th October 2015.

BINGO – he read the bulletin from Louise's death which was big news in the town.

She was a respectable member of the community and most locals, especially her close friend Agnes Newey were shocked by the decision to take her own life.

Agnes had known her for many years according to the chronicle and couldn't think of any reason why she would commit suicide, she couldn't believe it.

Her body was found in bed by the local police sergeant after they were alerted by a neighbour that she hadn't been seen for five days. She was on annual leave from work, so they wouldn't have known she was missing.

The paper also mentioned that she was on tablets for depression from her GP after both her mother and father had died earlier in the year.

Her husband had left her, and her only son had immigrated to New Zealand four years earlier.

It painted a sad image, of a sad woman, at a sad time for her and her family.

Chris thought this was an unfortunate set of circumstances, poor woman – case closed.

Sam was still beavering away on his computer so Chris decided to try and find a coffee machine and surprise him. He found the library café but was advised that drinks were not allowed to be consumed beside the computers. Only in the cafeteria itself.

He attracted Sam's attention and waved him towards the café.

"Found anything?" Sam asked as he sat down beside him at the table.

Chris explained what he had found and decided that it was an open and shut case.

"The friend doesn't seem to think so, does she?" Sam asked.

"I suppose not, but it's a close friend grieving her loss to the press. She's probably disappointed her friend didn't go to her for help," Chris pointed out.

"Maybe, maybe not," Sam said, "go see her and get her take on it, you've got nothing to lose, right?"

"Yeah true, I could do," Chris agreed, "even if it's just to put the whole thing to bed. Are you coming with me?"

"I'm mega busy on my guy," Sam told him, "you go, it will put your mind at rest."

"As long as you don't mind."

"Of course I don't mind, I will fill you in with my findings when you get back."

"Let me finish my coffee first."

Chris headed towards Keswick in the C4 Picasso.

He loved his satnav; he typed in Keswick and then listened to the robotic voice directing him from the 6" x 4" screen stuck onto his windscreen.

It took him onto the M6 as far as Penrith, and then redirected him onto the A66 towards Keswick, perfect he didn't even have to think.

He parked the car and looked around for the local paper shop. They would know where Agnes Newey lived he thought.

There were two female assistants behind the counter.

"Good afternoon ladies," he said politely. "Do you know where I can find a lady called Agnes Newey?"

"Agnes? Yes of course we do young man," the older of the women replied. "Go out of the shop, turn right to the traffic lights, turn left and you will find her at number 26 Low Road."

"Thank you very much madam, I appreciate your help," he said, "have a lovely day."

"So Agnes wasn't just her friend, she was also her next door neighbour," Chris thought.

He walked the short distance to Low Road and found number 26. The houses were lovely, they looked similar to the five-bedroom detached houses where he lived, but more posh and slightly larger.

He knocked on the door and stood back waiting for a response. After the third time of knocking, and being about to walk away, the door was answered by a gentleman in a grey suit.

"Can I help you?" he asked.

"I'm looking for Agnes, Agnes Newey," Chris replied.

"Is she expecting you?" the gentleman asked.

"No she's not actually," Chris answered, "I just wanted to ask her a couple of questions about her late friend Louise Tausney."

"Can you hold on a second please, I will see if she's available," he said closing the door.

It was at least 10 minutes before the gentleman returned to the door.

"Come in," he said signalling with his hands, "Agnes is in the back room; sorry about the wait I had to take her to the toilet."

Chris walked through the hallway into the lounge where there was a door leading into a converted bedroom. She was lying in a bed that had all sorts of gadgets and controls fitted to it.

"Hello young man, this is Doctor Latham he's come to give me my weekly check," she explained, "it's lucky he's late today or you wouldn't have got in, my carer doesn't start for another hour or so."

"I didn't think there was anybody at home as it took a while to answer the door," Chris chuckled.

"He didn't want to answer it," she said, "but I made him. What's this about my good friend Louise?"

"My name is Chris Higgins," he told her, "I work for the Department of Work and Pensions in the Special Investigations Department."

"Special Investigations," she shouted. "It's about bloody time. I knew somebody would come to find out the truth."

"Find out the truth about what?" Chris asked.

"Louise's death," she said. "It was a lot of cobblers what was written in the papers."

"What makes you say that?"

"Louise didn't kill herself, I told them that at the time but they didn't believe me, she was murdered I'm sure," she shouted struggling for breath.

"Calm down Agnes," Doctor Latham told her, "you will have a heart attack."

"Okay, okay," she replied leaning back on her puffed up pillows.

"So why do you say she was murdered?" Chris asked.

"They wrote that she was depressed because of her parents passing away and her husband leaving her," she explained. "Her mother had been suffering with cancer for the past six months and when she died it was like a blessing."

"I see," Chris responded.

"Her dad wasn't in good health anyway, all he wanted was to be with his wife, so it wasn't a surprise when he passed away two months later," she told him. "Louise saw this as a blessing in disguise and was so happy that they had gone almost together," she continued.

"As far as her husband leaving her was concerned, he was an absolute asshole. He had affair after affair after affair, he didn't leave her, she kicked him out. He hadn't worked for over five years and had been sponging off her all that time, she was glad to see the back of him."

"What about the depression tablets?" Chris asked.

"Ask the doctor, he's here," she said pointing to Dr Latham.

"I don't normally discuss patient's cases due to confidentiality, but her father was on depression tablets, not Louise," he told him. "His name was Leonard Tausney. L. Tausney was the name on the bottle which was where the papers got the wrong information from."

"It had L Tausney on the bottle and they put two and two together and made five, bloody papers," Agnes said cursing.

"I thought Tausney was Louise's married name?" Chris asked.

"They always told people they were married but they never were," Agnes told him. "It stopped the gossip."

"She allegedly overdosed on tablets with a bottle of brandy," Chris commented.

"Someone could have made her take them or forced them down her throat," Agnes suggested.

"Who would want to do that?"

"I thought it would have been her husband but apparently he was out of the country at the time."

"So it's possible she did take them herself?" Chris asked.

"No way, it was me that called the police in the first place," she said, "and I was with them when they went into the house. On the table beside the computer downstairs there were 2 etickets to and from New Zealand. The outgoing flight was from Edinburgh airport on 21st October 2015," she explained.

"She was always talking about going to see her son and his family but she could never afford it with her husband scrounging off her all the time. Now that she got shot of him she had the chance to go. So why would she kill herself when she was going to see her son in less than 2 weeks?"

"Did you tell the police all this?" Chris asked.

"Of course I did, when they found out her husband was out of the country and that any insurance would be void when she committed suicide they dropped it."

"What do you think Agnes?"

"I don't know to be honest, but I don't think she killed herself," she said with tears now streaming down her face. "Plus she hated brandy, that would be the last thing she would wash tablets down with."

Chris told Agnes he would keep in touch and let her know if they found anything.

When he was driving back to Carlisle he was so glad he had taken Sam's advice and came to see Agnes Newey. "She didn't commit suicide," he thought.

His satnav told him he would be arriving back to Carlisle at 3pm; he couldn't wait to tell Sam what he had found out. Sam should have just about finished what he was doing by then.

When he walked back into the library Sam was still sitting by the same place at the computer, but there was printouts scattered all around the desk.

Sam's nickname at work was "Mr Statistic", he always had stats for everything. Chris gave Sam the news about his visit to Keswick and he was speechless.

"How are you getting on with your guy?" Chris asked.

"So far I've found out through studying articles in several newspapers that James Cooper had been seen in at least four bars on the afternoon and early evening of his death," he said. "The peculiar thing is that he was remembered because he wore a ridiculously bright yellow shirt."

"Why is it peculiar?" Chris asked.

"Because the four bars that remember seeing him were all gay bars. The press jumped on this and labelled him as being homosexual," Sam said. "But friends and family denied it saying it was total nonsense."

"Did they follow it up?"

"Yes, nobody remembers him ever being in any of the bars before, so they put it down to him being drunk and not realising he was slap bang in the middle of the gay community in Govan."

"Yeah right, with a bright yellow shirt on?"

"That's what I thought," Sam agreed.

"Why don't we have a trip to Govan and see what we can find out," Chris suggested, still overwhelmed with his findings in Keswick.

"Did you know that there are 10 gay bars within a one mile radius of Govan tube station where James was killed?" he informed Chris. "And only four people were killed in Glasgow on Christmas Eve 2015, of which only 2 were alcohol-related."

"Slow down Mr Statistic what's this got to do with James Cooper's death?"

"Nothing, just giving you some facts," Sam joked. "I contacted all 10 bars, and just like it said in the papers he was only seen in four. The staff are only on duty in the evening so I suggest we go tomorrow night and stop over, see what we can find."

"That's fine by me but we are going together on this trip, I don't want any rumours starting through the department grapevine," Chris smiled.

Sam gave Chris a rundown on James Cooper's background. He was single, wasn't in any serious relationship before his death, was born on 08/08/63 and lived in Penrith, 21 miles from his workplace. He had lived there all his life. He dedicated his life to his work and was ideally suited to his role as social fund manager. He wasn't a member of any social clubs and tended to keep himself to himself.

They were hoping to find out a bit more about James Cooper from their trip to Glasgow.

Chapter Four

Chris and Sam contacted Tony with an update at half past three in the afternoon.

He was well impressed with what the lads had found out but wasn't sure whether it was linked to the phone call about Hessler, after all these deaths happened almost two years ago.

They arranged to meet in the Gretna office at 09:00 on Friday morning and see what they had all found out by then.

Tony advised them that it would be better if they travelled to Glasgow in the morning and have a look around in the afternoon.

It would give them chance to look at the scene of the accident and see where James Cooper fell onto the track.

They could try to contact the police and get some background on what happened with the investigation etc., you never know, they might be helpful.

Meantime Tony had been doing a bit of digging into the Hessler family. Ray and Jenny had been married for 24 years and had 2 children.

Adam, who was 24, and still in the armed forces based in Malta. Amy was 22 and had her own veterinary practice in London, both were in what looked like happy marriages and neither of them lived at home.

His sister and brother-in-law Helen and James McCabe were killed in a road traffic accident on the M74 in May 2007 after a lorry had ploughed through the central reservation.

It also killed four members of a hockey team that were travelling in a mini-bus on the way home from a competition in England.

It was all over the papers at the time.

The transport company were found liable due to inaccurate service records being held for the vehicle, and the driver being an illegal immigrant.

The families were awarded £350k each in compensation. This was split between the two McCabe daughters Anna and Michelle.

Still nothing stood out as far as the enquiry was concerned on Ray Hessler, so Tony called Heather to give her an update.

She was obviously aware that the two guys from SID had been sent to assist with the investigation, and was impressed when Tony filled her in on their findings.

Heather told him that in some cases they had to get the police involved in serious situations. They have an officer assigned to them called Joseph Livingstone. He used to work for the fraud team years ago before joining the police force, so he knew most of the procedures of the DWP. "He's been involved in a few arrests," Heather told him, "so keep that in mind."

"Let's see what tomorrow brings Heather," Tony said. "Then we can take it one step at a time."

"I'm concerned that Louise Tausney's death wasn't treated as suspicious if what her friend told Chris is true," Heather said. "And if James Cooper's death gives rise for suspicion it will open up a can of worms in the department, take my word for it."

"Yes, I'm sure it will," he replied, "but I still can't find a link with the phone call. Ray Hessler looks as clean as a whistle, and there's nothing obvious about his family either."

"Just keep digging, I'm sure something will eventually turn up, it always does when you're not expecting it," Heather told him.

The only thing that was baffling him was the fact that he couldn't find James McCabe's record on the database. If he had a national insurance number then he must be on there. He would try to find out his N.I. number, it had to be registered somewhere.

***

Tony decided to have a Chinese meal that evening. He sat in the restaurant as he didn't fancy eating it at the office or in his room at the hotel. Sweet and sour chicken, Cantonese-style with egg fried rice and a pint of Chinese lager.

When he finished his meal he phoned Becky.

She was surprised as it was only half past six. She thought he was making amends for yesterday.

He gave her the usual flannel about the new teams, little projects and stuff, told her how much he loved her and how he was looking forward to seeing her on Friday, which was true.

They arranged to go out to the cinema on Friday night, and then Tony remembered he promised Lucy he would have Mellissa.

So it would be a pizza followed by *101 Dalmatians* instead; it was his daughter's favourite.

They agreed and sealed it with a kiss, well another over the phone kiss that was.

He had organised a hotel for Chris and Sam in Glasgow for the following night.

Heather had organised a credit card for him to pay for his hotel, and for any unforeseen emergencies, sorted.

He booked them into a twin room between them, he was sure they won't mind. He couldn't wait to hear their response.

***

Lucy was reading Mellissa her bedtime story before tucking her up in bed.

She had a date tonight and Nanny and Granddad were looking after their little treasure. It had been two and a half years since she had split up, and this was her first date since.

It wasn't quite a blind date but not far off. Her brother had pestered her for months to go on a date with his colleague at work, Iain Logan.

She knew him briefly from past work functions with Tony and her father, but she wasn't exactly blown over with his charm or his stares in her direction.

Iain had always fancied Lucy and was envious of her and Tony's relationship for years.

When he found out they had split up he had started to drop hints with Lance to try and set him up on a date. Lance finally persuaded her. "It's only a date," he said, "see how it goes."

"So now we have arrived at the day of reckoning, life after Tony Lodge" she thought.

10 years they had been together, one beautiful daughter and plenty of memories.

Her father was the biggest influence in Lucy's life and certainly played a major role in her relationship and then split with Tony.

She still loved him with all her heart and wished until recently they could make amends and get back together.

Then she found out about Becky and realised it was just a dream.

Tony had moved on so she must do the same, but she couldn't. She found it difficult especially as Mellissa had her father's eyes, his ears and his hair colour. She was a miniature Tony Lodge.

Why did her dad have to get involved, she hated him for it, then loved him as he had cancer, then hated him again.

She just had to grin and bear it and hope everything would turn out okay.

The only thing that did turn out okay was her dad fighting off the cancer, it had gone, but so had her relationship with Tony.

Mellissa couldn't sleep, her nose was running, a cough had suddenly appeared and the tears came. The night out with Iain was cancelled, for the time being anyway.

Lucy wasn't sure if this was an act or if her daughter was truly poorly as she knew Mummy was going out. Being a mum, she gave her daughter the benefit of the doubt and stayed in.

Iain Logan put the phone down after Lucy's call and cursed her. "She's still in love with that knobhead Lodge," he thought. "I can't get away from him, now he's joined our department he will probably get all the good jobs and I will get the crap."

This had been his chance to get one over on him by sleeping with his ex-girlfriend.

He would have definitely made sure he knew, and rubbed his nose in it.

Now surprise, surprise she's cancelled, *bitch*, he held his head in his hands.

Lucy's mum and dad were relaxing in the study when she told them Mellissa was sick so she wouldn't be going out.

Her mum laughed and told her it reminded her of when she was little, Mummy's girl she was, Mummy couldn't go anywhere.

In the end they had to leave her in her bedroom until she learnt to respect her parents and stop being spoilt.

"Tony's got her on Friday night," Lucy told them. "So I can go out then instead. I might even stay out for the night"

"With Iain Logan?" her dad asked.

"Yes Dad why?" Lucy replied.

"I'm just not sure about him, that's all," he said.

"Here we go again," Lucy shouted, "I'm sick of you getting involved in my personal life, I'm going out with whoever I like whether you like it or not," she slammed the door on her way out and ran upstairs to her bedroom.

She text Iain and told him to get prepared for a drunken Friday night out, and to book a hotel for the night as she didn't intend to go home.

Iain was totally shocked when he read the text; maybe he was wrong after all.

Tony Lodge eat your heart out.

***

"What do we do now?" asked Angela.

"About Lucy?" John asked.

"No silly about us, and Ray and the rest of the crew," she said.

"Well Louise and James ain't in the crew anymore, so it just leaves us, Fiona Jacklin, Ray Hessler and their families."

"No way," she said. "We agreed that if anything happened to any of us the families would still get their cut."

"We haven't contacted any of them since 2012."

"Then it's time we did," she told him, "and get the ball rolling before it's too late."

"We can't, we need to make sure this can't be traced back, that's why you made the call remember."

"So how long do we have to wait?" Angela asked, getting impatient.

"I would say, give them a couple of weeks. If they don't find anything by then they never will," John assured her.

"Let's hope so."

"Six months is a very long time," he said. "We will have everything sorted out before I'm dead and buried, don't worry."

***

Tony arrived at the make shift office in Gretna at 7am, it was going to be a long day.

This time he knew he would be on his own, so he had to try to make an impact on the case and find something to chew on.

The feedback from the SID lads had opened his eyes yesterday; it gave rise for suspicion on one of the pack of five managers' deaths.

He could have more suspicions if the lads brought something else back from their visit to Glasgow, but was there a link between the deaths and the phone call? That was the leading question he needed to answer.

He contacted Jenny Hessler at 9 o'clock and arranged to meet her at her home at 10:30.

She was obviously aware that her husband would be with the DWP for 25 years in January, so he decided to stick with the surprise party theory.

He arrived at the Hesslers' at quarter past ten; there was a ramp that ran from the entrance gate all the way up to the front door. When she answered the door he understood why, Jenny Hessler was in a wheelchair.

"Come in please Mr Lodge," she said turning the wheels around to face back into the house.

As Tony walked in she clicked a remote control that automatically closed the front door.

She told him that she had had an accident at work six years ago and badly damaged her spinal cord. Since then she had been confined to a wheelchair.

She was concerned that her husband might leave her after the accident as she felt useless, but he turned out to be an angel and had been tending for her ever since.

"How can I help you this morning Mr Lodge?" Jenny asked.

"Tony, please call me Tony," he said. "As I'm sure you're aware your husband will have been with the DWP for 25 years in January."

"Yes I am aware of that, have you got a special prize or something for him?" she asked jokingly.

"Not quite, we are looking to improve the way we reward long-term members of the team as there has always been management thinking we don't do enough," Tony waffled. "Obviously they have spent almost all of their working life with the department and been loyal members of the team."

"That's true but I'm sure they've been really well paid for doing so and look forward to a reasonable pension," she said.

"The reason I'm here is to let you know that we are looking to hold a presentation on your husband's 25th anniversary and are looking to invite all his colleagues and family on the day," he said looking away, "I just need the details so I can finalise the numbers with the department."

"I'm sure you can find all of his colleagues better than I can Tony, you have a database that can help you with that."

"Yes I'm aware of that but I'm sure your husband could have certain colleagues that he would rather not attend," Tony said.

"As far as I'm aware my husband hasn't had a major falling out with anyone he's worked with, so feel free to invite as many of his colleagues as you like," she said confidently.

"What about family, is there anyone we could contact on his behalf?" Tony asked.

"There are only our children really," she informed him. "His sister and her husband passed away a few years ago, we only have a small family really."

"Is there no-one else in the family then?" he asked again.

"Not that I can think of at the moment," she replied.

"What about his sister's kids Anna and Michelle?" Tony asked.

"Crikey you don't miss much do you?" she said with a smile. "We will contact the girls directly when you give us a date. Thanks for asking," she said moving her wheelchair towards the door.

Tony looked to have overstayed his welcome; it was time to go he thought.

"Thank you for your time," he said. "We will be in touch."

"I'm sure you will," Jenny said waving him goodbye.

What a waste of time that was Tony thought, apart from finding out Jenny Hessler was in a wheelchair there wasn't a lot more to report.

He headed back to Gretna and set one of the offices up like a police incident room.

Maybe if he put things where he could see them it might trigger something in his or the guys' minds.

He put posters on the wall and set everything out so it was easy to follow and staring you in the face. He quite liked that.

He called Heather again and gave her an update, not much more than before to be honest but she was always reassuring and gave him confidence, he needed that at the moment.

Heather told him that she was getting pressure from her bosses and they thought something concrete might have come up by now, she thought they just wanted the accusation to disappear onto the back burner, but she couldn't allow that to happen.

He was hoping Chris and Sam found something in Glasgow but it wouldn't help towards the phone call. He still needed to find out why somebody made the call.

Tony decided to eat in the hotel and have an early night. He called Becky and wished her goodnight and told her it wouldn't be long until Friday and he would be back home, he missed her so much.

Chapter Five

Chris and Sam took Tony's advice and decided to make a visit to the underground station in Govan.

They asked for someone in charge so they could ask relevant questions if they needed some assistance, but found a solitary guard on duty instead.

Luckily he remembered the incident and was really helpful.

He informed them that after the accident happened the station had put additional safety measures in place to try to eliminate a similar occurrence.

They had drawn a thick yellow line two feet from the platform edge, and on busy periods a uniformed guard with flag and whistle was always on duty to make sure nobody crossed the line.

They were shown the point where James Cooper had fallen onto the track and realised it was an accident waiting to happen.

They also spoke to the officer in charge of the inquiry and he assured them that the witness statements had been checked out and were evidence enough that it looked like it was indeed an accident.

Afterwards they made their way to the hotel Tony had booked them in for the night.

"Thanks Tony, a twin room between us, I'm sure the DWP would have released enough funds to give us a room each," Chris thought.

They had listed the four bars in Glasgow that James Cooper had been confirmed in visiting the day he died.

Dalmonicas – Virginia Street

AXM – Glassford Street

Speakeasy – John Street

The Riding Room – Virginia Street

They were all in Merchant City close to Govan underground station, and not far apart.

They decided to visit Dalmonicas and The Riding Room first as they were on the same street.

Delmonicas was pretty quiet for 8 o'clock in the evening they thought. They asked for Maxime who Sam had spoken to on the phone the day before.

"Hi guys I'm Maxime," the guy behind the bar said with a feminine voice.

"Hi Maxime, I'm Sam I spoke to you yesterday about the guy that died on Christmas Eve 2015," Sam said.

"Yeah, it's Jonah you need to talk to," he said "*JONAH* over here boy."

A skinny looking bloke with long hair came wandering across the room.

"Jonah, these guys want to talk to you about Mr yellow shirt."

"Yo, what do ya wanna know?" Jonah said in rhyme.

"I'm Sam and this is Chris from the special investigations department for the DWP," Sam told him.

"Hi guys, what do you want to know?" he said.

"Just what you remember really," said Chris.

"Well he had a bright yellow shirt on," Jonah said smiling, "you couldn't miss him."

"Was he drinking with anyone?" Chris asked.

"He was drinking with lots of people, the clientele are friendly in here," he answered.

"Anyone in particular?" Chris asked.

"No, but I remember he kept looking around all the time," he said, "as though he was looking for somebody."

"Did anyone show do you think?" asked Sam.

"Normally in these places if someone is on a blind date, or meeting someone they haven't seen before, they will wear something to get themselves noticed," Jonah said, "he stayed for 2 drinks, then went."

"Are you sure?" Sam asked.

"I'm positive mate, we had a bet what his date would look like," he confirmed, "I said an office guy with money, but we didn't get to find out because he left."

"Okay, thanks for your help," Chris said. "Come on Sam let's try The Riding Room."

Charles from The Riding Room had the same story to tell. James had showed up in a bright yellow shirt, kept looking around, stayed for a couple of drinks then disappeared.

John Joe from Speakeasy had a slightly different story.

He seemed to think he actually came in with somebody; the stranger had one drink with him, and then went.

He said the guy with the yellow shirt stayed, had a few more drinks, then he left.

"Did you see what the guy was wearing that came in with him?" asked Sam.

"Well it wasn't a yellow shirt," he laughed, "just an ordinary guy by the look of him, but he did wear a trilby, cream with blue motives on it."

"Do you think it might have been the signal for a blind date?" asked Sam.

"It could be but trilbies are not unusual in gay bars, though a bright yellow shirt is," he said.

This could have been the person he was looking for in Virginia Street, they thought.

Last but not least they visited AXM; this bar was really busy with booths where you could have some privacy if you wanted it.

A dance floor with flashing lights and dedicated staff to serve you where you were sitting.

Sam asked for Sandy and was directed to a rather fat guy standing at the end of the bar.

"Sandy?" Sam asked.

"Who's asking?" he said.

"Sam, I spoke to you yesterday," Sam said.

"Of course sexy Sam," he said looking Sam up and down.

"Is the member of staff on duty you told me about?" Sam asked.

"Yes, she is, her name is Samantha not as nice-looking as you Sam," he said.

Sam was getting a bit nervous and kept looking at Chris for support. Chris was chuckling inside and thought it was funny but eventually stepped in.

"Which one is she then Sandy?" Chris said in an aggressive voice.

"The little blonde girl over there," he said backing off.

"HEY Samantha, have you got a minute please" he said in a much more disciplined voice.

Sandy led them to a corner table and left them to it after offering them a drink, "No thank you," the guys said.

"Hi Samantha, this is Sam and I'm Chris."

"Sandy told me about Sam's call so I was expecting you," she said.

"What can you tell us?" Chris asked.

"The same as I told the police really," she said, "the two of them came in and found a corner table out of the way."

"There were two of them?" Chris asked.

"Yes, the bloke with the yellow shirt, he was probably in his early fifties," she explained, "and a younger guy wearing a trilby hat."

"Cream with blue motives?" Sam asked.

"Yep, how do you know that?" she asked.

"He was spotted in Speakeasy as well," Sam told her.

"The older guy was already well-oiled before he came in here, I had to ask Sandy if it was okay to serve him any more drinks," she continued, "'it's Christmas,' Sandy told me, 'drink and be merry.' I felt so guilty for ages after that when I found out he had fallen under a train," she said sniffling.

"So you think he would have had enough to lose his balance," Sam asked.

"Yeah definitely, but the strange thing was the younger guy wasn't drinking," she said, "well he had one drink and made it last until they left but he kept ordering more drinks for his mate."

"So they left together?" Chris asked.

"Yeah, the young guy more or less had to carry him to the door," she told them, "they left to catch the last tube from Govan."

"Did you tell the police all this?" Chris asked.

"I did, but apparently there was nobody with him when he fell in front of the train according to witnesses," she said, "there were people on the platform apparently but no-one with a trilby hat."

"You can miss seeing a trilby," Sam said, "but you can't miss someone in a bright yellow shirt."

This didn't prove or disprove anything, but it created an element of doubt as to whether this was an accident or not, the guys thought.

Sam read through the police report when they got back to the hotel, at least two witnesses came forward at the time saying that he fell in front of the train.

The platform was packed as it was the last train before the Christmas holiday on the underground; it brought the service into chaos.

Originally they thought it was a suicide, and the selfish bloke wanted to cause disruption on the line.

Then they thought he may have been pushed or nudged by people jostling for a place in the queue, and then finally it was deemed an accident due to too much alcohol being consumed on Christmas Eve.

The video surveillance system in the station was faulty, so the police could only go on witness statements to determine the cause.

The guys came to the conclusion that it could have been a suspicious death or it could have been an accident, they couldn't prove anything either way, but there was definite doubt.

They ordered something to eat on room service and decided to have an early night. They had the meeting with Tony Lodge at 9 o'clock in Gretna, it would take them at least a couple of hours at that time in the morning to get back, so shower, then bed.

They woke up at six and discussed the previous evening's events, as they got dressed.

"What should we tell Tony?" asked Chris.

"Tell him what we think," answered Sam, "we can't prove anything one way or another, and neither could the police."

"It just seems so dodgy to me," Chris said.

"That's only because you're taking Louise Tausney's case into account as well," Sam said, "take away that case and this one would also be an open and shut case just like you said Louise Tausney's was," he laughed.

"Smart arse," Chris chuckled, "it's amazing what you can find out if you ask the right people the right questions."

"Exactly," confirmed Sam.

They had breakfast before taking the road to Gretna, as usual Chris was driving and the satnav was directing, nothing changes.

***

Tony got into the office at 7:30am, he wanted to do a couple of changes in his new incident room, he felt that his part of the investigation wasn't getting anywhere and maybe he needed some help from the two guys from SID.

He filled up the kettle as he had bought coffee, tea, sugar, hot chocolate and fresh milk. The coffee machine was okay but it was slow, and the coffee was lukewarm when it eventually dropped the last drip into the cup.

Tony checked his watch, it was 08:50 and still no sign of Chris and Sam. "They did have to travel back this morning from Glasgow, on a Friday. Chances are they left late and got caught in the main traffic, which would be unusual as they always seemed well organised," he thought.

It's just Tony being paranoid, looking at his watch every five minutes.

08:55 on the dot the door opened and in came the guys.

"Morning Tony," said Chris, "how you doing?"

"Okay, thank you Chris," Tony answered, "I've set the middle room up as a type of incident room."

"Sounds good, good morning Tony," Sam said.

"Good morning Sam," he replied, "I've had a call from Heather yesterday, she's getting pressure from upstairs to make some sort of movement on the investigation."

"Bloody hell Tony, they only had the call on Friday, less than a week ago," said Chris, "I know it's important to them, but crikey give us a chance."

"I know, I know, it's my first case on fraud and I started the same day as it was passed to me," he said.

"Don't stress out, we will get there," Chris said, "we just need a bit more time and we will crack it."

"I like your confidence; I just wish I felt the same way," Tony said, "so far I can't find anything to point a finger at Hessler for fraud."

"Okay, so today we will spend all day going over everything that we have found," Chris said, "I don't mean to take over but we will have to all work together and do what we have to do, to solve this mystery one way or the other."

"Okay guys, let's organise a drink and sit in the incident room and thrash this out," said Tony.

They spent all morning going through everything that they had done, where they had been, who they had talked to, what their individual thoughts were and where they would go next in the case.

The first thing it highlighted was it raised questions:

1. If Louise Tausney and/or James Cooper was killed, then why?
2. Who was the caller that left the message?
3. If Raymond Hessler did commit fraud, how could he have done it – opportunities etc.?
4. Is it possible that the five members of the management team who started on the 5th November 2006 are involved?
5. Is there really a case to be solved or is it just a hoax as the hierarchy think?

Tony wrote the questions on a flip chart. He put each question on an individual sheet.

"Okay guys, let's brainstorm each question individually," Tony said.

They went through each question slowly and made relevant notes beside each one.

1) They could have been part of a group, they were having an affair with someone else's partner, and they upset or annoyed an ex-employee.
2) A scorned lover of Hessler, a hoaxer, the killer of Louise and James.
3) He was finance manager so he could have paid himself or family released payments not due and take a cut, he didn't do it.
4) Maybe one of them is getting rid of the others, could the fraud be linked to all of them, there isn't a fraud at all.
5) Could be, no it isn't, yes it is.

It took all day to scrutinise what was already done and still they had nothing concrete to go on.

It was now 16:30 and everyone was brain dead and tired, they all went home and Tony gave them his personal number in case they thought of anything else over the weekend.

If not they would meet again in Gretna at 9am on Monday morning.

Tony phoned Heather and gave her the news about the guys visit to Glasgow and the brainstorming exercise.

"Look Tony, if there's nothing to find, then there's nothing to find," Heather told him, "to be honest I was hoping that would be the outcome as it would create so much aggro in the department if something was found."

"Can we have another couple of days Heather?" Tony asked. "Then if we don't find anything we will call it a day."

"Okay Tony, I will give you till the end of play Wednesday," she said, "if you don't find anything by then you pack up and come back."

Tony wasn't going to arrive home until around 7pm, so he phoned Becky and asked her to collect Mellissa from Lucy.

She was due to be dropped off at six, he knew Becky wouldn't let him down, so he called Lucy to let her know.

He arrived home at 18:45 and his little princess was waiting for him with open arms.

Becky had already ordered the pizza and had the film ready to go in the DVD player. They didn't mind Mellissa staying up until 9pm as it was the weekend, but she didn't normally last that long anyway.

She fell asleep at ten to nine and Tony carried her upstairs and tucked her in, with a nice kiss on the cheek.

When Tony got back downstairs the DVD and television were switched off, and Becky was sitting on the settee.

"Come on then Mr Lodge, tell me all about Gretna Green," she said.

So he did, he told her everything, he apologised for not telling her the truth before but explained what Heather had told him.

She understood completely, so he told her all about the case, the two deaths, and the interviews with Archie McPhee and Jenny Hessler. Becky sat there shaking her head.

"What's wrong?" Tony asked her.

"So the department get a call about one of their senior managers committing fraud and they put a "new kid" on the case," she said, "these two guys from SID, have they dealt with a case of this magnitude before?" she asked.

"I don't think so; as far as I'm aware all their cases have been small and mundane," he said, "they were over the moon being put on this case with me."

Becky sat for a few minutes in deep thought, then got her wine out of the fridge and poured a glass.

"There's no red left, you drank it all," she said, "would you like a glass of white?"

"No thanks, I've got a bottle of Stella in the fridge," he said going to the fridge and popping the top off the bottle.

"From where I'm sitting it looks like one of two things," she said.

"What's that?" Tony was intrigued.

"They either think this accusation is a load of baloney or they don't want this guy caught," she suggested, "otherwise they would have put their major players on the case."

"So what would you suggest?" Tony asked her.

"Investigate it as a fraud," she said, "at the moment you're tiptoeing around the edge."

"What do you mean?" he said curiously.

"You keep going back to the five original managers, right?" she asked.

"Yes," he answered.

"But you haven't actually spoken to any of them," she explained, "two are now deceased and for some reason you are trying to investigate their deaths that might or might not be linked."

"It looks like their deaths could be suspicious," Tony said.

"Maybe they are, but until you find the fraud you won't know that," she snapped, "find the fraud, that's what you were asked to do in the first place wasn't it?"

Tony knew she was right and yes maybe Heather was told from above to put him on the case, but now more than ever he was determined to get to the bottom of it.

"If it was you on the case what would you do next?" Tony asked her.

"Well it's not me on the case and you need to think about a strategy yourself," she told him, "but I would talk to your three managers from the original five."

That answered Tony's question, Monday was going to be very interesting. They sloped off to bed just after midnight. They had a kiss and a cuddle on the settee beforehand. Nothing else, while Mellissa was there.

Chapter Six

After Lucy dropped Mellissa off with Becky, she drove home to get ready for her date.

It had been a long time since she had a proper night out, so she was feeling a bit nervous.

She already had her choice of what to wear hanging up on the closet in her bedroom, and had had her hair done that afternoon.

The red dress that came just above the knee was her final choice after changing her mind three times.

Iain was picking her up at 7:30 so it gave her plenty of time to dress to impress.

He was 10 minutes early when he drove through the gates at the entrance to the estate; he hadn't seen her house before, he was rather shocked.

Iain was nervous as well as he took a few deep breaths before walking to the front door, and knocking firmly.

Lucy's mum answered and invited him into the study and explained she was not quite ready yet.

"Are you going anywhere nice?" Angela asked him.

"West Wall Theatre," he replied in a nervous voice, "to see Blood Brothers, it's had an excellent review."

"Sounds perfect, Lucy loves the theatre, good choice," she said, rather impressed.

"Then maybe for a bite to eat or a drink," he said feeling a little more comfortable.

"We haven't got Mellissa this evening, so there's no reason for Lucy to rush back," Angela told him.

Lucy then walked into the room. Even her mother looked in disbelief, she looked absolutely stunning.

"Lucy Palmer," her mum said. "You look fantastic, where have you been hiding for all this time?"

"Wow!" Iain gasped. "Lucky me."

"Okay don't overdo it," she said blushing. "Let's go, we don't want to be late."

Lucy thoroughly enjoyed the show, but Iain spent most of the night staring at her, he was hypnotised.

"What shall we do now?" he asked her. "Would you like to go for something to eat?"

"I'm not really hungry to be honest," she replied, "shall we go for a drink instead?"

"Do you prefer a quiet or a lively bar?" he asked.

"Quiet please," she replied. "I would prefer to hear myself think without music thumping in my ears."

"How about the piano bar?" he suggested. "Soft music and somewhere to relax."

"Sounds great, piano bar it is," she agreed.

The bar didn't close until around 1am. During this time Lucy drank two cocktails but Iain managed to consume eight pints of Strongbow cider. The conversation was like an inquest into Lucy and Tony's relationship the whole night.

The more he had to drink the more personal the questions would get, Lucy felt really uncomfortable.

"Look Iain, forget Tony Lodge. He's history," she told him.

"Okay I'm sorry, I wasn't sure if you still had a thing going for him, that's all," he said slurring his words.

"Tony moved on a long time ago, it's taken me a bit longer because of my daughter," she explained.

"Okay point taken," he said smiling "I've booked us into the Ibis hotel."

"Oh, just one room?" Lucy asked.

"Yes, sorry I didn't realise you wanted a room to yourself," he said confused.

"It's been a long time since I've been out on a date Iain and I'm certainly not the kind of girl to hop into bed with someone on the first night," she said.

"Of course, I understand I must have got my wires crossed," he said, "we will get another room when we get there."

"I will pay for my own room," Lucy said "it's only fair."

When they got to the hotel they found that all the rooms were reserved. Most of the reservations were taken by the cast of the show they had just been to see the receptionist told them.

She also pointed out that the room Iain had reserved was in actual fact a twin, and not a double.

After debating whether or not to find another hotel at that time of the night they decided to share the twin room. Lucy wasn't keen on waking her parents up, so that swayed her decision in the end.

They both had a shower and got ready for bed, Lucy chose the bed closest to the door and Iain had the bed beside the window. It was slightly ajar as it was a warm night.

Lucy was tired as it had been an eventful night, and she felt better when she heard Iain snoring on the other side of the room. Now she could relax, she thought.

She was awoken by the touch of Iain's hands massaging her breasts; he had climbed into bed with her.

"What the hell do you think you're doing?" she said pushing him away. "Get off."

He carried on and started to move his body closer to hers.

"If you don't stop I'll scream," Lucy shouted.

"No you won't," Iain said putting the masking tape over her mouth that he had prepared earlier.

He then turned her onto her stomach and tied her hands behind her back, and then turned her back around and spread eagled her legs tying them individually to the legs of the bed.

"Now you're all mine," he said licking his lips.

***

Tony and Becky were fast asleep and Mellissa was cuddled up with her toys in the spare room.

Becky prodded Tony in the side.

"Tony....Tony wake up," she whispered.

"What?" he said rubbing his eyes. "What's wrong?"

"There's someone at the door," she said. "They've been knocking for about 5 minutes."

They jumped up, got dressed, and made their way downstairs. The knocking was getting harder and more frequent by this time. Tony unlocked and opened the door, it was Lucy.

"What the…." Tony started to say.

"I'm sorry," Lucy said crying her eyes out, "I'm so, so sorry."

She looked terrible. Her hair was everywhere and she had makeup smudged all over her face, where she had been crying.

Becky stepped past Tony, put her arms around her and helped her inside.

"Come in and sit down Lucy," she said getting some handkerchiefs out of the box, "let's go into the dining room, I don't want us to wake up your daughter."

"I'm sorry," Lucy said again.

"What's happened?" Tony asked. "You look terrible."

"It was horrible," she said starting to cry louder, "he's an animal."

"Who's an animal?" Tony asked.

"Iain Logan," she confirmed, "he raped me."

"Iain from the office?" Tony screamed.

"Yes Tony Iain from the office," she said. "I should never have let Lance talk me into it."

"Oh shit," Tony said, "I will kill the bastard."

Lucy told them everything that happened. He had fallen asleep afterwards and she managed to undo the tape and get out.

"You need to report him to the police straight away," Becky said.

"I can't," she said, "he said if I did he would deny it and tell them it was my idea to book the hotel."

"You've got marks on your wrists and ankles," Becky told her. "You don't get them from consenting unless you're stupid."

"Exactly," Lucy said, "I was stupid, I should have listened to my dad he said he wasn't sure about him."

"Your dad tries to protect you Lucy, he was the same when we started going out," Tony said.

"It would destroy my parents and what would it do to my daughter," Lucy said bursting into tears again.

"Our daughter will be fine," Tony reassured her.

"All he did all night in the bar was talk about me and you," she told him, "it was like he had been stalking us for years, I didn't realise it till now."

"Weird guy," Becky said.

"Very weird guy," Lucy agreed. "I should have gone home, got a taxi, I was too bothered about what my dad would say."

"You still need to report him, this type of guy needs locking up for good," Becky told her.

"If you don't report him I will snap his arms and legs in two," Tony said.

"It was like some sort of revenge. Even when he was raping me he was saying, take that Lodge, it was really scary," she said.

"I don't even know the guy," Tony said, "I've only just started working in the same office as him, what's his problem?"

"Well it must be serious for him to rape your ex-girlfriend. I hope he won't be looking for me next," Becky pointed out.

"Oh no," Tony thought, "I'm away till at least next Wednesday; you're going back to your mum's Becky Doyle."

"Do you want me to call the police?" Tony asked.

"Can I sleep on it please?" Lucy said. "I'm not sure what I want at the moment."

"Don't take too long," Becky reminded her, "the police will need to take samples for evidence, and examine you."

"Okay, can I sleep in with Mellissa?" she asked.

"I would rather you didn't disturb her tonight," Tony said. "I'm sure she wouldn't want to see you in this state."

"Okay I will sleep on the settee so I don't disturb anyone," Lucy said.

"No way," Becky told her. "You're coming in with me."

***

Iain Logan woke up in the morning and looked across at the empty bed on the other side of the room.

His head was throbbing and he was trying to remember what happened the night before, it was all a blur.

***

Lucy was in Tony and Becky's kitchen preparing breakfast. She was looking forward to seeing the look on Mellissa's face when she saw her.

"Have you decided what you're going to do?" Becky asked.

"I'm going to leave it Becky, I don't want to upset my parents and I've got my daughter to think about," Lucy replied.

"You've also got the women he's probably already done this too, and the women he's likely to do it to in the future to also think about Lucy," Becky said getting annoyed. She was getting flashes from her past.

"Let me deal with this my way please," Lucy said.

"I just think you're making a big mistake, but it's your choice," she said, seeing images of her ex-boyfriend's face.

"Mummy," Mellissa shouted running into the kitchen and jumping on her mum. "What are you doing here?"

"I've just got back from a crazy night out and forgot my keys," she told her winking at Becky, "so Daddy and Becky kindly let me stop here."

"I like your dress Mummy," she said touching it.

"Yes it's nice darling," she said sadly, "but it won't be coming out again for a while."

Lucy called a taxi, said her goodbyes to everyone and thanked Tony and Becky for having her. Then she headed home for a shower, and get changed.

When Lucy had gone Tony looked at his girlfriend's face, he could see the pain in her eyes. She had gone from his happy little Becky Doyle to what looked like a frightened child. This incident had hurt her more than it hurt Lucy; it brought back traumatic memories from her past.

Memories that had been buried at the back of her mind until now. They had re-emerged.

She didn't have to say anything, he just knew, why did Lucy have to bring her problems to their door, what a selfish cow.

All she had to do was to report him to the police and get him sorted, and then all the problems would have disappeared.

They had spoken many times about her relationship with Robert Cowie. She couldn't even mention his name, she always referred to him as "IT".

She blamed herself for not reporting or telling anybody sooner because after time they escalated beyond imagination or belief.

She wasn't sleeping or eating. She was trying to make herself look undesirable so that nobody else would look at her, then he wouldn't have a reason to punish her when they got home.

Her life was a living hell and if it wasn't for her mother reporting him, who knows, she could well have still been there now.

It took almost three years of therapy before she got back to what she considered to be normal, and another two years before she could trust having another man in her life.

Tony was pleased to say that man was him, and nobody would hurt her again, not while he was around.

***

Lucy arrived home and had a nice long shower. She still ached in parts she hadn't used for a while, and a hot shower eased the pains from the night before.

It had been a while since she last had sexual intercourse, and she didn't imagine the next time would have been against her will.

The smell of his cheap aftershave had gone, and the taste of his cider breath had been replaced with the taste of fluoride.

It wasn't the police she was going to make contact with, it was Iain Logan himself.

***

After breakfast Tony and Becky took Mellissa to the Urban Adventure playground in Carlisle.

They went there two weeks before and she loved it.

She had met a couple of new friends and played with them for hours. To their surprise, when they got there the sun was shining and the same friends were there again.

It gave them chance to talk without being disturbed.

"Don't," Becky said straight away. "I don't need a lecture."

"I wasn't going to lecture anyone," Tony said, "what Lucy chooses to do is up to her, we've got no influence over her."

"I know I made the wrong decision once," she said, "but that's in the past, I get flashbacks now and again but I can deal with them."

"Good," Tony said with a smile, "I just need that infectious smile back."

Becky gave him the biggest smile he had ever seen; now he knew why he had fallen in love with her.

Becky had already made her mind up she was going to go and see Lucy by herself, and soon.

***

Iain Logan was back at home at his parents' house. He had lived there all of his life and had just one or two relationships that he could call serious in his 32 years.

He wasn't exactly a handsome looking guy, but not what you would call ugly either. He had worked for the fraud department since 2010 after applying through an advertisement in the local press. The favourite part of his role was following the fraudsters without them knowing he was there; it gave him a thrill when he caught them and they were prosecuted.

The case would then be passed across to the detective team at the police for the final conviction and he wouldn't be identified at any time, that's what he liked.

He had seen an attractive looking girl that he took a fancy to coming out of the Edinburgh office in 2011. After a bit of investigation work he found out her name was Lucy Palmer. Her dad was the benefits manager in the Carlisle office and she was dating one of the clerks at Edinburgh. She didn't work for the DWP.

He thought she was beautiful and wondered what she was doing with a dickhead with no future, she should be with him.

He wasn't brave enough to confront any of them, so he just used to follow them now and again. He saw her gain weight, lose weight, carry a baby for 9 months, walk the baby in a pram, then a pushchair. He watched her grow from a young woman to a mature mother in the 6 years he had been infatuated by her.

Her brother started in his office a year after him, so he would get some gossip from her relationship from Lance when he could. When he told him she had split up from her partner over 2 years ago he kept pestering him to get her a date. Then eventually she had agreed, he thought it was Christmas when she called him back and told him to organise a hotel after they would have a drunken night out. She looked like a million dollars when she walked into her parents' study at her mum's house, he couldn't wait to get her into bed. All through the night he couldn't take his eyes off her, he couldn't believe she was with him. Then when he started drinking heavily the memories came back when she was with Tony Lodge, he had to make sure she didn't have any feelings for him anymore.

Then she rejected him, didn't want to be with him, but somebody up there was looking after him and she stayed in his room anyway. The bag he took with him had his painting things in and he remembered he had some masking tape in the side pocket.

He had lay there for ages with her in the bed opposite, she turned round a few times when she was asleep and the duvet had slipped to one side. It revealed her beautiful figure that was only covered with a flimsy top and a pair of laced underwear. Her nipples were erect and her bottom was perfect, he could feel himself getting aroused. He wasn't sure if he would be up to it anyway after having too much to drink, but after she turned around a few more times he felt he was definitely ready. He took the tape out of his bag and tore a couple of lengths off in preparation.

He was hoping she would want him, but he already knew what her reaction would be before he started. He couldn't remember finishing; he must have fallen asleep half way through.

Just as he was going over it again in his mind his phone rang.

It was Lucy Palmer. "Oh my god," he thought. "Shall I answer it or not?" He was shaking all over.

"Hello," he said quietly.

"Hiya Iain," Lucy said, "I was just calling to say thank you for a great night last night," she continued. "I'm sorry I didn't wake you up when I left, you were fast asleep."

He was gobsmacked and couldn't believe what he was hearing.

He expected the police to knock on his door any minute, his job would have gone, and he would have been locked up for years. He certainly wasn't expecting this.

"Thanks Lucy," he said with a little more confidence.

"We will have to do it again sometime," she said, "just let me know when you're available."

"I'm available anytime," he said.

"I will call you when I can get a babysitter," she told him "I can't wait."

"If I don't answer please leave a message," he said overjoyed.

"Bye then Iain, hope to see you soon," Lucy said before hanging up.

Lucy's phone rang 10 minutes later. "Shit," she thought, "he isn't calling me back?"

It was Becky, she arranged to bring Mellissa back on Sunday to give her a bit of time to think, and maybe they could arrange to go for a coffee or something to get to know each other.

"You've got my man, and now you want to be friends," Lucy thought, "NO WAY sister."

Chapter Seven

Ray and Jenny Hessler woke up at 6:30am and Ray carried out his normal routine.

He helped his wife to get out of bed, took her to their walk-in washroom where she had a shower fitted with handrails and a seat under the shower spray.

She always dried and dressed herself before she called him to help her out of the washroom into her wheelchair. It had become so routine he could do it in his sleep.

Love making had come to end after the accident, not that it was that frequent anyway after he was transferred to the newly-built Carlisle office in 2006.

He thought back to when it all started in Carlisle 11 years before.

Archie McPhee had employed five managers to be the heart of the operation. There was himself, Fiona, John, James and Louise.

They used to have regular meetings to get to know each other and share their new responsibilities.

They were all newly promoted into the roles by Archie himself. It had been difficult for a couple of them to adjust to the job, but with the support of the others everyone felt confident.

Archie would chair the monthly meeting and they would all go for a couple of drinks after, Archie came to the first one or two social nights then he made his excuses and ducked out. The five of them got on really well to the extent they called themselves "The Wicked Five".

If they sent internal mail to each other they used to put "W5" at the bottom of the page. It became their trademark and they thought it was quite amusing, even Archie had a laugh.

He said that was why he eventually dropped out of the social side, as "W5+1" didn't quite sound so good.

He didn't know who suggested it first, but they arranged to have a weekend away for just the five of them without their partners.

They found a country hotel in Brampton, Cumbria and made a reservation for two nights. The first night had been slow, nobody quite knew what to do or say, or if it was formal or informal.

Louise looked elegant and beautiful for a woman in her early forties, and Fiona didn't look too bad either.

On the first night they all had a meal, a few drinks and went back to their own rooms for an early night.

The second night was like a total transformation, everyone let their hair down and they all ended up in one room at the end of the night. They had consumed a few drinks and the girls were a bit giggly at times.

They all felt like teenagers again and played games until the early hours of the morning.

Louise asked everyone if they had ever played spin the bottle. Of course most of them had in their younger days but not for a few years.

"Let me spin," Louise said merrily, "whoever it lands on has to give me a kiss."

She spun the bottle and it landed on Ray, so he gave her a peck on the cheek.

"That's not a kiss," she said grabbing his head with both hands and kissing him passionately for a few minutes. "That's a kiss."

Everyone laughed. This time Fiona spun the bottle and it landed on John, this time John knew what to do so there was no peck on the cheek.

"This time I will spin it twice," Louise said, "and the two it lands on have to spend the night together," she said.

"What if it's two male or two female?" Ray asked her.

"Then it's up to them what they want to do," she said. "Don't knock it until you've tried it."

"There goes a voice of experience," James said smiling.

73

She spun the bottle twice and it landed on John and Fiona.

"See you in the morning," Louise said ushering them out of the room.

She spun another two times and this time it landed on her and James.

"I want a re-spin," she said, "it was in between you two guys."

The next spin landed bang in the middle of Ray's chest, so there was no argument this time.

"Goodnight James," she said opening the door, almost pushing him out. She looked Ray in the eye, "It's just me and you."

Ray and Louise had fancied each other from a distance since they first met, so this encounter was inevitable.

They had another drink and chatted for a while about their relationships with their partners. They were both reasonably happy, but not quite 100%, they told each other.

"What about sex?" Ray asked her. "Is your sex life good?"

"He's a bit like a wham bam, thank you mam type of guy," she told him. "He just wants a quickie to get it over with."

"I see," he said, "and what are you actually after then?"

"Love, passion that's what a woman always wants isn't it?"

"Sometimes I suppose but my wife has to be in the mood for anything like that, so that's probably once in a blue moon," he said laughing.

They undressed each other and made love almost until the sun came up; they both gave everything to each other and more.

Fiona and John had also made love, but not with half the passion of Ray and Louise.

Unfortunately James ended up as gooseberry on this occasion.

The weekends away became a monthly occurrence and over the next three months the bottle had a busy time.

They got more promiscuous as time went by.

They started off with one on one sex, then tried threesomes and even a foursome.

Louise hated it when Ray was with somebody else, but it wasn't an affair she was after at the moment, it was just to fulfil her lust and was sure it was the same for everyone else.

The five had an understanding with each other and vowed that whatever happened in Brampton, stayed in Brampton.

Ray remembered that it all changed then for a while when Archie retired and Charlie Grant took over, the weekends away stopped.

***

Lucy called Iain back at 11am.

"Hi Iain, I've managed to get Tony to look after our daughter again tonight," she told him, "do you fancy another night out?"

"When, tonight?" he asked.

"Of course," she confirmed, "it's not very often I get the chance to get out, it's up to you."

"What do you fancy doing?" he asked.

"Well I would rather you didn't drink so much this time," she said, "so maybe a meal would be nice, and we can take it from there."

"Sounds good," he answered, "what time shall I pick you up?"

"I'll meet you in town, I've got to get some things anyway," she said, "dress casual as I fancy an Indian or a Chinese, what do you think?"

"I prefer Chinese if you don't mind," Iain said.

"Perfect, do you know the Lucky Dragon on London Road?" she asked.

"Yeah I've been there a couple of times, it's alright," he confirmed.

"Okay I will see you outside at 7 o'clock if that's okay," said Lucy.

"No problem, see you at 7."

Iain couldn't believe his luck, two nights on the spin with his dream girl – wow, especially after last night when he thought he had blown it once and for all. Roll on 7 o'clock he thought.

***

After the urban adventure ground Tony and Becky took Mellissa back to the apartment in Scotby.

"I hope Lucy is feeling alright today" Becky said.

"I'm sure she will make the right decision in the end," Tony told her. "If not it's on her shoulders not ours"

"How can you be so cruel?" she said. "She's the mother of your child for crying out loud."

"What do you want me to say Becky?" he asked. "She was the one that ended up back in a hotel room alone with him."

"It doesn't give him the right to rape her does it?" she asked.

"No it doesn't, but it gives him the opportunity" Tony said annoyed at the situation.

"Why do men always blame the woman?" she asked.

"I'm not saying it was her fault, but on her first date, she doesn't know the guy and she's in a hotel room with him. Come on Becky, that's bloody stupid don't you think?" Tony emphasised.

"I suppose so, but still, it doesn't give him the right to abuse her now does it?" she said getting irate.

"No it doesn't," he said, "can we leave it now, Mellissa is coming back downstairs."

They had pizza and *101 Dalmatians* the night before, so it would be Kentucky Fried Chicken and games tonight.

Mellissa liked Snakes and Ladders and Guess Who, so here he went again. Another night of acting as a child, but at least it took his mind off Mellissa's mum for a while.

***

Iain waited outside the Chinese, had been there for 15 minutes.

He was early as usual, an eager beaver waiting to apologise for his stupidity the night before.

Lucy came walking around the corner bang on 7 o'clock, dressed in jeans and a dark blue hoodie. Iain now felt overdressed with his smart trousers, shirt and tie.

"Lose the tie," he thought as he undone it and put it in his pocket.

"Hiya," Lucy said, greeting him with a kiss on the lips.

"Hi," he replied trembling all over.

"Let's eat," she said opening the restaurant door.

Lucy was famished.

She had a starter, main course and a glass of house wine with her meal.

Iain was that nervous he hardly touched his food. He didn't even have an alcoholic drink, choosing orange and lemonade instead.

This time it was Lucy looking at him, and he could hardly bring himself to make eye contact.

"Have we got a plan for after our meal?" Lucy asked.

"I'm not sure," he answered, "what do you think?"

"Can we finish where we left off last night?" Lucy asked him.

"I can't really remember," he said, "I think I may have had a couple too many."

"You fell asleep before we finished," Lucy reminded him.

His mind was racing; did he dream that he raped her? Why wasn't she angry? Why wasn't she screaming at him?

"I was a little disappointed," she said, "it's been almost three years since I made love, and when you started being aggressive it really turned me on."

"I'm sorry," he said.

"What for Iain? I loved every minute of it," she told him. "Can we finish off tonight please?"

"Are you sure?"

"I've never been so sure of anything in my life," she said. "Phone up and book the same room at the Ibis."

Iain reserved the room. He was not sure whether he was excited or scared, he was shaking like a leaf.

"Iain go and get the key. I don't want anyone to see me going in," Lucy said "I will take my car to the rear car park and walk to the fire exit at the end of the corridor."

"Why?" he asked curiously.

"One of my mates works there on a Saturday evening," she told him, "I don't want her to see me."

"Where does she work?" he asked.

"On reception, if my parents find out I'd never be able to see you again," she said winking.

"Okay, give me 10 minutes then I will open the exit door."

"Sounds good, have you got the tape?"

"Yeah but there's not a lot left."

"I'm sure there will be plenty," she said winking again.

Iain walked into the reception area and paid in advance. He picked up his key and made his way to the room.

After checking there was nobody around he opened the fire exit door.

Lucy came in and closed the door quickly behind her and entered the all too familiar room.

Iain was standing there not sure what to do next.

Lucy closed the bedroom door and put her arms round his shoulders and started to kiss him tenderly on the lips.

She started to undo his shirt while he pulled the hoodie over her head.

She then undid his belt, took his trousers off and threw them on the floor. Iain promptly undid her jeans and pulled them down over her thighs, he was now getting aroused.

She sat him down on the bed as he unclipped her bra and let it fall onto the bed.

All that was left was his boxers.

He was reaching for her knickers.

"Stop," Lucy said. "Have you got the tape?"

"It's in my bag," he said reaching over to get it. "Do you want me to tape your mouth first?"

"No silly, it's your turn tonight! Then I can do things to you instead."

"Like what?" he asked.

"It's a surprise but you will be impressed," she said.

Lucy pulled down his boxers, and then kneeled down in front of him.

He closed his eyes in anticipation.

"Tape," she said.

He passed her the tape and she tied both hands behind his back. She made sure they were secure and he couldn't move them. She then asked him to lie on his back while she tied both his feet to the legs of the bed, again she made sure he couldn't move or wriggle free.

"This is great," he said. "Now I see why you enjoyed it last night."

She then put the tape over his mouth, and then taped his eyes so he couldn't see.

The room went silent.

Iain was confused, where had she gone? Then the tape was pulled away from over his eyes.

In front of him were two men, naked apart from wearing Halloween masks.

"Hello Iain," one said.

He recognised the voice immediately, it was Lance Palmer.

"It's party time," Lance said setting off a party popper.

Lucy closed the fire exit door on her way out. She did what her brother had asked and got him back to the hotel.

Lucy couldn't sleep after she went to bed at Tony's last night, her mind was going round and around, reliving what he had done to her.

"If you tell anyone I will say it was your idea," he had said, "you will have to prove it."

She was mad at Lance for getting her into this position in the first place, so she rang him at 6am from Tony's kitchen.

Lance went absolutely ballistic on the phone, he couldn't believe it.

Lucy told him everything that happened and Lance kept apologising again and again and again.

"What should I do?" she asked him.

"Let me call you back in 15 minutes," he told her.

When he called her back he told her that him and Geoffrey had a plan. Could she try and get him back to the hotel tonight?

"You're joking," she said. "How the hell am I going to do that?"

Lance told her exactly what to do and see what reaction she got. The plan worked a treat, and now he was at the mercy of

Lance and Geoffrey. She couldn't even imagine what would happen to him, and didn't care.

"Two years you've been pestering me to get you a date with my sister you bastard," Lance said, "and this is what you had in mind."

Iain was watching the two of them while they unpacked a holdall onto the dressing table. Rope, tape, baby oil, a vibrator, a truncheon and two whips.

Lance took out a CD player and plugged it in.

"Music maestro please," Geoffrey said cracking one of the whips.

There was sheer terror written all over Iain's face.

***

Tony and Becky sat cuddled up in front of the television; Mellissa was fast asleep after an entertaining night tired her out.

"Have you decided what you're going to do about the fraud case?" Becky asked.

"Yeah sweetheart, as you suggested we need to talk to John Palmer, Fiona Jacklin and Ray Hessler," he said.

"What reason will you give for questioning them?" she asked.

"I think maybe about the deaths of James Cooper and Louise Tausney," he told her, "we can say we've had a tip off and after looking closer into their deaths it looks suspicious. See if it ruffles any feathers."

"You mean ask them if they know of anyone that would want them out of the way?" she asked.

"Exactly," Tony replied. "If they know anything it could generate a reaction."

"Okay, it's a start," she said.

"I'll get the two guys to interview John Palmer, I couldn't look him in the face after what happened to Lucy," Tony said. "I'm sure she won't tell them."

"It's Saturday night, let's relax and forget about work and issues we can't do anything about," Becky said. "Which film do you want to watch?"

"*Along Came a Spider*," Tony suggested. "It's my favourite."

"Coming up," Becky said slotting it into the DVD player.

They watched the film and had a couple of glasses of wine before retiring to bed; it had been a long day.

***

Sunday was a quiet day for everyone. Tony and Becky had breakfast with Mellissa, then went to the local park with a bat and ball and played some rounders.

Becky then contacted Lucy and arranged to meet her with Mellissa at the nearest McDonalds for lunch. Lucy agreed so they made it for 1 o'clock.

Lance and Geoffrey stayed at home and had Sunday lunch. Lance liked to play chef on a Sunday and always made a fuss.

John and Angela went out to the pub and had a carvery; they liked to have an easy day on a Sunday. Normally Lucy and their granddaughter would come with them, but they had made other plans.

Ray and Jenny Hessler visited Jenny's parents on a Sunday, and always had lunch with them.

Iain Logan always had Sunday lunch with his mother, but she was still waiting for him to get home. "Another night out with the new girlfriend," she thought with a big grin.

Becky met Lucy with her daughter at 1 o'clock as planned. McDonalds was really busy, "Don't people eat Sunday dinner anymore?" Becky thought.

They managed to find a table and Lucy ordered the food. Six chicken nuggets extra value meal for Becky, some fries for Lucy, and a cheese burger happy meal for her daughter.

Becky found some colouring sheets and crayons to keep Mellissa occupied while her and Lucy had a chat.

"Have you made up your mind what you're going to do about Friday night?" she asked Lucy.

"I'm just going to let it go to be honest," she said shrugging her shoulders.

Becky told her all about her past and the volatile relationship she had with her ex-partner a few years ago.

"I made the wrong decision then by bottling things up and not telling anyone. By doing that it just escalated," she told her.

"I'm not in a relationship with him Becky, and I don't intend to be. It's finished, all over."

"It probably will be for you, but it won't be for his next victim," Becky said, getting upset and annoyed.

"Then let the next victim report him," Lucy said. "I'm happy the way things are at the moment so let's forget it please."

"What a selfish bitch," Becky thought.

"Bloody leave it," Lucy was also thinking, "it's already been dealt with."

The two women parted company after half an hour. The atmosphere between the two of them wasn't very pleasant, especially with Mellissa being there, so it was better to separate as soon as possible.

Iain Logan arrived home just after midday.

He went straight upstairs to his room without even saying hello to his mother. He wasn't feeling well, he felt sick and ached all over, especially in parts he shouldn't be aching.

It was painful to stand up; it was painful to sit down. The only position that was manageable was to lie down on his stomach. So he lay there all day and all night. He won't be raping any more girls in his lifetime, he thought.

Lance told him that if he even as much as looked at his sister again, next time he wouldn't be going home. If they hear of him touching another girl without consent, he would get the same again if not worse.

He blamed Friday night on the amount of alcohol he had consumed in a short period of time. So no more excessive drinking for him, he promised himself.

"I've been caught and punished without the law being involved," he thought. "It's going to be a nightmare at work looking at Lance every day, but that will be better than looking at four walls in a prison cell."

He tried to have a hot bath, but couldn't, he was still losing blood. It might have to be a trip to the hospital.

Chapter Eight

Heather was passed the message when she got into the office at 8 o'clock on Monday morning.

Iain Logan wouldn't be in work for at least 3 to 4 weeks. He had had an accident and had emergency surgery during the night.

***

Tony arrived in the make shift office at half past eight closely followed by Chris and Sam. They congregated in the "incident room" where Tony chaired the meeting.

"This is the plan for today guys. We need to organise meetings with the three members of the original five and try to rock the boat," he said.

"That's fine," Chris said. "But what do you propose we say?"

"We've got until the end of play Wednesday, then if we don't find anything concrete, the case will be closed and deemed as a hoax," he told them.

"Crikey, we know there's something going on somewhere," Sam said.

"Then let's find it," Tony told them, "let's tell them we've had a tip off about the two deaths and they are now being treated as suspicious."

"Then what?" Sam asked.

"See what reaction we get, let's take one each," he suggested.

"I don't think that's a good idea," said Chris, "I've always found one to one interviews are non-productive, it's better with two. Firstly it's easy for one person to miss something and secondly with two, it puts them under pressure, two against one scenario."

"Okay, let's start with John Palmer, you two can interview him. You're probably aware that I was going out with his daughter for 10 years and he knows I've been transferred to the fraud team."

"Yes we are aware, and yes it's better if we speak to him," Chris agreed.

Chris pulled a pocket notebook from his jeans pocket and opened it up to reveal a list of numbers. He then dialled John Palmer's number from his mobile phone.

"Good morning John, it's Chris Higgins from SID," he told him. Chris knew John would know who SID was, so he didn't need to elaborate.

"Morning Chris, how can I help you?"

"Are you available this morning John, we are just investigating a tip off and need to have a quick chat if possible."

"What time are you looking at?"

"Say ten o'clock if that's ok."

"Yeah that's fine, see you at ten."

"That was easy enough," Tony said rising from his chair.

"Normally they would ask about the tip off, but he didn't."

"He knows you're seeing him in an hour, so he will find out then."

"Human nature Tony, your mind always wants to know, especially after having a call out of the blue."

"So you think he knows something then?"

"My gut reaction is yes, but I will find out at ten if there's anything we need to follow up, won't we Sam?"

"Yes, boss," Sam said laughing.

This was normally the point where Chris would take over, he loved to take control. Sam only ever remembered one case where he read things wrong and blew it, but apart from then he had always been right in the three years they had been together.

Tony switched the computer on in the back office; he wasn't as organised as Chris.

He had to go online to get the numbers for Fiona Jacklin and Ray Hessler. Tony decided to target Fiona and suggested that he and Chris see Ray Hessler.

After all he's the alleged fraudster.

Chris agreed and asked Tony to arrange an appointment with him for this afternoon.

Chris and Sam arrived at the Palmers' residence at ten o'clock.

Like others before them they were impressed with the house.

It was fantastic they thought, there was definitely money there. It was actually left to Angela Palmer as the only grandchild of her late nan and granddad in their will, they moved in January 2002.

Chris was expecting a butler to let them in, but instead it was John's daughter Lucy that showed then into the study.

"Gentlemen," John said walking into the room carrying a tray with a pot of tea, three cups, milk and sugar. There was even a side plate with half a dozen or so cookies, they were being spoilt.

Chris was surprised at how frail he looked; if he lost any more weight he would resemble a skeleton. He knew John was in and out of work over the past three years, and had been recently signed off again by his doctor for at least another month.

Chris was also aware of his cancer treatment from 2014 to 2016 until he was given the all-clear, but if this was him being better, then he wouldn't have wanted to see him at his worst.

"A tip off you said, sorry which one of you is Chris?"

"I'm Chris, and yes John a tip off from an outside source," Chris said putting sugar in his tea and stirring the contents of his cup.

"I apologise for my short and sweet telephone conversation earlier, my wife was on her way out and she was after some help to put things in the car."

That would explain why he didn't ask about the tip-off, Chris thought.

"Anyway help yourself to some cookies, they will only go to waste if you don't eat them," John said sitting himself down and poured himself a cup.

"What was the tip off about then lads?" he asked.

"You obviously remember Louise Tausney and James Cooper?"

"Of course I do, what about them?"

"The caller suggested that we should look a little bit closer at their deaths," Chris said watching John's face.

"Didn't Louise commit suicide?" John looked puzzled.

"Allegedly but Sam here followed it up, he interviewed a couple of people close to her and came up with the conclusion that it definitely wasn't suicide," Chris didn't want to say it was his enquiry on this one.

"And James?"

"This time we both followed this one up, and again there is rise for suspicion around his death."

"I hope the police get involved then, I really loved those two, we all did," John looked genuinely upset.

"Can you think of anyone or anything that might cause someone to want them out of the way?"

"No, definitely not, they were wonderful people. I know Louise was in a relationship for years with someone she didn't love as far as I was told, but I wouldn't say it was a reason to kill her."

"She kicked him out a couple of months before her death."

"Well that wouldn't make sense, if she committed suicide he wouldn't be entitled to any insurance, it would be void."

"That's what the police said."

"Sorry I haven't got a clue on that then, Louise was an extremely pretty woman, and had a heart of gold. So I can't think of anyone that would have a reason to harm her."

"James Cooper fell in front of a train," Chris said looking again for a reaction from John.

"So I heard, he must have been visiting some friends of his in Glasgow."

"He had friends in Glasgow?"

"James had friends all over the place, he was bisexual."

"Oh, we didn't know that, he actually visited at least four gay bars on the night of his death," Chris told him, so now that was confirmed.

"That doesn't surprise me."

"He was seen drinking with someone just before he died, when they left the pub they were heading to catch the last train home, his drinking partner hasn't been seen since."

"Crikey, that does sound suspicious, and so does Louise's death," John looked confused and bewildered. Chris came to the conclusion that John Palmer didn't know anything about these deaths.

Just as they were about to get up out of the comfortable chairs his wife came back.

"Honey I'm home," she shouted in a weird voice. "I'm coming to get you," she went bright red when she put her head around the door and saw them sitting there.

John hadn't had time to tell her they were coming as she was in a rush to get to her exercise class.

They had parked their car round the back which was out of site.

"Gotcha," Chris thought, "I would recognise that voice anywhere."

They said goodbye and thanked John for his hospitality. On the way back to the office they both confirmed that the voice on the tape belonged to Angela Palmer. What they couldn't figure out was why?

***

Tony was on his way to meet Fiona Jacklin.

He had an appointment with her at the Carlisle office at 10:30.

When he arrived he went through the normal security checks before being sat in a waiting area in the main administration office.

"Mr Lodge?"

"That's me."

"Come through please," he was led into Fiona's office tucked away in the corner on the 1st floor.

"Good morning Mr Lodge, how can I be of assistance?"

"Tony...please call me Tony. As I said on the phone we had a tip-off from an outside source regarding the deaths of two of your ex–colleagues."

"I presume you're talking about James and Louise?"

"Yes that's correct."

"So how can I help you?"

"It's just to ask if you know of any reason why someone would want to kill them?" he waited for some sort of a reaction.

"As far as I was aware Louise committed suicide and James died in an accident."

"That's what we thought to until we received the call, so we sent two investigators to look into their deaths in more detail."

"And?"

"Both deaths have been confirmed as being suspicious."

"I see," she said looking puzzled, "I would never have thought anyone would have reason to kill them."

"No reason at all?"

"No Tony, no reason at all, they were both lovely people and not the type to attract enemies I wouldn't have thought," she said "we knew each other since 2006 when we all started here when it opened, and if anything was unusual we would know, we all got on so well together."

"Okay, thanks for your time Fiona," Tony said as he left her office.

He had planted the seed, but he was under the impression that she didn't know anything about these deaths.

"NO WAY," Tony said as he was told about the guys' suspicions. "What reason would she have to make that kind of call?"

"We both thought the same as soon as we heard that voice," Chris told him. "She wasn't expecting anyone to be there, so she slipped up playing around with a silly scouse accent, just like on the tape."

"It could be anybody on that tape."

"No Tony, it was her on the tape, believe me."

"But why?" Tony asked disbelieving.

"That's a good question, it's totally stumped us."

"I can't do this," Tony said feeling physically sick.

"Don't pull out now mate, we've only just got started making progress, we only need to find the reasons behind it," Chris tried to assure him. "Anyway the fraud department are already a body down for a few weeks."

"Why?"

"Iain Logan had an accident over the weekend and is in hospital, he had to have an operation last night, it was critical at one stage apparently."

Tony couldn't believe he was hearing this, he just wanted to curl up into a ball. "What have you done Lucy?" he thought.

Tony managed to convince Chris to take Sam with him to the meeting with Ray Hessler at 2pm. He said he wasn't feeling in the right frame of mind, and wouldn't be able to concentrate properly.

"Hello," Tony said when Lucy answered the phone.

"Hi Tony, how's things?"

"Never mind how's things, what the hell have you done?"

"What are you talking about?"

"Iain Logan, that's what I'm talking about."

"What about him? I told Becky yesterday I was going to leave it," she said crossing her fingers.

"I'm not stupid Lucy. I don't know what you've done but I'm sure I will find out."

"I don't know what you're talking about."

"It's now 1 o'clock in the afternoon and I'm sure your loving brother would have told you that Iain Logan is off work for at least a month."

"No he hasn't actually, what happened?"

"He had some sort of an accident and needed an operation last night. Apparently it was critical at one stage, he could have died."

"Oh no, that's a shame, but please forgive me for not giving a shit. I don't feel sorry for that jerk."

"Maybe not Lucy, but I hope I don't find out you had anything to do with it."

Lucy put the phone down and then called Lance. He told her not to worry, everything was sorted, and he won't be saying anything to anyone if he knows what's good for him.

"Let's hope so," Lucy said.

Chris and Sam arrived at the Carlisle office of the Department of Work and Pensions at 13:45. They had to follow the same procedures as Tony had earlier, but this time they were taken to the top floor which was currently being renovated, so there was no staff there at all. There was a large meeting table and six chairs in the room, nothing else.

Ray came in five minutes later with a mug of coffee in his hand.

"Good afternoon gentlemen," he said in a sarcastic manner, "What can I do for you today?"

"It's simple," Chris said, already pissed off with his attitude, "we want to know what your involvement was in the deaths of two of your ex-colleagues."

"You what?" he said with a wicked look on his face. "What two ex-colleagues?"

"Louise Tausney and James Cooper."

"Hold on a minute you two; I don't like your accusations."

"Sit down then Mr Hessler, you know where we are from, so cut with the attitude and answer the question."

"Louise committed suicide and James was killed on Christmas Eve when he fell onto a rail track when he was drunk."

"That's what we thought until we received a call telling us otherwise," Chris said staring into his eyes.

"That's all I know I'm afraid, I haven't heard anything different."

He doesn't know anything about the deaths either, Chris was positive about Ray Hessler too.

Chris contacted Tony and arranged to meet in Gretna at 4 o'clock. They went straight into the incident room and updated each other after the day's events.

"Shall I tell you what I think?" Chris asked the other two guys.

"Yes please," they both replied.

"I think Angela Palmer definitely made the call," he reminded them, "I also think John Palmer has the cancer back as he doesn't look very well. This could be the reason why."

"Maybe John found out something about Hessler but doesn't want to get involved himself," Tony suggested.

"Let's look at your breakdown on the board Tony," Chris said flipping back the wall chart to the beginning.

"This message is for your National Fraud manager"

"What Angela is saying here is that the fraud is national, not just at a local level; otherwise why ask for the National Fraud manager. Right?" Chris said looking for feedback.

"We agree," the guys also nodded.

He skipped past the next statement to number three.

"It's too risky for me to identify myself"

"If Angela identified herself it could have repercussions for John and Lance within the DWP… right?"

"Agreed," the two nodded again.

"It's important this is resolved as soon as possible"

"If John Palmer has got the cancer back I'm sure he would like it completed before his time runs out. Right?"

"Absolutely," agreed Tony.

"Don't ignore this call it's not a hoax"

"This speaks for it guys, Angela knows there is a fraud somewhere, which leads us back to number two."

"Investigate Raymond Hessler, especially his past and family members"

"There's only one way forward guys, and that's to talk to Angela Palmer. Agreed?"

They both agree, but Tony was now part of the investigation that included family, his daughter's family.

"What about the deaths of Louise and James?" Tony asked curiously.

"I've came to the conclusion that surprisingly I don't think any of the three that were interviewed have anything to do with the killing of the other two," Chris said confused. "They never showed any signs that they were trying to hide anything. I'm sure they would all pass a lie detector test," he laughed.

"Can we keep this under our hat until we are sure?" asked Tony.

"We can't, Heather has daily updates remember and we only have officially two days left on the case," Chris reminded him.

***

Raymond Hessler went back to his office after the meeting with the two guys from SID. The conversation brought memories flooding back from their past again.

It had taken a couple of months after Archie had retired for them to settle down again. Charlie Grant had set them higher targets and cancelled their monthly meetings. The W5 had eventually started meeting on their own on a monthly basis, and rekindled their weekends away. They had all missed them especially Ray and Louise.

"I didn't think we would ever be here again," Louise said when she was alone with Ray in her room.

"Neither did I," he agreed, "I've really missed you."

It was really weird as even though they saw each other on a daily basis at work, this was a different environment and like a different planet. Carlisle was Carlisle, and Brampton was Brampton. Carlisle was reality and Brampton was fantasy. All five of them used to live the fantasy while they were there, but went back to reality when they got back to Carlisle. An odd hello and smile in the office, but ripped the clothes off each other in Brampton.

Ray even remembered when they found out about James Cooper's sexuality. It was when the bottle had landed on Ray and then James.

"Don't knock it if you haven't tried it," Louise said. "In for a penny, in for a pound."

He didn't enjoy the experience but went along with it in case they decided to drop him out of the group if he refused, after all, what happened in Brampton stayed in Brampton.

They hated Charlie Grant with a vengeance.

"Stitch the bastard up," Archie had said one night when they all met him for a drink.

"How do we do that?" they asked.

"If you all work together I'm sure you will think of a way," Archie said before staggering home from his local.

For the next few weeks all Ray could think about was how they could stitch up Charlie Grant.

***

Tony phoned Heather and told her they were carrying on with their enquiries and making progress slowly but surely. "Roll on Wednesday," said Heather, "let's get this put to bed."

Tony didn't tell her what he was sure she didn't want to know anyway, that there was definitely a case to answer, but it could be at the sacrifice of someone important in his daughter's life. He couldn't even tell Becky, he stayed in the office.

Lance was told by Heather about Iain Logan, he wasn't particularly bothered to be honest. If you screw around with a Palmer then you're going to get your fingers burned.

Lance was worried about his dad, he had lost a lot of weight recently and looked extremely ill. The family had got very close since he was cleared over a year ago, and everything was going fine. He just prayed it wasn't bad news again, he was tired of trying to put things right for the family – not again he hoped.

Chapter Nine

Tony did the un-thinkable, he phoned John Palmer and told him he was coming around at 8 o'clock that evening.

"Any particular reason why Tony," he asked.

"I need to have a chat urgently, can you make sure Angela is there as well."

"Crikey it must be serious," he said. Tony would never stay in the same room if John and Angela were there. It would be as if they were fighting over whether Tony was accepted into the family, he hated it.

Tony took the CD with the phone call on it, and headed for his ex-girlfriend's parents' house.

"Come in Tony," John said waiting at the door. "Would you like a drink?"

"I'd better not thanks, I'm driving."

"What's this about Tony?"

"I think you probably already know John. The two SID officers will be with me when I come tomorrow, so I thought I would come first to forewarn you"

"Warn me about what?"

Tony took the CD out of his jacket pocket, walked to the CD player he had used a million times over the years and pressed the play button.

When it has finished he turned to Angela.

"Chris recognised your voice, I couldn't believe it. I didn't want to believe it and I won't ask you about it."

"Then why did you come then Tony?" Angela asked him.

"Because I care, I care about your family and I care about my daughter's future. Just make sure you've got a good story for tomorrow," Tony said heading towards the door. "If we say 10 o'clock is that too early?"

"No that's fine," Angela said. "Did you know John's got the cancer back, they give him six months maximum."

"Chris guessed that, he told me he was looking frail, and he was right, he said he thought he must have it back."

Lucy must have heard the voices, she came into the lounge where they were standing.

"Hi Tony is everything alright?" she asked moving her eyes towards the kitchen. She always used to do that when she wanted Tony to get away from her parents.

"See you in the morning," Tony said walking towards the door.

"Don't forget this," Angela said rejecting the CD from the unit and passing it to him.

"Thanks, that could have been awkward."

Tony and Lucy walked into the kitchen and she flicked the kettle on.

"You haven't come to tell tales on me have you?"

"Don't be silly Lucy I'm not like that and you know it."

"Then why are you here?"

"Just some personal business with your parents."

"Fraud squad business?"

"I didn't say that just business that's all."

"At 8 o'clock in the evening, yeah right."

"I didn't say anything about you Lucy, I promise."

"Okay I believe you, would you like a coffee?"

"Yes please if you don't mind."

"I never mind you being here, I've missed you, and so has Mellissa."

She moved to put her arms around his neck.

"Don't please Lucy," Tony said moving away. "We both know that would be a bad idea."

"It was worth a try, you do realise I'm still in love with you?"

"I can't believe you ended up in a hotel room with Iain Logan."

"That was a combination of Lance, my dad and me being downright stubborn Tony."

"I thought you had more sense."

"I have, that's why I told him to get off and he decided to tape my mouth, arms and legs."

"I'm sure you've got something to do with the fact he's in hospital."

"Maybe or maybe not, it doesn't matter he's got what he deserved Mr Lodge."

"Okay I'm just worried if anything happens to you Mellissa will suffer."

"She won't Tony, she's always got you and Becky remember."

"True, but I would rather she had her mum."

Tony couldn't put his finger on it, but he felt comfortable standing in the kitchen with Lucy and trying to protect her parents.

What was going on he wondered.

He eventually dragged himself away from the Palmers' house at 11pm.

Lucy ended up being good company and they talked about the past and what had happened to make them split up. In the end they decided they were both at fault and the influence of her parents didn't help either.

At the end of the day Tony found out in his mind which one was the "Love", and which was the "Lust".

***

Tony didn't wake up till 07:30, the day before must have drained him. The day was going to be challenging to say the least, *here we go*.

He walked into the office just before nine, Chris and Sam were waiting patiently in the back office.

"Are you ready for it Tony?" Chris asked giving him a high five.

"As ready as I'll ever be," he said with butterflies moving around in his stomach.

They decided to make the trip in one car. They set off in plenty of time to get there by 10 and face the music.

John and Angela were standing at the door when they arrived.

"Good morning gentlemen, come in please," John said escorting them to the study. "I'm sure this is Deja-vu guys."

"Yeah it seems that way," Chris said. "I presume you know Tony Lodge?"

"I should think so, I've got his daughter staying with us at the moment," he laughed. "For what do I owe this pleasure so soon?"

Tony took the CD from his pocket.

"Do you mind if I play this on your CD player?"

"Be my guest," John said pointing to the corner unit.

Tony followed the same process as the evening before and pressed play on the tape.

When it had finished he asked if he could play it again, which was granted.

He then took it out and put it back in his pocket.

"I'm confused," John said looking at Chris, "I thought you were investigating the deaths of Louise and James."

"We are, it all came about after we received this call," Chris said stuttering.

"What's this call got to do with me?" he asked.

"Don't you recognise the voice?" Chris asked him looking in Angela's direction.

"Should I?" John asked in a questioning tone.

"It's your wife," Chris said looking at Sam for support.

"My wife? Are you joking?"

"I heard her yesterday when she came back from her exercise class," Chris said. "She sounded exactly like that."

John started laughing.

"My wife inherited this house from her grandparents who were originally from "Birkenhead", have you heard of "Birkenhead" young man?"

"Of course."

"As a family tradition every time we enter the house we take off the accent of her ancestors as a standing joke. I can assure you this is not the voice of my wife on that tape."

"The accent sounds exactly the same."

"If you get 100 women to try and impersonate a scouse accent that are not from Liverpool, they will all sound the same."

"Brilliant," Tony thought. "Absolutely brilliant." It was like watching Shakespeare.

They left the Palmer's estate with what seemed like a smacked behind and went back to the office.

Nobody spoke in the car on the way back, Chris was just stunned, he was sure he had it right.

John looked at Angela and almost burst out laughing when they left.

"Do you think I convinced them?" he asked his wife.

"I'm not sure but they looked totally confused when they left."

"We will see, hopefully Tony will guide them in a different direction from now on," he said, " but we will have to tell him the truth at some stage."

When the three of them arrived back in Gretna Tony was the first to break the silence.

"It looks like we are back to the old drawing board lads"

"I was sure we had it wrapped up," Chris said slouching back in his chair.

"He's right though, how can we be 100% sure that was his wife on the tape?" Sam asked.

"True, it wouldn't stand up in a court of law, that's for sure," Tony said, "we need to look at it from a different direction."

"Circles comes to mind," Chris said. "We are going round in bloody circles, going over the same things again and again."

"Maybe it was a hoax and we are looking too much into the two deaths because we want them to be connected," Tony asked.

"Possibly," said Chris. "But it just looks too suspicious to be a coincidence."

"Okay so let's say she didn't make the call and none of the three remaining managers know anything about the two deaths, where does that leave the investigation?" Tony asked.

"Good question," Sam answered.

"Circles," Chris said repeating himself.

"Let's have a couple of hours' break and see if anything comes to mind," Tony suggested.

"Okay," Sam agreed, "I'm getting out of here."

"Me too," Chris said as he disappeared out of the door.

When the lads left Tony called Becky, she would be on her lunch break by now. He gave her the rundown on the case thus far and apologised for not calling her last night. He didn't tell her he was with his ex till 11 o'clock.

But he did tell her about Iain Logan.

"You're joking?" she said. "What the hell did Lucy do to him?"

"That's what I thought but she denies all knowledge."

"Bullshit, it was her guaranteed."

"I wouldn't say it was her personally, but I'm sure she's probably behind it."

"Four weeks in hospital, it must have been something Iain won't forget for a while."

"He said it was an accident according to Heather."

"Well he isn't going to say it was revenge after I raped someone, now would he?"

"Very true Becky, very true."

"What's going to happen now with the fraud case?" Becky asked, she was curious.

"It might just dissolve into oblivion, who knows?"

"But you thought there was something going on didn't you?"

"I'm not sure now, Chris thinks we were just going round in circles and I tend to agree."

"Oh well, let me know."

"Will do sweetheart, talk to you later, and bye."

"Goodbye," Becky said hanging up.

Tony didn't really tell her anything, not about Lucy, not about the tape voice, not about anything that would implicate the Palmers.

When Becky put the phone down she arranged with her manager to have the next two days off. She had something planned after her conversation with Tony, and she would keep it a secret. Her face was beaming from ear to ear and she was excited thinking about her devious plan.

Tony's next call was to John Palmer. He told him he would be there in 30 minutes, and he agreed.

When Tony arrived John had arranged the comfortable chairs in the study so they were facing each other, he thought he was going to take part in *Mastermind*.

There was a coffee table in between the chairs with a teapot, a coffee percolator, milk and sugar. There was also one teacup and one coffee cup on saucers with separate spoons, John preferred tea and he knew Tony liked coffee.

"Two cups," Tony thought, "obviously there was just going to be the two of them," and with the amount of caffeine on display, it could be for a while.

John explained the reason he got Angela to make the call was because he wanted to make sure everything was watertight before the cancer finally finished him off.

He then told him about the five managers' monthly meetings away from the office after Archie McPhee retired, and about their weekends away.

He also told him about Ray Hessler's obsession to get one over on Charlie Grant, and when it all started.

"Ray would rack his brain for weeks on end on how he could get one over on him," he explained, "then he came up with a plan. His sister hadn't long been killed in an accident along with her husband Jake. He used to have a double-barrelled name before they got married. His mum had remarried and added her new husband's name onto the kids. He was known as Jake McCabe Murdoch, but dropped the Murdoch just before they got married, Helen didn't want a double barrelled name."

That was why Tony couldn't find him on the databases.

"Ray's plan was to make a claim for benefit in Jake's name as he had never been on benefits before. He completed the paperwork to claim jobseekers allowance in the name of Jake McCabe Murdoch from his mother's address where he lived before they got married.

"He ran through how it could be processed with the other four managers at one of their monthly meetings, and explained that we would all have to get involved to ensure the claim went successfully through the system.

"Fiona would deal with the administration of the claim; I would ensure the benefit would be administered as a jobseekers allowance claim; James would process a budgeting loan against his name; Louise would set a housing benefit claim up and Ray would make sure it went through finance.

"Louise and Fiona were concerned in case they got caught, but Ray was excellent at convincing them otherwise."

He also explained that the maximum length of time for each claim would be under 6 months. After this the system would generate an automatic instruction for the advisor to call them in for an interview, so after 22 weeks the claim would have to be terminated.

Each manager followed their part of the process.

It was estimated that each claim would generate a total income of just under £9k over the period.

They couldn't believe it when his claim went through without a hitch.

The proceeds were then put into a pot just in case it was found.

In the next meeting Ray had a list of 10 people that had died in the area that was covered by the Carlisle office.

They all agreed to process those and again they went through without a problem.

The following month he appeared with another ten, then so on and so forth.

He changed the benefits claimed to suit the individual's background and put a lot of time and effort into making sure it worked.

He gave them a monthly report of the totals accumulating in the pot.

"What was going to eventually happen to the pot?" Tony asked.

"I will get to that, be patient," John said. "On one of the weekends away it was decided to make a deadline date or amount when we would stop, and then look at how they would split the proceedings.

"We worked out that by 2012 they would have accumulated approximately £15m.

"The agreed date to stop was set at the 25th July 2012."

"Crikey," Tony gasped, "and did they stop?"

"Yes Tony we did."

"And you had your split?"

"No, it was invested."

"Invested in what?"

"Property Tony, one property," John said smiling, "it was a golden opportunity. Ray knew a property developer that had a location going for a song, and as we always did, we sat down and had a vote on what to do."

"What property was it?"

"It was an old castle in the highlands, it had over 10,000 acres of land. Previous owners had been given planning permission to develop the land into a golf course, but the castle could only be renovated as it was a listed building"

"What happened to it?"

"We bought it," he said grinning. "It cost us £12m for the property and £2.5m to develop and renovate the castle. The last valuation we had on it was £83m."

"Wow…you're joking. Right?"

"I'm not joking Tony."

"Who else knew about this?"

"As far as I'm aware, just us five and the property developer – why?"

"Don't you think that would be a good reason to kill off two of your five managers?"

John laughed. "No, whatever happens all five will get 20% of the stake. If they pass away it goes to their next of kin, so there would be no reason to pop each other off, we all loved each other."

"Whose name is the castle registered in?"

"We created a private company in the Seychelles. We called it W5, as in The Wicked Five as we were known."

"Do any of your partners or kids know about this?"

"I told Angela the last time I was diagnosed with cancer, she was worried about her and the kids when I had gone."

"What about Lance or Lucy?"

"No, they don't know anything."

"Why did you risk losing all that by getting your wife to make the phone call, don't you trust Ray or something?"

"I just wanted to put my mind at ease I suppose."

"You could have disturbed a hornet's nest John."

"I know Tony, What do you think?"

"At the moment the hierarchy and Heather think, and I'm sure hope it's a hoax."

"What about Chris and Sam from SID?"

"Chris isn't convinced the call wasn't made by Angela, I'm not sure what his next step could be."

"And what about you, what's your next step?"

"I don't honestly know," he answered, "at this moment my daughter comes first, and she loves her Nan and Granddad."

"Don't forget, her future will be secure."

"Her future will be secure whatever happens as long as I'm around. If I don't say anything and we all get caught then there will only be one future. We will be locked up and Lucy will be on her own."

"There's nothing for them to find."

"I'm not sure," Tony wasn't convinced.

"It's been five years since we stopped and nothing's been detected."

"And probably never would have if you had kept your insecurities to yourself."

"I realise that now."

"Hopefully by the end of play tomorrow Heather will pull the plug on the investigation, unless someone finds something."

"Then just make sure they don't."

"We will see."

"One more thing Tony," John told him. "When we stopped and bought the property we locked the deeds in a safety deposit box."

"What deeds?"

"The deeds for the castle silly, it's got all our five names on them."

"Yes, and?"

"We all wrote down a five letter/digit password and put it into one of the five envelopes Ray gave us on the day. We went to the vault together and secretly put in our code into the digital locking system. Without all five codes, we can't open the vault to access the deeds."

"What difference does that make if it's in the name of the company?"

"The company details are in there too proving who the owners of the company are," John explained, "and before you ask, no it wouldn't be a reason to bump each other off, same rule applies, next of kin etc."

"So why the envelopes?"

"If something happened to one of us, the stamp addressed envelope would go to the vault company manager for safekeeping until the agreed date to open the vault."

"Do you have an agreed date?"

"Yes January 1st 2020, all five of us were hoping to be around at the time."

"And now at most just the two of them."

"Unfortunately, but at least all the families will be looked after."

"Let's hope so John, let's hope so."

Tony contacted Sam and Chris and asked them to meet him in the Gretna office at 9 in the morning. He reminded them this could be their last day.

Chapter Ten

Ray Hessler finished work early as his wife had an appointment at the hospital.

Some more tests, another waste of time as far as he was concerned.

He arrived home from work at 2:45pm, her appointment was at 3:30pm and the hospital was only half an hour's drive away.

Jenny was well prepared as usual, waiting at the door with all her necessities in her bag.

"Hello dear," he said opening the front passenger side door. "All prepared as usual?"

"You only moan if you have to wait," she replied.

"How long will these set of tests take this time?"

"They said about an hour and a half in total."

"I will have a drive into town after I've dropped you off while you're being poked and prodded if that's ok with you?"

"Yes Raymond I don't mind, you don't have to do anything when you're there anyway."

Ray took her to the hospital, got Jenny out of the car and slotted her into the NHS wheelchair provided.

It wasn't as comfortable as her own but saved packing and unpacking hers every time.

"See you around five dear."

"No problem, can you get some cranberry sauce? We've run out and I'm making a roast for later."

"Will do."

"Don't be late, the meat is in the oven."

"Okay see you later."

Jenny's tests were completed and she was waiting in the hospital reception to be wheeled to the car.

It was five o'clock and still no sign of her husband.

"Where is he?" she wondered.

It then became half past five, then six o'clock and still he hadn't turned up.

She didn't possess a mobile phone as when she left the house Ray was always with her.

This was unusual, he was always a stickler for time and hated being late.

When half past six came she decided to call a taxi, her two kids lived too far away to help out.

She asked to borrow the wheelchair and promised to return it the following day, which was granted.

When she arrived home Ray's car wasn't on the drive.

"Sorry driver you will have to trust me and come back later, my husband's not back yet to pay you."

"That's not a problem madam," the driver said as he took the wheelchair out of the boot and helped her to get comfortable.

He then pushed her to the door.

Jenny told him where he would find the spare key, "That will need a new hiding place," she thought.

She could smell the burning meat from the oven and switched it off, forget dinner.

After Ray left the hospital he headed straight for town. He parked his car in the multi storey car park and walked into the centre where he stopped at a café for a cappuccino.

He then went to the supermarket and bought cranberry sauce for his wife, and some apple sauce for himself "still only half past four" he thought looking at his watch.

"No way," he said to himself. "That's not Fiona Jacklin in the supermarket?" It was and she recognised him too.

"Good afternoon Fiona."

"Mr Hessler, it's been a long time since we've been able to talk just the two of us," she said smiling.

They arranged to meet back at the café where Ray had been earlier.

Time just evaporated, before they knew it they were being asked to leave so the girl behind the counter could go home.

It was now six o'clock and Ray would be in trouble, it was great to see and talk to Fiona about old times.

Although he saw her at work most days, it wasn't appropriate to chat on a one to one basis.

He tried calling the hospital but spoke to an answering machine, and it was the same at home but he left a message at five past six.

Fiona asked if he had a visit from Tony Lodge the new member of the fraud team, but he told her he had been seen by two damned rude members of the Special Investigations Department instead.

"I can't believe they think James and Louise may have been killed," Fiona said.

"Nor me, who would want to kill them?"

"Beats me, I'm sure they have got something mixed up somewhere."

"Probably, have you spoken to John recently?"

"Not for a few months, he's been bad especially after the cancer scare, I didn't want to disturb him," Ray said, "but we might need to."

"Why, what's wrong?"

"I don't like the idea that fraud and SID are sniffing around, we might need to bring forward the date for cashing in our inheritance."

"Wouldn't it be better to keep our heads down? If they catch wind of anything we could attract unnecessary attention," Fiona advised him.

"Yeah you're probably right but we should consult John and get his opinion."

"Why don't you both come round tomorrow night for dinner at my house?"

"What time?"

"Six o'clock would be perfect, Henry will be out at his lodge meeting."

"Okay, I will inform John, if there's any problems I'll call you, can I just confirm your number?"

She did, then Ray called her back so she could register his number on her phone.

It was half past seven when he eventually got home. Jenny was livid.

"I was just about to call the police and register you as a missing person" she shouted.

"I'm sorry I was captured again by the two guys from SID, they asked me to go into their office for questioning," he said, not thinking of any other excuse.

"What's their problem? What have you done?"

"Nothing, their investigating a tip-off about the deaths of Louise and James. Our colleagues that started the same time as the rest of the managers in 2006."

"What's that got to do with you?"

"Nothing dear, absolutely nothing. Didn't you get my message?"

"What message?"

Ray walked across to the answering machine. There were 10 messages on the machine, dating back 3 months.

"I don't know how to use that thing," his wife said.

"Fantastic, it's just as well I hadn't been in an accident or something," he said wiping off the messages.

"Dinner's ruined, we will have to get a takeaway unless you want a sandwich."

"I'm not hungry," he said taking his phone out to the reception area to call John Palmer.

He organised for them to be at Fiona's house at six o'clock on Wednesday evening, she still lived at the same address.

Ray texted her to confirm and walked down the local chip shop for fish and chips for him and Jenny.

***

Becky left home at 6am and headed south, she was on her way to see Tony in Gretna Green.

"I'm sure he won't mind," she thought, "it will be a nice surprise."

She arrived at the same time as Tony, Sam and Chris. Tony's face was a picture.

"What are you doing here?"

"I've booked a couple of days off," she told him, "I thought I would come and see where you're working in case it's your last day."

"I've got to go into a meeting with Chris and Sam," he said introducing them, "I'm not sure how long we will be."

"That's ok I will wait out here, have you got a computer I can play on until you finish," she asked.

Tony took her into the back room and switched the computer on.

"You can get into Google and stuff, but not any of the DWP databases, they are password protected," he told her, "so don't try putting any codes in as it's monitored by head office and you will get me into trouble."

"I won't, don't worry," she said with fingers crossed.

Tony had always told her he used the same password for everything as he didn't have a good memory for codes, "Mellissa12", his daughter's name and year of birth, easy for him to remember.

Becky was flicking through the databases after inputting Tony's password correctly for over an hour.

She found what she was looking for then logged off, left Tony a note telling him something came up and to come back to their weekend apartment when he finished, and headed out of the Gretna office.

Her next stop was to meet Lucy Palmer at her local coffee shop.

Tony, Chris and Sam were in the "incident room" with flipcharts, walls littered with information, and notepads in front of them. They started going through things for what could be the last time.

From what was in front of them they still didn't have anything concrete on the fraud accusation aimed at Raymond Hessler.

They couldn't prove conclusively that Angela Palmer was the woman on the voice tape.

Even the suspicious deaths of James Cooper and Louise Tausney were inconclusive.

All this time and effort had come to nothing. Was there anything they could do for the rest of the day that might change things?

"Nothing," Tony said, "I can't see anywhere else we can go, or anyone else we can see to change what we already have."

"All this hard work for what?" Sam asked. "Maybe we should contact the police forces involved in the deaths and try to get them to reopen the cases."

"We didn't find anything more than the police already looked at," Chris reminded them, "it's just because we may have wanted to find something, and they didn't."

Heather called at 12 o'clock and asked all three of them to be at the office in Edinburgh for 4pm.

"The final countdown," Chris said and Tony agreed.

"Better luck next time."

Becky met Lucy in Carlisle. She didn't want to go to Lucy's parents' house as she would have felt uncomfortable, so the local coffee shop was fine.

"Can I ask you something?" Becky said looking at Lucy.

"Try me," Lucy answered.

"What's it like to get your revenge on someone?"

"I'm not sure I know what you're asking me."

"I think you do Lucy, what happened to Iain Logan?"

"I told you, he raped me."

"Yes, you told us, and it looks like you got your revenge."

"I don't know what you're talking about Becky."

"I just want to know what it felt like."

"I wasn't upset when I heard the news if that's what you meant."

"You know exactly what I meant Lucy."

"Okay it felt great, I wasn't going to sit back and let him get away with it. The police would have taken ages to do anything."

"It looks like you did him good, he's in hospital for 3 or 4 weeks apparently."

"I don't know to be honest, and I don't really care. He won't be raping anyone again though."

"Let's hope not."

"Exactly."

Becky finished her coffee and said goodbye.

Tony tried to call her to let her know he had to go back to Edinburgh for a meeting, but she wasn't answering her phone, so he left a message.

They arrived back in the Edinburgh office and were immediately summoned into the Directors' meeting room. They were then joined by Heather, Edward Foster – MP secretary of state for DWP, Andrew Snead – Internal Communications and James Patriot – Deputy Director for News/Media/Press.

The meeting was short, sweet and to the point.

They were relieved that nothing was found to implicate Raymond Hessler in the accusation, and were unanimous in the decision to close the investigation with immediate effect.

They thanked all three of them for their time and efforts in the investigation, and told them to have the next two days off as a gesture of goodwill from the department.

Chris wasn't happy the he didn't have the opportunity to voice his concerns about the deaths of James Cooper and Louise Tausney, but it was obvious that they just wanted this episode behind them.

Heather met them outside and apologised for the abruptness of the meeting. She was shocked, but could understand the relief felt by the department heads.

She told them to enjoy their two complimentary days off, and to report back at their normal offices when they returned.

Tony said he would clear out the offices in Gretna as soon as he could and return the key to the I.T. department in Carlisle.

Tony tried Becky's number again, but now it was going straight onto the answering services, so he left another message.

He arrived home about six o'clock to an empty house, there was no sign of Becky.

He got her note that she left in Gretna asking him to go back to the weekend apartment, but he left her a message to say he was coming back home.

Maybe she had decided to stay south of the border after all as she had booked a couple of days off work.

They didn't have a landline connected as they spent little time there, so they didn't see the point.

***

Ray and John arrived at Fiona's for dinner just before six, she had made a chilli-con-carne with garlic bread knowing they all liked it, and her husband could have some when he got home.

"You're looking a bit thin John," Fiona told him.

"Unfortunately my cancer has come back," he told her. "The point of no return."

"I'm sorry to hear that," Ray said sadly.

"I've had a good innings to be honest, I can't complain," he said with a smile.

"I don't know what I would be like in the same boat," said Ray.

"Thin," John said and they all started laughing. At least he hadn't lost his sense of humour.

"As long as my family are going to be okay I can deal with it."

"I was going to suggest we brought the date forward for cashing in our little venture," Ray suggested, "especially with this investigation going on."

"That's finished now," John told them, "it was shelved this afternoon."

"How do you know that?" Fiona asked.

"Let's say I've got eyes and ears everywhere," John laughed.

"You mean Lance?" she asked.

"Amongst others, yes. We don't have to worry about that anymore."

"That's a relief," Ray said. "Shall we bring the date forward or not?"

"Yes I think we should," Fiona said, "at least there will be the three of us before John goes."

"I agree," said John, "it will make me feel so much better knowing it's done and dusted."

"How about Monday August 14th?" Ray suggested.

"Yes, that's fine," the other two agreed.

Ray phoned Glasgow Vaults while the other two were there, it was open until 9pm, and made an appointment for 10am on 14th August.

Julia Webb wrote the appointment in her diary.

She had been with Glasgow Vaults for 15 years and was the organiser of the contract for W5 in the Seychelles.

She opened up the safe in her office and retrieved the two envelopes marked W5 and placed them in her diary beside the date.

These had been received via recorded delivery from a solicitor's office shortly after the two clients had passed away.

Julia had a list of the five names related to W5 on file and was told that in case of death she would receive a sealed envelope with the name of the client.

She was then to check whether their deaths were linked to anyone else in the group, if so and the person was found guilty, the envelopes already received were to be destroyed without the seal broken.

She was aware of the company and its members, but wasn't aware of what was in the deposit box.

***

Tony was getting worried, it was now half past seven in the evening and he still hadn't heard from Becky.

He decided to drive to the weekend retreat in Scotby to see if Becky was there. When he arrived there was no sign of Becky being there since they left on Sunday. Everything was exactly as they had left it.

"Where could she have gone?" he pondered. "And why hasn't she returned my call?"

Tony called her mum but she hadn't spoken to her since the last night. She had told her she was going to surprise him but didn't say how. Now her mum was worried.

When she put the phone down to her mum, Lucy rang.

"Hello handsome," she said happily, "how's the case going?"

"It's been cancelled surprise, surprise," he told her, "I don't suppose you've heard from Becky by any chance?"

"Yeah I saw her today, why?"

"She's disappeared, I can't get hold of her."

"No way," she said, "she was a bit weird today. I don't know if it's related but she was asking me what it felt like to get revenge on Iain Logan."

"You didn't tell her did you Lucy?"

"She kept pestering me, so I told her it felt great, why?"

"Bloody Robert Cowie, that's why."

"Oh shit," Lucy said realising now why she was asking her about Logan.

"Bollocks I will have to call you back," Tony said rushing out of the door.

He drove straight to Gretna Green and opened up the office, it was lucky he still had the keys.

He switched on the computer and logged onto recently accessed files.

In the DWP database was the file for Robert Cowie, the file had been accessed at 8:43am the time that Becky was in the office while he was in his meeting.

He noted the address and locked up sharply before racing 2.6 miles to Cowie's listed address in Mossband.

The light was on in what looked like a front room of the house, but the curtains were drawn.

It wasn't quite dark yet but not far off so Tony knocked on the door.

It was opened by an elderly woman.

"Hi I'm looking for Robert," Tony told her, "Robert Cowie?"

"Bloody hell," she said, "two people in one day I can't believe it. His ex-girlfriend, Becky I think her name is called earlier looking for him."

"Is he here?"

"No, he moved out two months ago, got his own place"

"Did you tell Becky where he lives?"

"Yes, but I told her he doesn't finish work till 10 o'clock and won't be back until about half past."

"What's his address?"

The woman gave Tony his address, and he scribbled it down. It was 15 minutes away by car according to his satnav, so it should get him there just before 10:30pm.

Tony got there at 10:25pm and saw Becky's car parked on the corner of the road.

He pulled up behind her and jumped out of his car.

Becky was sitting staring at the road in front of her, waiting.

She had a baseball bat on the front passenger seat beside her, and a can of legal pepper spray.

Tony opened the passenger side door and jumped in.

"I hope they're not for me," he said smiling.

Becky burst into tears and threw her arms around him.

"I'm sorry Tony. I'm so sorry," she said with floods of tears.

Just then a car pulled up and parked directly outside the address Tony had scribbled on his piece of paper.

The driver inside shuffled around for a while before opening their door.

He then slid out what looked like a wheelchair, and gradually managed to manoeuvre himself out of the car, close the door and sit down.

"Is that him?" Tony asked.

"My god, yes it is," Becky's face changed. "The lord moves in mysterious ways."

On the way back to Scotby, they visited who turned out to be Robert Cowie's mother.

She told them he had become disabled two years ago when he was diagnosed with Becker Muscular Dystrophy.

It was inherited from his granddad, he refused to do exercises or have treatment and just gloats in his own self-pity, his mum told them.

Tony told Becky that unfortunately for Cowie the disease had a much better result for her than the baseball bat could ever have had, she agreed.

They sat and talked for hours when they got back and he made her promise never to pull a stunt like that ever again.

She hadn't answered her phone because she knew she wouldn't have been able to lie to him, and knew he would have talked her out of it.

"What Lucy did was wrong Becky, I'm sure the police would have been a better option," Tony told her.

"I understand what you're saying, but I can also sympathise with Lucy, she was devastated I'm sure."

"I know but it still doesn't justify what she did."

"Okay let's just agree to disagree," she said laughing.

"When do you go back to work?"

"Friday," she said. "Why do you ask?"

"I'm not back until Monday, let's find a flight somewhere and go away for a long weekend."

"Sounds great, let me call my boss in the morning, it shouldn't be a problem."

They flew off to Crete from Edinburgh airport on Thursday morning, due back on Sunday afternoon. When they landed Tony was tempted to switch off his phone, but realised he couldn't, he had a four year-old daughter who might want to say hello.

***

Thursday night and off goes Henry to another one of his lodge meetings.

Fiona's husband joined the Masonic Lodge 20 years ago and was recognised in their command as an acting officer. It was a matter of life or death for Henry, he loved the commitment and dedication he gave to the Freemasons.

Fiona on the other hand loved watching the soaps and was up to date in Albert Square, the Rovers Return as well as Emmerdale.

She was settling down for a quiet night in front of the TV.

They lived in a small village called Monkhill, 5.2 miles from Carlisle in a bungalow all on its own, purpose-built.

It was lovely and quiet and far enough away to not be bothered by neighbours. They both enjoyed living there.

Fiona heard what sounded like a banging noise coming from the kitchen.

It sounded just like when she had left the back door open and it got caught in the wind last week.

"It doesn't sound windy outside," she thought, "and I'm sure I locked the door when I took the rubbish out."

It was 11:30pm when Henry pulled onto their driveway.

"She's left the bloody lights on again," he said mumbling to himself.

The front door hadn't been locked either, as it opened when he turned the handle.

Henry found his wife's body in the kitchen with what looked like a head wound. He called an ambulance and the police, but it was too late.

He tried to wake her up before the emergency services had arrived, he thought she might have just knocked herself out when she fell.

There was no evidence of a struggle, or any weapons lying around if she was hit by someone, so he presumed she must have fallen over and banged her head.

The police asked him the usual questions and searched inside and outside the bungalow. They had spotlights at the back and at the side of the house, so it was now illuminated like a football pitch.

No sign of forced entry and as far as Henry could see at first glance there was nothing missing. The officer said they would carry out a post mortem to confirm the cause of death. He thought she may have hit her head on the corner of the work surface as there was some blood in that area.

Chapter Eleven

Chris Higgins was called into Heather's office on Friday just before lunchtime. He received the call at half past 10 in the morning and was told to get there as quickly as possible.

"What the hell has happened now," Chris thought to himself.

He was on the way to Torquay with his wife and son for the weekend, so he had to make a detour back and drop his family back at home.

"Give me time off, then take it back, nice one," he thought, "now I'm in the doghouse with my wife and kid."

When he walked into the office he was taken straight to the boardroom.

Waiting there were Heather, Edward Foster, Andrew Snead and James Patriot. "Snap," he thought. "Exactly the same gang as before."

"Sorry to call you back from your day off," Heather said.

"That okay, it wasn't my day off anyway," he said smiling.

"I know you were involved in looking into the deaths of James Cooper and Louise Tausney," she explained, "can you tell the guys what you found and why you weren't happy with the outcome?"

Chris explained in detail exactly what he and Sam had found and what reasons they had for it to raise suspicion in both cases.

He told them that he wasn't impressed with the sloppy police work, and what he would have done differently.

Edward Foster was the Secretary of State for Work and Pensions and was as cute as they come. He was only recently given the role and wanted to impress the Prime Minister.

"All this starts from an anonymous phone call into the department," he said, "and then three of you try to investigate a fraud, but come up with a potential murder enquiry, interesting."

"One just led onto the other sir," Chris said respectfully.

"I understand that Chris, and given what you have told us I tend to agree with you, it does seem to smell a bit."

"Which leads us to why you're here Chris," Heather said. "We've been informed this morning that Fiona Jacklin was found dead by her husband when he returned home last night."

"What?" Chris was shocked. "It doesn't make sense."

"What doesn't make sense Chris?" Edward asked.

"I interviewed the other two managers Ray Hessler and John Palmer and none of them have any reason to kill anyone."

"Nobody said Fiona was killed," Heather said. "But I'm sure it's a possibility."

"Maybe you've all missed something," said Edward, "I want you to go through everything again and see if anything less obvious jumps out at you."

"Circles, bloody circles," Chris mumbled. "It's all we did for almost two weeks was go round in circles."

"Then get off your merry-go-round and bloody find something."

Edward was losing it, he knew he would be the one under the spotlight when this became public knowledge.

"I presume that I am working on this by myself since nobody else is here?" Chris asked.

"No Chris, you will have the assistance of Sam and Tony again, but this time you are in charge," Heather said.

"You mean it's my head on the block?"

"No, you're the most experienced and you've got a good head on your shoulders."

"Thanks for that vote of confidence," Chris said as the pack left the boardroom at the same time.

***

Henry Jacklin picked up the phone and dialled John Palmer's number. Lucy answered and told him her parents had gone shopping.

Henry asked her to pass the message on after telling Lucy about his wife, and asked her to get her dad to call him back as soon as he was free.

John and Angela were unpacking the shopping from the car when Lucy gave her dad the news.

"You're joking," John said.

"I don't think Henry would joke about something like that Dad."

"I just can't believe it," he was distraught. "It's like the five of us were jinxed."

"What will happen to the money?" Lucy asked.

"What money?"

"The money you swindled from the DWP?"

"We didn't swindle any money Lucy."

"I'm not stupid Dad, I've known for almost six years."

"Known what for six years?"

"About the "Wicked Five" and your nest egg," Lucy told him.

"How the hell?" he said looking at his wife.

"It's news to me too," Angela said. They both then looked at their daughter.

"It must have been the night you all had a meeting and you'd had a few drinks," she said, "you came home drunk and all the paperwork fell out of your jacket pocket, including a sealed envelope. There were notes on pieces of paper that didn't make sense, but when I opened the envelope and found a password with your next of kin and a date in 2020 I kind of put two and two together."

"Have you told anyone?"

"No Dad, not even Tony," she said, "I was going to but I told Lance instead. He looked through everything and couldn't make 100% sense of it, so that's when he asked you to get him into the fraud section at DWP. He wanted to find out exactly what was going on."

"And did he find out?"

"He said not, but the more I think about it the more I think he knows something, but won't tell me."

"I thought the seal had broken because I had dropped it," John said thinking back.

"No Dad we put it back in your pocket after we read it."

"It cost me £100 to get that resealed back to its original state," he said grinning.

"You can afford it now it will just be split between two of you," Lucy told him.

"Who told you that?" John asked.

"Well it's obvious, the fewer left of the five of you the more you will share."

"It doesn't work like that Lucy, we will all have 20%. If anything happened to any of us, it goes to the next of kin. That's why they were listed in the sealed envelope," he explained.

"Oh. Okay now I know," Lucy said puzzled.

John Palmer's mind was racing, he wasn't aware both his kids knew about the fraud.

If they thought the money was only being shared with surviving members of the group, and then he was diagnosed with cancer?

Both James and Louise were killed when he had it the first time, and when he had the all clear, nothing happened afterwards.

Now that he looks ill again maybe, just maybe they guessed he's got it back.

"Oh shit, what am I going to do?" John was worried.

Lucy phoned Lance to let him know about Fiona Jacklin, he didn't sound surprised. He remembered visiting her with their dad once and noticed it was in a rural part of the country.

Chris Higgins decided to head for Fiona Jacklin's house and see what he could find out. When he got there most of her close family were there, including her husband.

He introduced himself then asked Henry if it was okay to have a look round, he didn't mind.

Chris thought he was probably still in shock.

He looked in the kitchen first to see where she was found, then started looking to see where access could be made to the kitchen from the outside.

Apart from someone walking in through the front door, the only other access to the kitchen would be through the back door or one of the downstairs windows.

He noticed that all the windows had internal latches fitted, and they were all in the closed position. Henry confirmed they were always set like that as they never had to open the windows.

So the only other access point was from the back door.

He checked the door, no damage, and then walked outside to see if there were any tell-tale signs of an intruder.

He couldn't find anything obvious and his only other thought was that somebody might have had a back door key.

This looked like an accident on this occasion as far as Chris could see, but three out of three deaths in a fraud-related case all accidents? He didn't think so.

He contacted both Sam and Tony and gave them the heads up on what was happening on Monday.

They would meet back at Gretna Green as before but this time they would have Sergeant Lee Monk from Cumbria Police Force in their presence.

Tony was completely dumbfounded.

"What's going on?" he thought.

They must have missed something, surely this wasn't another coincidence? He was going to have another chat with John Palmer.

He told Becky about Fiona Jacklin and told her he was driving straight to their weekend apartment when they got back from Crete.

He had the key to get into Gretna and they wanted to start early on Monday morning.

He then phoned John and arranged to meet him at his apartment in Scotby on Sunday evening.

He couldn't stop thinking about it all weekend, he was pleased they had put Chris in charge this time, especially now he knew about the fraud himself.

He needed to be extremely cautious on how he handled the situation from now on, but was serious about finding out who and why someone was killing off the original five.

Maybe John was next, or even Ray Hessler, or was it one of them that was the guilty party?

***

Tony and Becky flew back from their short break and Tony kissed her goodbye before driving to Scotby.

John turned up at 8 o'clock and was looking even frailer than before.

"You're really looking ill now John," he told him. "Are you feeling okay?"

"Not really, I'm just tired all the time, somehow I don't think I will last too much longer."

"More reason to get this sorted as soon as possible."

"It's getting worse Tony," John said.

He told him about his conversation with Lucy, and about Lance.

He also told him about his concerns on whether or not his kids could actually be at the bottom of the killings.

"I would have said no up until about a week ago, but now I'm not so sure," Tony said.

"Why until a week ago?"

Tony told him all about Lucy being raped by Iain Logan, who ended up in a hospital bed for four weeks.

He told him he suspected Lance would have been behind the revenge attack, probably with his boyfriend Geoffrey.

John was horrified and couldn't understand why she didn't tell him.

"She said you advised her not to go out with him, and she didn't listen to your advice."

"There was just something about the creep," John said.

"She felt guilty and blamed herself, and she also blamed Lance for setting her up in the first place."

"He always did like to interfere, especially where Lucy was concerned."

"That's why I think he got revenge on him for his sister."

"Do you think they could have killed Louise, James and Fiona?"

"I'm not sure to be honest, it's possible, let me make a few more enquiries."

"I hope not, I will never forgive myself if it ruins my family, this was supposed to set them up for life."

"Who else knew about this apart from the five of you and the property developer, can you think of anyone else?"

"Not that I can think of, unless Lucy or Lance told someone."

"I can't believe Lucy never even told me, so she would definitely not have told anyone else," Tony said.

"That's true, what about Lance?"

"I'm sure he would have told Geoffrey, otherwise why would he give up a promising career in accounts to join the DWP?"

"That's true, I didn't think of that."

"Could the two of them be capable?"

"Makes sense I suppose, especially in James Cooper's death."

"Will you tell your Sergeant and Chris Higgins tomorrow?" John asked with a sad-looking face.

"Not yet, I will let the enquiry take its course before I get involved. I will stay in the background now I know I'm not in the spotlight."

"Just another thing while I remember it," John said. "Each time we met up with Archie McPhee in his local, it was always Archie that was feeding Ray Hessler with ideas on how to stitch up Charlie Grant. I'm not sure if he was enjoying the wind-up or had something against him."

"Did Archie know about the deception in the end?"

"I'm not sure, I don't think so. Ray would have told us if he did."

"Okay maybe something to look into," Tony said. "I will have to tell Ray Hessler I know what's going on."

"To be honest you've got no choice, otherwise we will all be dead, and nothing will be collected," John joked.

Tony wasn't laughing, he was convinced someone else was involved in this fraud.

Either directly or indirectly and it was costing the others their lives.

"This isn't a coincidence," Tony thought, "if this isn't solved quickly someone else could be rich at the Wicked Five's expense."

John Palmer left and headed home, he was tired and was looking forward to a hot bath, then bed.

Lucy was waiting for him when he got back.

"What did Tony have to say then Dad?"

"Who?"

"I just followed you earlier, and surprise, surprise you went straight to the apartment where I drop my daughter off at the weekends."

"Why are you following me Lucy?"

"Because I'm worried about you, you look terrible."

"I'm fine darling, stop worrying," he lied, he felt awful. "Tony knows everything, he guessed before, and me and your mum had to tell him. Don't worry though he's not going to tell anybody."

"Of course he will stupid, he's head of the investigation, he'll get into serious trouble if he doesn't tell them," she said sobbing.

"He's not in charge of the case now Lucy, Chris Higgins is and they've got the police involved as well," he told her. "So Tony's keeping a low profile and will let us know what's going on."

"This is a disaster Dad, we are going to end up with nothing and in a lot of trouble."

"You're not involved Lucy, and I wish we had never got involved in the first place, it seemed like a good idea at the time," he said, "three colleagues are dead and it's getting worse, we would be better off out of it anyway, you don't need the money or the stress."

"It's a bit late for that," Lucy was petrified.

"Why didn't you tell me about that scumbag Logan?"

"Bloody big mouth Lodge," she scowled, "he got what he deserved, he won't do it again in a hurry."

"Was it Lance that sorted him out?"

"Yes Dad it was Lance, he was the one that persuaded me to go on a date with the jerk in the first place."

"Tony was right then," he said. "Tony's always right."

John was worried now, he thought Lance and his partner Geoffrey could be responsible for what was taking place, and Ray Hessler could be his next target.

Even though it was late Tony took a chance on calling Ray Hessler.

His wife answered the phone, Ray was asleep but she woke him up as Tony said it was important.

He was due in Gretna at eight, so he arranged to meet Ray at his house at 7 o'clock in the morning.

When Tony arrived Ray was still in his dressing gown.

"I'm in no rush this morning," he said. "I will get there when I get there. What's so important that it can't wait till office hours Mr Lodge?"

Tony told him everything that he knew and told him that he was concerned that he was now a potential target.

"I wondered why all this attention started," he said, "I thought it was supposed to be for my 25th anniversary with the department, or that's what my wife was led to believe."

"Yes, sorry about that we couldn't exactly say we had a phone call could we?"

"I suppose not, but what's John Palmer playing at, we are almost home and dry. The date has been brought forward so we could put things to bed once and for all."

"I know, we had put things to rest as well until Fiona Jacklin died, then the alarm bells started ringing again in head office."

"What happened to Fiona?" Ray asked.

"Apparently an accident, no suspicious circumstances or anything to say otherwise."

"Then why the alarm bells?"

"It just doesn't add up why three of the managers in the loop have passed away and your name was linked to a possible fraud."

"It's like I told your two cronies, none of us had any reason to take the others' lives, and it was all tied up. As you know the 20% of the inheritance would go to the next of kin if anyone passed away, so why bump each other off."

"That's what I don't understand," Tony emphasised, "It doesn't look logical, but doesn't look natural if you know what I mean."

"Yes I do, maybe it is just sheer coincidence and it's being blown out of proportion."

"Maybe, maybe not. Did anyone else know about the fraud or even have an inkling in what was going on?" Tony asked.

"Not that I can think of," he answered.

"What about Archie? John said he was involved in some of the conversations."

"In the early days yes he was involved, he wasn't happy with the way Charlie Grant treated us. As far as Archie was concerned we were his team and Charlie was destroying what he had put in place, so he suggested we stitched him up."

"In what way?"

"He said if we worked together we would find a way."

"Obviously you did, but did Archie know?"

"Not really, but he had lots of ideas on different things and even came up with the idea of having a safety deposit box so we couldn't rip each other off," Ray laughed.

"So the eventual fraud was your idea?"

"Yeah, I think so but obviously it was discussed over a few different meetings before I came up with a definite plan."

"Were you all at the meetings?"

"Mostly yes, maybe an odd time one of us couldn't make it."

"And Archie?"

"We met at his local pub, so he was only five minutes' walk away. Sometimes he wasn't there for the whole time, he couldn't hold his drink, so when he had enough he went home."

"So Archie was part of the decision on the final plan."

"No, we didn't discuss this when he was there, we organised the final points when he had gone, we didn't want him to be involved."

Time was getting on so Tony said his farewells and made his way to meet the guys in Gretna.

Tony had most of the information about the fraud that he needed and knew he couldn't share it with any of the guys or the policeman that was meeting them in the office.

He wondered what the plan was going to be in the next steps of the enquiry, Tony was planning a trip to see Archie McPhee whenever he could sneak away.

Chris had swapped the rooms around to suit his way of working, they were now convened in the front office.

He had brought a table from the back office into the room and put it together with the existing table to replicate a meeting room. He had placed six chairs around the desks and there was paperwork beside each place in preparation for the meeting.

It looked well organised, but Tony thought this was for the sergeant's benefit, to impress.

When they had all arrived and made themselves a drink Chris started the meeting.

"Good morning gents, just to let you know what our instructions are: to re-open the case with regards to the accusation of fraud directed at Raymond Hessler," Chris started. "As you are aware, after several days of investigation there was nothing found to substantiate the claims. However, what was found and became a matter of suspicion were the deaths of both James Cooper and Louise Tausney."

Chris had found recent photos of both of them and had pinned them onto a freshly prepared notice board in his new office, their names were labelled above the photos.

"Now in addition to these two we have unfortunately received the news of the further death of Fiona Jacklin late last week," he said pointing to a photo of Fiona placed next to the other two. "Our briefing now is to investigate all three deaths and to try and find a link if there is one."

He went through his and Sam's findings from their visits to Keswick and Glasgow, and his visit and findings when he went to see Fiona's husband.

He did emphasise that he didn't find anything suspicious while he was there, but was waiting for the results of the post mortem.

"So none of the deaths have been listed as suspicious by the relevant forces," Lee Monk asked.

"Not at the moment," Chris replied.

"Two of the deaths were in 2015, right?"

"Yes, but we looked carefully at both as we said, and found they were suspicious, that was the opinion of all three of us," he said looking in Sam and Tony's direction.

"Don't you think the police looked into all the areas of doubt before they closed the investigation?" Lee said shaking his head.

"It's just what we found, it looked suspicious."

"An opinion is an opinion, with suspicion you need proof, was there any proof?"

"Well no, not concrete proof."

"What am I doing here?" Lee commented "just because a bloody Member of Parliament feels under pressure, we have to scrutinise three different police force investigations to make sure they were handled correctly?"

"My sentiments exactly," Tony laughed.

"Okay let's get on with it," Lee snapped. "Where are we going first?"

Chris asked them to read the itinerary that he had placed on the table before they came in. he had split them into two teams, Chris and Lee in one team, who were going to Glasgow to revisit the death of James Cooper and Tony and Sam who were back on the case for Louise Tausney.

Tony was going to squeeze in a visit to see Archie along with this one, he just had to lose Sam for a while.

***

Lucy loved her dad, looking at him she knew he was definitely not in good health so she asked her mum.

"Dad's got the cancer back hasn't he?" she said with tears in her eyes.

129

"Yes darling he has," her mum answered her bursting into tears.

"He looks so frail and ill, how long has he got do you think?"

"He was given a maximum of six months if he was having treatment, but he refused. He seems to have deteriorated over the last couple of weeks since this fraud thing started," her mum said, "he just wants to get it out of the way and go in peace, but it's getting to him I'm sure, especially after Fiona dying as well."

"He's lived with this on his mind for 10 years now, it must have had an impact," Lucy said. "Why did he have to get you to call Mum?"

"Guilt I think Lucy, he felt so much guilt and remorse and didn't want you and Lance to brunt the backlash if he was caught after he'd gone."

"We should have told him years ago that we knew, maybe that would have made a difference."

"What's done is done, as long as you and Lance are okay that's all that matters to your dad now."

"We will be fine Mum, we will be fine," Lucy said crying into a tissue. She then contacted Lance to tell him about their dad.

"I guessed that weeks ago," he told her, "he hasn't looked well for ages."

Chapter Twelve

Chris and Lee set off for Glasgow's main police HQ on Stewart Street.

Lee had contacted them and arranged a briefing with Sergeant Joseph Beckett, he was one of the officers in charge of the enquiry when James Cooper died.

On arrival they were escorted into one of the interrogation rooms close to the main entrance where they were greeted by Sergeant Beckett.

He had already pulled out the file on the case before they got there. It also included photographs from the scene, and witness statements.

"What do you think?" Lee asked.

"Confusing," the Sergeant replied. "It took us a while to come to a final conclusion to be honest, it could have been a multitude of reasons why he fell."

Chris looked through the photos of the scene from Christmas Eve 2015.

Some were extremely gruesome, especially as he had been hit by a train. There were also photos of where he had fallen from on the platform. This was confirmed by Chris as it was still exactly the same. He told the Sergeant he had visited the station recently with his colleague.

"So what swayed the decision to call it an accident?" Lee asked.

"Witness statements mainly," Sergeant Beckett told him.

"The platform was busy wasn't it?"

"Extremely, shoulder to shoulder apparently."

"So how could anybody have a clear view of what happened?"

"The two main witnesses were standing side by side with the deceased," the Sergeant said, passing Lee the file.

He read through each statement carefully then handed them back to Sergeant Beckett.

"Who interviewed these two?" he asked.

"I did," said the Sergeant.

"Had either of them been drinking?"

"Probably, but neither of them were drunk, they were more in shock than anything else."

The two witnesses were Andrew Clarke, 45 years old, civil engineer from Renfrew and Jonathan Ellis, 25 years old, student living in student accommodation in Glasgow. "There was no reason for either of these two to lie," Lee thought.

"Who interviewed the pub staff where he had been drinking?"

"My colleague Malcolm Croft, the statements are there as well. There was nothing to say this was suspicious to be honest Lee, it was probably the usual bumping and barging to get closer to the edge when the train was coming. Mr Cooper had too much to drink and couldn't keep his balance."

"Looking at these I would say you were right," Lee said passing everything across the desk to the Sergeant.

"So that's it?" Chris asked.

"Yes Chris, what else is there?"

"What about the man in the trilby?"

"Come on mate, it's a gay community on the day of celebration. James Cooper probably copped for a blind date, got drunk as a skunk and fell under a train on the way home," Lee told him. "There's absolutely nothing else here that tells me different."

"I don't know, I'm not sure about this," Chris said.

"Get over it mate, let's go, I've seen enough," Lee said shaking Sergeant Beckett's hand on the way out "Thanks for your time."

He went absolutely mad with Chris on the way back to Gretna Green.

"So come on then Mr Higgins, tell me where the police investigation was sloppy, that's what you told them at head office wasn't it?"

Chris went bright red, he didn't realise they would have repeated what he had told them. He felt stupid and apologised to Lee but he didn't want to know.

***

"Keswick here we come," Tony thought as he joined the M6 heading south.

"Didn't Chris get a telephone number for Agnes Newey Sam?" he asked.

"Yes, I tried it but it's just ringing out," he replied.

"Okay let's hope she's at home and her little helper is with her to answer the door," Tony said putting his foot down.

They arrived on Low Road just before 11 o'clock and everywhere was quiet. Tony knocked on the door several times but got no reply.

"Now what?"

"Let's try the paper shop," Sam suggested. He remembered Chris telling him that's where he got her address from.

The same crew were on duty as before and were extremely helpful.

"She's in hospital," the elderly assistant told them. "Private apparently, getting her bones fixed."

"Which hospital?"

"She's got Fibromyalgia, it makes you tired all the time and can make you bedridden," she explained. "Agnes paid for a private course of treatment over a two-week period to help her to deal with the symptoms and hopefully get her active again."

"How do you know all this?" Tony asked.

"She's my sister," the elderly woman informed them. "I don't know how she can afford it. She said she found a wealthy sponsor," she laughed.

"Where's the hospital?" he asked again.

"She found it through the London Pain Clinic on Harley Street, London."

"Crikey, that will be expensive," Tony commented.

"That's what I thought," she said, "but Agnes said she didn't have to worry about expense, it would all be paid for. Good luck to her, she's in the Manor Hospital in Carlisle."

"Nice one," Tony thought, "I'm getting closer to Moffatt to see Archie McPhee."

They arrived at the Manor Hospital 50 minutes later, it was only 36 miles away and there was hardly any traffic.

"Good afternoon," Tony said to the girl behind the reception desk. "We are here to see Agnes Newey."

"Is she expecting you? We don't have anything in the diary about visitors," she said, "we normally only have visitors by appointment only, people like their privacy in here."

"I understand," Tony said. "Tell her it's the DWP guys to see her about her friend Louise, she will know what you mean."

The girl disappeared through some swinging doors and came back two minutes later, "This way please."

She led them back in the direction from where she came, into a private room the third door on the left.

Agnes was sitting up comfortably in her bed with pillows supporting her back and hips. She had flowers and chocolates on her bedside unit, and the place looked like a million dollars, "That's what it probably cost," he thought.

"That was quick," Agnes said, "have you found her killer?"

"No Agnes, not yet. We just wanted to ask you a couple more questions to try to find out who would want to kill her, or if she did actually commit suicide," Sam told her.

"This is nice Agnes," Tony said looking around. "We hear you've found yourself a sponsor for all this."

"Yes, I couldn't believe it either to be honest," she explained, "two days after your colleague came to see me I got another visitor out of the blue."

"Who was that then? Richard Branson?" Tony laughed.

"No silly, Jake."

"Who's Jake?" Tony asked.

"Jake Tausney, Louise's son from New Zealand."

"Okay," Tony said looking at Sam. "Why did he come to see you?"

"He heard about my illness and wanted to come and help if he could," she said smiling, "he knew me and his mum were good friends and said he would help me as much as I needed. He's my sponsor, no expense is too much he told me, so here I am, Lady Newey."

"Is he still here?" Tony asked. "I mean in the UK?"

"No, he went back to New Zealand two days after."

"Confused-dot-com," Tony said to Sam, "I wasn't expecting this."

"Nor me," Sam said. "What does it mean?"

"From the outset nothing, but it could mean something if we look a bit deeper, who knows?"

"What did you want to ask me?" Agnes asked.

"I can't remember now," said Tony. "Can you Sam?"

"No, I think you probably covered everything the last time," Sam said nodding towards the door.

When they got outside they just looked at each other.

"He must have a good job in New Zealand to foot the medical bills from Harley Street," Tony said.

"A fortune comes to mind," Sam agreed. "Why come back to the UK just for that, or was he here for something else?"

"This gets more complicated every time we turn a corner," Tony told him. "Let's head back to Gretna and see if the other two are coming back today."

Chris and Sergeant Monk were due back in Gretna at four o'clock, so it gave Tony chance to visit Moffatt and get back before them.

He gave his excuses to Sam and headed on his way to see Archie McPhee. He called him and arranged to meet in the pub at 2pm, then half an hour with Archie, then back by half past three, lots of time.

Archie was eating lunch when Tony arrived at the pub.

"Sorry to disturb your meal," Tony said. "Do you mind if we talk while you eat?"

"Carry on," Archie said. "I'm starving, the wife's at her sisters so I've got to fend for myself for a couple of days."

Tony attracted the barman's attention and ordered an orange juice.

"No ice or cherries this time, and definitely no umbrella, it's not raining," Tony joked.

"What can I do for you Mr Lodge?" he asked.

"Somehow I probably think you know Archie."

"Know what?"

"About the scam set up by your five managers in Carlisle" Tony said sipping on his orange juice.

"I know as much as they wanted me to know and that's it."

"And how much is that Archie?"

"It depends who I'm talking to," Archie said. "If it's Tony Lodge of the Fraud Department or Tony Lodge related to my good friend John Palmer."

"You're probably aware I already know the majority of what's happening, but I can't understand why anybody would want to kill them off when there's no benefit in doing so."

"John and Ray assure me 100% that they are not involved whatsoever in any of the deaths," Archie confirmed.

"I believe that completely," Tony agreed. "But it could be family that misunderstood the agreement, or someone like you that found out about it and wanted a cut."

"I don't think so," Archie disagreed. "I've been fed information at different times over the years, and from what I can gather none of them told their partners or any of their families."

"Lucy Palmer found out about it on the same day they made the agreement about the safety deposit box scenario."

"Yes I know, then she told her brother and he then joined the DWP on the fraud section to find out more about it," Archie said, "John told me all this."

"Lucy thought it was going to be shared with the surviving managers on the agreed pay out date."

"Again I know, John told me."

"So that's a bloody good reason for Lance to try and ensure their family weren't going to miss out if John died of cancer."

"I know, I know, I know," Archie said louder and louder.

"I appreciate you and John were good friends long after your retirement Archie, but you must admit Lance looks favourite to have committed the murders?"

"He didn't Tony, believe me," Archie said looking him in the eye.

"How can you be sure of that?"

"A few months after Lance started with the department he came to see me. He was worried about his dad and told me what Lucy had found," Archie said. "I didn't know a lot then but I knew enough to tell him that even in the event of any of the group passing away, their families would inherit their share."

"Did he believe you?"

"Yes Tony, he believed me and the subject never came up again."

"Wow…" Tony gasped, "is there anything else I need to know?"

"No, you probably know far too much as it is. Let's hope your counterparts don't pick up on what's going on as well."

"They haven't got a clue, don't worry about that."

"Let's hope not, keep your ears open and your mouth shut," Archie advised him.

Tony started back to Gretna. He couldn't stop thinking about Lance Palmer.

After all he had gone through with his father's illness, the saga with the fraud and now his sister being raped by someone he had set her up with on a date.

Tony felt respect and admiration for this guy, with Lance his family would always come first.

Tony arrived back in Gretna just before the other two landed, that was close.

Lee was still furious with Chris and was even more annoyed when he found out that Tony and Sam hadn't even asked Agnes Newey anything about the suicide.

They were side-tracked with the news that her friend's son arrived in the UK and paid her hospital fees.

For some reason Sergeant Monk was not a happy chappy and threatened to quit the scene.

"Good bloody riddance," the others were thinking.

Chris touched base with Heather and told her the situation, she told him to ignore Lee Monk and carry on with his own work.

Chris shuffled round partners for the next day, that was if Lee turned up.

"What exciting adventure do we have lined up then?" Lee asked sarcastically.

"You will find out, if or when you get here," Chris told him in a firm voice. He asked Tony to stay back for 10 minutes to have a chat.

"He's driving me mad," Chris told Tony.

"It looks like it," Tony laughed.

"I can't believe Heather told him what I said about the police investigations."

"It wouldn't have been Heather, more than likely our member of parliament rocking the boat."

"True, but it's put me right into his line of fire. It looks like anything I say or do will be scrutinised by the police Sergeant."

"You've done the right thing by keeping him out of your way."

"I can't see this leading anywhere either Tony."

"Me neither, but it's what they want so you just need to knuckle down and keep them happy."

"Okay I'll see you in the morning and decide what to do then," Chris said shaking Tony's hand.

Tony phoned Lance when he arrived by in Scotby.

He had decided to stay somewhere familiar rather than in a hotel.

"Hi Tony, how's things, to what do I owe this pleasure?" Lance said when he answered the phone.

"Just saying hello and finding out how my little girl's uncle is?"

"Cut the bullshit Tony, the answer is no."

"The answer to what is no?" Tony asked surprised.

"I didn't and wouldn't get rid of any of my father's colleagues from work," he scowled, "but yes I did sort out our work mate, Iain Logan for raping my sister."

"Slow down Lance," Tony said. "I was only calling to say thank you for looking after my daughter's mum, even though it was a bit harsh."

"Nothing's too harsh after rape."

"Okay, point taken, but the police should have been your option."

"I'm not after a lecture, thanks for trying," Lance said.

"Okay Lance. Take care see you soon," Tony said hanging up.

That didn't go down as well as he meant it to.

He then called John Palmer.

"Hi John, sorry to call you again at home. Nothing urgent, I didn't get the name of the property developer you told me about. Have you got his number?"

"Hold on Tony I will just get it from my notebook."

John came back on the line and gave Tony the name and contact details of the company that had dealt with Ray Hessler.

Elite Properties Nationwide Limited.

The development manager was Dominic O'Sullivan. He could only be contacted online on their website, no number was listed for either him or the company.

John told him Ray had his direct number as they kept in touch regularly regarding the property value over the years. Tony called Ray for his number and Ray told him Dominic was on holiday until the middle of August, another four weeks. Tony took his number anyway in case of emergency.

John Palmer was feeling terrible, so he asked his wife to make him a drink and he would head off to bed.

Lucy had just taken her daughter to bed and tucked her in, she was on her way back downstairs when her father collapsed.

Lucy screamed and her mum phoned an ambulance straight away. The emergency services were there within minutes and put him on oxygen to help his breathing, then took him to the hospital.

He was taken into a private room and they waited for the consultant to come and check him over. Meanwhile the nursing staff took some samples including blood and gave him some medication to help him sleep.

Angela phoned Lance and told him to get to the hospital, she wasn't sure how long her husband would last.

He hadn't eaten a proper meal for days and his liquid content had gone to almost zero, it was as if he was giving up.

Lucy called Tony to ask if he could have Mellissa for a while after explaining about her dad.

"Of course I will have her," he said. "I will come and pick her up, I'm staying in Scotby anyway."

Tony went to the Palmers' house. Lucy was standing outside with tears running down her cheeks.

"I will come and pick her up as soon as I can," she said sobbing, "don't tell her anything please, not yet anyway."

"Of course I won't, give your dad a big hug from me please Lucy," Tony said with tears in his eyes too.

They had a massive cuddle and held each other tight, "It's just like the old days," Lucy thought.

Mellissa came out after packing her night things along with her cuddly toys.

"An extra night with Daddy!" she said. "Yippee!"

Chapter Thirteen

Archie McPhee put the phone down after arranging to meet someone at 8 o'clock at the usual place.

"It was getting closer to the deadline date," he thought," now was the time to start the ball rolling."

Ray Hessler decided to go for a drink at the local working men's club, his wife was tired and was having an early night.

He enjoyed the 25 minute walk to the club, it gave him a chance to get his thoughts in order.

This was normally a once a fortnight event, but recently it was getting more frequent as his wife wasn't exactly exciting company. There was always somebody he knew at the club to pass the time away with until closing time.

It was someone's birthday party tonight and the place was pretty busy with a few strange faces in the bar. The music was definitely to Ray's taste as it was from the '70s and '80s with some Northern Soul in between.

He was enjoying himself and had a couple more drinks than normal before setting out for home.

He thought about taking the club steward's advice and getting a taxi, but decided to walk instead. "It would do me good," he thought.

Part of the walk home took him along a stretch of country road with no footpaths. It was dangerous during busy periods, but he had made this trip on many occasions. Normally you wouldn't see one car at this time of night, so he felt comfortable and safe to walk.

On this occasion he was wrong, so, so wrong. As he walked along the road a car came speeding up behind him and took him by surprise.

It hit him with such force that it knocked him about 20 feet into the field. He couldn't move, blood was pouring out of his head and he felt faint, then he passed out.

Jenny Hessler had taken a couple of sleeping tablets the night before, it was just before 9am when she was awoken by the telephone ringing continuously.

"Hello," Jenny answered.

"Hello it's Joanne," the girl said. "Is Ray there please?"

Joanne was Ray's personal assistant from the office in Carlisle.

"What time is it?" Jenny asked.

"Just before 9am. Is he there Jenny?"

"Let me check, I've just woken up," she said rubbing her eyes.

"No problem," Joanne replied. "I'll wait."

Jenny checked the spare room and downstairs, but there was no sign of her husband. It took her about 10 minutes to check everywhere as she had to get herself onto her wheelchair and manoeuvre around the house.

"Hello Joanne?"

"I'm still here."

"He's not here. He should be at work shouldn't he?"

"That's why I'm calling, he hasn't turned up yet so I thought he might be ill or something."

"Not that I'm aware of, he went out last night and I had an early night with a couple of sleeping tablets, so I didn't hear him come back."

"Okay can you ask him to call me when he comes in? I will tell him to call you if he turns up here."

"Okay, sounds good. Bye for now," Jenny said putting down the phone.

She checked around the house again and came to the conclusion that her husband hadn't come home.

His bed wasn't slept in, and the casual clothes he was wearing last night were nowhere to be seen. "I hope he's not been arrested," she thought.

She called the local police station to find out, but nobody had been arrested, so that ruled out that theory.

"Would you like to report your husband missing Mrs Hessler?" the on duty officer asked.

"No, he's probably stayed at a friend's or something after having too many to drink," Jenny told them.

"Okay, I hope he turns up safe and sound."

"Thanks I will call back if there's any problem."

There was a problem, a serious problem. Ray Hessler was dead, the head wound from the impact of the car had almost killed him instantly. He probably survived another couple of hours, but no-one would have heard his cries for help.

***

Tony contacted Heather and Chris in the evening and explained the situation with John Palmer. This meant he had to have his daughter for a couple of days while the family were at the hospital.

Heather authorised him to have the rest of the week off, but to keep in touch in case there were any developments.

He watched a movie with Mellissa, but he was more concerned about Lucy and her dad.

He kept in touch with Lucy during the night via text. John had slept most of the evening and night due to the amount of medication they had given him, so he would rest.

He was in good spirits when he woke up, and had eaten most of his breakfast as well as two pieces of toast. That was the most he had eaten for days, her mum told her.

So hopefully he was on the mend, even if it was only temporarily.

Lance was also at the hospital and hadn't left his father's side all night. Geoffrey was there giving him moral support, and Lucy was there with her mum, they needed all the support they could get.

Becky asked Tony if he would like her to have a couple more days off and travel down to Scotby, but he said it was fine and it would be nice to spend some daddy time with his daughter.

All the family were rallying together to support one another, it was nice but they all knew what the ultimate conclusion was going to be.

At 4pm on Tuesday afternoon Jenny reported her husband missing. The police sent an officer round to get some information of his whereabouts the night before.

Jenny explained that her husband went out and she had taken a couple of sleeping pills as she was having trouble sleeping.

Then after the normal formalities the officer left to follow up the information he had been given.

They contacted the steward at the club who confirmed that Ray left at approximately 11:30pm slightly the worse for wear.

He told the officer that he had tried to persuade him to catch a taxi, but he refused as he had walked the route a hundred times and could do it in his sleep.

The officer took a slow drive from the club to the Hessler house and back again a couple of times, but couldn't see anything obvious from the car.

He was given permission by his sergeant to walk the route on foot after they closed the road off. He was given another two officers to speed up the process on the one and a half mile trek.

The road was then closed off for the rest of the day after they found the body, as they had to complete detailed enquiries into what they suspected was a hit and run.

Jenny was mortified and was uncontrollable.

She blamed herself for being such a bitch she told the female officer.

They weren't on speaking terms for the past couple of weeks, especially after a friend told her that she had seen him with a female work colleague in a café. This was on the day that he was supposed to be picking her up from the hospital, and left her stranded. He told her he was pulled in for questioning by the Special Investigations Department which she found out was a blatant lie.

She called Joanne at the DWP office on Wednesday morning and asked her to pass the message on as she didn't really want to talk to anyone at this particular moment as she was too upset.

Heather Mooney was numb.

She couldn't believe what she was hearing. She immediately contacted Chris Higgins who in turn called Tony Lodge. Tony couldn't get his breath, four out of the five original managers in Carlisle were dead, and the fifth one was in hospital dying of cancer.

"What is the connection?" he wondered. "Who the hell is involved in all this?"

Tony didn't have to pick his daughter up from school until 3pm, so it gave him a few hours to work on any actions he could come up with.

This most recent death appeared to be a hit and run, so it could have been anyone on that stretch of the road waiting for Ray to appear. The police hadn't really started their enquiries yet so Tony phoned Chris to ask him to get Sergeant Lee Monk to see if he could find anything out.

"The case was closed," Chris told him. "We were told to go back to our normal roles and shut up shop in Gretna."

The instruction had come from above and they were told emphatically not to discuss the case with anyone, it was over.

Tony didn't know whether to laugh or cry.

It was a relief in respect of his adopted family the Palmers, and a disaster as far as the deaths of nearly all the crew of the "Wicked Five".

It looked like John Palmer would have to conclude affairs, no matter how ill he was, all by himself. It would be up to him to make sure the families got their share of the spoils. Would he be up for it, or could he pass it on to someone else?

John took the news of Ray's death badly, he was devastated.

Tony wasn't sure why they had to tell him while he was trying to recover from his latest bout of cancer treatment. He thought they should have given it a couple of days to see how he progressed. But he knew maybe it was better under the circumstances.

He lay in bed thinking, he wasn't sure what to do next. Even if someone had killed his colleagues they wouldn't gain anything financially, so why would they do it?

Only he and Ray Hessler knew everything, and now it was only him. Even his wife and family didn't know. He decided to confide in Angela and explain what they had arranged and why.

Angela said she was shocked, but not surprised as she thought Ray was a devious bastard at the best of times. She had never trusted him especially after John told her about the fraud when he had cancer before. What John told her made sense, and it had definitely been the right thing to do. She was now sworn to secrecy and couldn't even tell her children, well not until her husband passed away.

***

Archie McPhee called his daughter Julia to organise seeing her in the morning.

Julia married Edward Webb 12 years ago and became known as Julia Webb, the manageress of Glasgow Vaults. She made a note in her diary that her dad plus one are coming at 9:30am tomorrow morning. She always wrote appointments in her diary, even if it was family members.

Archie had the passwords of Fiona Jacklin, Ray Hessler, Louise Tausney and James Cooper, he only needed John Palmer's for the full set and open the box.

He intended to visit John in hospital that evening to get his code for the appointment in the morning.

The police scanned the road at the point they think Ray could have been hit by the vehicle. There were no skid marks anywhere on the stretch of road, so the vehicle didn't brake sharply at any time. The chances were that either the driver didn't see Mr Hessler or they intentionally ran him over.

The vehicle would have been damaged at the point where he hit the deceased, so they alerted garages to be on the lookout for vehicles brought in with front end damage of any kind.

An extract was put in the local paper about the accident and for anyone with any information to contact the police direct.

This was becoming a major police enquiry into the death of Raymond Hessler.

Tony Lodge received a call just before 7pm number withheld.

"Hello," Tony answered. "Can I help you?"

"Hello, is this Tony Lodge?"

"Yes speaking, who's this?"

"Hi Tony, sorry to bother you so late," the voice said. "This is Detective Inspector Glenn Thomas from the Cumbria Police Department."

"Good evening Glenn, how can I help you?"

"I've been given your contact details by Heather Mooney," he explained. "I'm investigating the recent death of Raymond Hessler. I wonder if I could come and see you to have a chat."

Tony told Glenn about the situation with his daughter and arranged to see him at the local Scotby police station at 9 o'clock in the morning. Tony was curious why Heather had given him his number without contacting him first to let him know, very strange.

Lucy called to let him know she was on her way to see her daughter.

"A little bit more notice would help," he told her.

"Dad's fast asleep so it gives me chance to get away for a breather, it's not exactly fun and games here," she said sadly.

"I'm sorry, of course it's alright, see you when you get here."

Lucy arrived around 8pm, Tony had let her stay up to see her mum when she got there.

"Mummy can we stay here forever, I love it? Me and Daddy watch films and have pizza and nuggets it's great," Mellissa was excited, it wasn't very often she has both her mum and dad together at the same time.

"No sweetheart," Lucy told her. "It's only for a couple of days then you're back home in your own bed."

"Ohhh...spoilsport," she said dropping her lip. "Come and play a game with me."

"Stay here with Mellissa and I'll go and see your dad for a while," Tony said.

"Oh, okay I will make myself at home if that's alright?"

"Yeah of course, I won't be too long," Tony said heading for the door. He wanted to tell John about his meeting with Glenn Thomas in the morning.

Tony arrived at North Cumbria University Hospital at quarter past eight. Lucy had told him the ward name and number and the best place to park his car.

When he arrived Angela was by the entrance to the ward.

"Is everything alright?" he asked her.

"Yes fine," she said, "he's just had another visitor turn up, so I thought I would leave them to it."

"Who's that then?"

"Archie McPhee, it was nice to see him again"

"Did he say why he's come?"

"Not really, he heard about his collapse and thought he would come and see him. Probably before he pops his clogs I suppose," she said thinking.

"They always got on really well didn't they?"

"Yes they did, I think John was his favourite"

"It's nice of Archie to come and see him, do you want to go for a coffee? Give them some time together?"

"Yeah go on then, but let me pay please, I insist."

They headed off towards the canteen, ordered their drinks then sat down at a table.

"I can't believe Ray Hessler's dead," Tony said.

"Nor me, it all seems so unreal, five managers started a new career, open a new department and now they are all dead apart from my husband, and he's not far behind"

"The jinx of the Wicked Five," Tony joked.

"What's the Wicked Five?" Angela asked.

"It was a title they gave themselves not long after they started. Archie McPhee was still there then."

"Crikey I didn't know that," she said.

"If they sent each other internal messages they always signed it as W5 at the bottom of the page."

"Well I'll be damned," Angela said thinking back. "I wondered what all those letters were in his study with W5 at the bottom."

"Important letters?"

"I didn't really pay much attention to them to be honest," she continued, "I thought they were from a society or something."

"Has he still got them?"

"I don't know, this was years ago."

"With only your husband left out of the five we need to make sure everything goes smoothly with the handover of funds to yourselves and the other relatives."

"Don't worry about that Tony, it's already been sorted."

"What do you mean already sorted?"

"I can't say for now, but everything is fine, honestly."

"Okay I believe you, I'm just wondering if Archie McPhee is trying to get in on the act and that's why he's appeared without invitation?"

"Don't worry Tony it's sorted, leave it for now please."

"Okay I don't want this to affect Lucy or my daughter."

"It won't. Well, only for the good of their future."

"I've got a Detective Inspector wanting to interview me tomorrow regarding Ray's death, and god knows what else."

"You don't know anything," Angela reminded him, "so you can't tell them anything."

"That's true."

"Can you do me a favour please Tony?"

"I'll try, what?"

"Make sure Lucy gets a good night's rest, I don't want her coming back to the hospital until the morning. I've already sent Lance and Geoffrey home."

"I will try, I can't promise anything, and you know what your daughter is like," Tony said. But he knew exactly what she meant.

It was a pleasant surprise for John when Archie turned up, he was pleased to see him.

"You're not the grim reaper come to take me to my maker?" John asked jokingly.

"I wish I was your fairy godfather come with a cure instead," Archie replied with a smile.

"I haven't seen you for a while, what brings you here?"

"I'm concerned to be honest, I can't believe Ray has also been killed," he said. "It's like a curse."

"It looks that way but my fate is down to illness, the other four I'm sure could have been avoided," John said sadly.

"Do you think they were murdered?" Archie asked.

"I didn't think so when Louise and James died, but now I'm not so sure," John told him. "It just seems too much of a coincidence, and too close together."

"Who do you think would kill them?"

"Who knows? I thought maybe Lance or even you Archie."

"Nope, you're wrong on both counts," he said. "Lance came to see me about the fraud five years ago, he was concerned about you and his family."

"And you? What about you Archie?"

"No John, you were like kids to me, there's no way in the world I would wish any harm on any of the five of you."

"Then I haven't got a clue, it could be anyone," John said shrugging his shoulders.

"I've made an appointment for 9 o'clock in the morning to get the deeds and documents out of the safety deposit box," Archie said. "I just need your code so I can open it."

Chapter Fourteen

When Angela and Tony got back to the ward Archie McPhee had gone. John was fast asleep and looked comfortable so Tony didn't want to disturb him.

"Tell him I will pop in tomorrow after I've been to the police HQ in Scotby," he told Angela.

"I will Tony, look after my daughter please she deserves a break."

Tony didn't reply, he just shook his head to acknowledge her as he left. Becky called just as he was leaving the front entrance.

"Hiya how's things?" she asked.

"I'm just leaving the hospital," Tony said. "Then going back to our place, are you okay?"

"I'm fine, how's Mellissa?"

"Great thanks, she's enjoying spending time with Daddy," he laughed.

"I didn't think you were going to take her to the hospital yet?"

"I didn't she's with her mum."

"Aha, she's gone back home?"

"No, at our place."

"Lucy's at our place?"

"Yes, she popped round to see Mellissa and I asked her to look after her so I could come and see her dad."

"So she's going home when you get back?"

"I expect so, why do you ask?"

"I just wondered that's all," she said lowering her voice.

Tony hadn't seen this side of Becky before, and he wasn't sure if he liked it.

"Don't you trust me Becky?" he asked.

"Of course I do, I'm not sure I trust Lucy that's all."

"Don't be silly darling, she will go home when I get back," Tony said hesitantly remembering what Angela asked him to do.

"Okay Tony, call me later so I know you got back safe."

"I will, talk later, love you."

"Love you too, bye for now."

It was after half past nine and Mellissa was still awake when he got back.

"I waited up for you Daddy to say goodnight," Mellissa said excitedly, "see you in the morning. Come on mummy, come and tuck me in and read me a story."

Tony took the opportunity to call Becky while the girls were upstairs and lie through his teeth.

He told her Mellissa was fast asleep and Lucy was on her way home. He didn't want an argument or for Becky to get stressed out.

"Goodnight sweetheart," he said ending the conversation. "Love you loads."

"Love you loads too, sleep tight."

Lucy came back downstairs at ten o'clock, she had found one of Becky's night shirts and slipped it on after she had a shower.

"I know," she said, "I shouldn't have but I'm too tired to drive home, it's been a long day."

"I understand," Tony said, "it has been for all of us, and each day is going to get longer."

"I hope not, I don't want my dad to suffer," she said fighting back the tears, "he deserves better than that."

They sat together on the settee and Lucy put her head on his shoulder. He put his arm around her to make her feel safe, and kissed her on the top of the head.

"What happened to us Tony?" Lucy asked. "Why did we split up?"

"It was lots of things in the end," Tony surmised.

"There must have been one thing that triggered it off in the first place," Lucy said.

Tony thought back to the conversation her dad had with him when he found out he had cancer. John pulled Tony to one side and told him that he wasn't the one for his daughter. If he didn't leave her he would take Lucy and Mellissa off the will.

They wouldn't get a penny when he died unless he called things off with her.

He thought they had a reasonable house and it was only him that worked, nothing in comparison to what she would have if he gave John his wish.

That's when he started the petty arguments to make it look as if he didn't care anymore, but he loved Lucy with all of his heart, it was broken in several places when he walked out the door.

"I think your dad's cancer didn't help, your patience and attention became minimal then," he said trying to justify what happened.

"Maybe, but that's when I needed your support and you pushed me away."

"I think I was jealous because I wasn't getting the attention I used to get."

"You mean sex?" she asked.

"That as well as other things I think."

"We've got a daughter that needed attention continuously, a parent who was dying of cancer and the worry about my dad pulling off a millions of pounds fraud with the DWP," Lucy said remembering back.

"I can't believe you never told me about that."

"I couldn't, I didn't know how you would have reacted," Lucy explained, "the way you two were with each other I was frightened you would tell on him."

"We had been together a long time Lucy, I wouldn't have done anything that would have affected you or my daughter."

"I can see that now, but I couldn't then I was frightened."

"I think our intimate side of the relationship took a dip after you had Mellissa."

"Lots of women have post-natal depression Tony," she laughed.

"I thought you were punishing me because I wanted a boy."

"Don't be stupid, I could see you loved our daughter as soon as you set eyes on her," she told him. "I think we should have talked to each other a bit more, we just seemed to clam up."

"Every time we tried to communicate we would start arguing, and I don't know why."

"That was the problem, we never gave each other a chance, and it was too easy to walk away without a fight," Lucy said starting to cry. "The amount of times it's played over and over in my mind. Wishing I had said the right thing."

"Stubborn," Tony said, "we were both too bloody stubborn."

"At least one good thing came out of it," she said, "and she is upstairs asleep in your new girlfriend's spare room."

Tony laughed, "And my ex-girlfriend is downstairs wearing my new girlfriend's night shirt." They both laughed out loud and held each other tighter.

Lucy looked into Tony's eyes.

"I still love you Tony Lodge."

"I love you too Lucy Palmer," he said. "I always have and I probably always will."

"What happens next," Lucy asked.

"I don't know, we will have to take it one step at a time," he said putting his lips against hers.

"This isn't a good idea," Lucy said.

"Why not?" Tony said "I hope you're not going to get your brother to pay me a visit."

"I don't think so," she said, "I was the sole prize possession of Tony Lodge, and Tony Lodge only until he raped me, he deserved everything he got."

"I agree, he definitely did," Tony said unbuttoning her shirt.

Lucy wasn't plump, or frumpy, she had looked after her body and looked gorgeous from head to toe, Tony was always wishing she was so that nobody else would be attracted to her.

They made love on the settee for what seemed hours and all the previous feelings and emotions came flooding back.

Now Tony had a problem, what would he do about Rebecca Doyle?

They got up together in the morning and took their daughter to school.

154

Lucy then went to the hospital and Tony headed towards the police station to see Glenn Thomas.

When Lucy arrived at the hospital her mum already had breakfast and was on her second cup of coffee.

"How did it go last night?" she asked her daughter.

"How did what go mother?" she replied with a smile.

"That good," her mum said winking.

"Behave, private is private."

"Okay point taken," she said. "Your father has had a fantastic night's sleep and is as bright as a button this morning."

"That's good news."

"The doctor said he was just lacking in liquids," she explained, "he's been on a drip for two days and all the nutrients etc. are back in his blood stream. They've given me an instruction manual on what he needs to take on a daily basis to keep his strength up."

"Meaning what?" Lucy asked. "He can come home?"

"Yes dear, but not until tomorrow all being well."

"That's excellent news, I bet dad's over the moon."

"He is, this time he will do as we say and maybe we will get another six months out of the old fool," she laughed.

Lucy went across and gave her father a great big hug, she loved this man so much, well almost as much as she loved Tony Lodge.

"We missed Archie yesterday, he had gone when me and Tony came up from the canteen."

"Was Tony here?" he asked. "I didn't realise he came, sorry about that"

"And Archie? What did he want?"

"My code," he smirked, "for the safety deposit box."

"Did you give it to him?" his wife asked.

"Of course I did, why shouldn't I?" John smiled from ear to ear, "I wish I could be there to see his face."

***

Tony arrived at the police station in Scotby and was greeted at the door by Glenn Thomas himself.

"Good morning Tony," he said opening the internal security door. "Come through."

Tony walked in past the reception area and along a corridor to one of the interview rooms at the rear of the building.

"Sit down," Glenn said pointing to a chair.

There was a table between them that contained a new technology recording machine that looked to be already plugged in.

Another uniformed officer came into the room and Glenn closed the door.

"This is Detective Inspector Darren Ashcroft, "Daz" for short," Glenn said. "Daz is currently working on two recent cases involving what could have been suspicious deaths. One is Ray Hessler's demise and the other a woman called Fiona Jacklin."

"As you're aware, both of these victims were involved in an ongoing investigation led by yourself via the fraud department at the Department of Work and Pensions," Daz commented looking in Tony's direction.

"Yes but the investigation has been terminated as far as I'm aware," Tony said, "and recently it was passed across to the Special Investigations Department to head the enquiry."

""Yes, but the initial investigation was headed by you, is that right?"

"Yes it was, what's that got to do with these deaths?"

"Everything, Mr Lodge absolutely everything."

"Meaning what?" Tony asked getting nervous.

"Your team, according to Heather Mooney were unsure about the two deaths of previous employees James Cooper and Louise Tausney," Daz pointed out, "and now another two from the same group are also dead."

"I understand that," Tony stressed, "but the findings were inconclusive, there was nothing definite to point the finger at the deaths being intentional."

"Unfortunately in the two recent cases there is evidence of foul play," Daz told him. "They are both being treated as murder."

"Which leads us back to the previous two deaths, these cases have now been reopened and are being investigated again as we speak," Glenn told him.

"Sergeant Joseph Beckett who previously investigated the James Cooper death has been assigned to the investigation," Daz told him. "He may want you to travel to Glasgow for an update on exactly what was found when you looked at the cases before."

"He would be better to speak to Chris Higgins and Samuel Wong from the SID. They were the guys that were involved in looking at the cases in Glasgow and Keswick," Tony informed them.

"We will pass that information on," Glenn said.

"You say the recent two cases are definitely murders?" Tony asked.

"Yes," Daz replied, "Fiona Jacklin's death was originally thought to be a fall onto the corner of her kitchen unit, but the post mortem shows two indentations on her skull that were administered by a blunt object, not a sharp corner as originally thought."

"It looks like someone smeared blood onto the unit to make it look like it was where she hit her head," Glenn informed him, "unfortunately no finger prints or weapon were found in or around the scene."

"And Ray?" Tony asked.

"There were no skid marks where a vehicle would have tried to brake quickly if they saw someone on the road," Daz explained, "and we found glass near where his body was found. The glass looks like it's from a car headlight which must have shattered on impact with the deceased. The vehicle looks like it could have been travelling at a fair speed giving the damage to the glass."

"If the glass was on the road, couldn't other vehicles have driven over it to incur further damage?" Tony asked.

"The glass was found on the grass verge at the side of the road, if there were other cars driving over the glass it would be evident on the road itself and the glass would probably ended up sticking to their tyres," Daz said.

"This most definitely would have happened to some of the headlight as we only found about half of what you would expect to find immediately after a collision," Glenn confirmed.

"We would imagine there is a good bit of damage to the vehicle and possibly a cracked or broken windscreen where Ray hit his head, that would have been the deadly blow I'm afraid," Daz said sadly.

"So why have you brought me here?" Tony asked.

"Mainly because you were brought into the investigation on a fraud that as far as we can see may have involved all of these people that have been killed," Daz said.

"Two were definitely killed," Tony corrected him, "I'm not convinced about the first two."

"Okay, potentially all of them were killed," Daz pointed out "we just wanted a feel for the organisation and a potential killer."

"Crikey, I don't know," Tony answered, "out of the five managers that started in the Carlisle office, there is only one left, and he is in hospital with cancer, so that rules him out."

"No-one else?" Daz queried.

"There is their original boss Archie McPhee," Tony told them, "he retired five months after they opened and was replaced by Charlie Grant who is still in charge."

"What are they like" asked Daz.

"I wouldn't say Archie has killing potential, and I don't really know Charlie Grant. You would have to speak to him yourself."

"What about any relatives or staff in the department?"

"Nope, nothing comes to mind."

"Okay Tony, thanks for your time, we will keep in touch and let Sergeant Beckett in Glasgow know about your SID officers," Daz concluded.

Tony left and headed in the direction of the hospital to see John Palmer.

"Hello beautiful," Archie said to his daughter as he walked into Glasgow Vaults. "How is my favourite girl?"

"I'm fine Dad, I thought there were two of you coming?"

"Yes there is, they will be here shortly."

"Would you like a coffee?"

"Tea please Julia, you should know that by now," he laughed. "When did I ever drink coffee?"

"Okay don't push it," she said sarcastically. "Tea it is."

As Julia made the tea a male figure walked through the door and joined Archie at the counter.

"Can you make that two please Julia?" he shouted to his daughter.

"Milk and Sugar?"

"Yeah, milk and two sugars please," the male voice answered.

Julia brought the two cups from the kitchen and guided them through to the back office.

"Julia," Archie said. "Meet Charlie Grant"

***

Tony eventually got to the hospital after being stuck in traffic for 45 minutes. Angela and Lucy were sitting by John's bed when he arrived.

"Good afternoon girls," he said joyfully.

"Hello Tony," Angela said winking at him.

"What's Lucy told her?" Tony thought.

"Hiya Tony," Lucy said. "Fancy seeing you here." She chuckled.

"Let's go and get a hot drink," Angela said grabbing her daughter's hand. "Let the boys have some time together"

The girls made a sharp exit.

"What's all that about?" Tony asked.

"You know what those two are like Tony," John replied, "I think they're hoping you're going to ask me for my daughter's hand in marriage."

Tony looked petrified.

"I'm only joking, sit yourself down," John said with a look in his eye. "What did the police want?"

Tony went through the conversations he had with Glenn Thomas and Darren Ashcroft. John wasn't surprised to find out they had been killed and wouldn't be surprised if they found evidence that James and Louise were killed as well.

"What makes you say that?" Tony asked surprised.

"I suppose it's the amount of money involved," John answered, "money is the root of all evil. That's why everything was tied up years ago. Both myself and Ray changed the original plan because we could smell a rat."

"What do you mean?"

"Time will tell Tony, I can't say anything yet but you will find out soon enough."

"You're the only one left, what happens if whoever it is comes for you next?"

"They won't, they know I've got cancer and haven't got long to live, so there's no point taking any more chances to kill someone who is almost already dead."

"So you know who it is?"

"Not 100% but I've got a good idea."

"Is it Archie?"

"No," John said smiling. "Even Archie doesn't know who it is."

"Oh, that surprises me to be honest."

"The world is full of surprises matey."

"Tell me about it," Tony said thinking about last night.

"All I can say is this," John told him. "If everyone involved keeps their head down and their mouths shut, everything will be fine. However, if anyone gets greedy or silly the whole thing will have been a complete waste of time."

"I wish you could tell me now John, I'm just worried in case anything happens to you."

"Don't worry Tony, Angela knows, I'm sure she will tell you when the time is right if anything does happen to me."

"Okay I won't ask again," Tony said. "Does Lucy know anything?"

"She knows about the fraud itself, but nothing else."

"That's okay then, I would rather keep her safe."

"She will be safe Tony, and your daughter will also be safe."

"As long as I'm around my daughter will always be safe," Tony smiled.

"As long as you're around, my daughter will also be safe Mr Lodge, look after her please. Don't let her get away from you this time, no matter what I say to you. I was wrong and I'm so sorry, I should have trusted you with Lucy but I was depressed and down in the dumps. It will never happen again, she was like a child with a new toy this morning, and you make her happy."

"I know," Tony told him, "two years down the road and I'm still as much in love with her now as I was when I first met her, I thought when I met someone else I could forget her, but it didn't happen. Every time she dropped Mellissa off my heart sank. I was dreading the day when I found out she was seeing someone else, and luckily for me that didn't happen."

Chapter Fifteen

"Let's put them in alphabetical order," Archie told Charlie Grant. "They've got to go into the de-coder in order."

"Okay let's work it out," Charlie said writing the names down in order.

"COOPER, HESSLER, JACKLIN, PALMER, TAUSNEY," he then typed in the password against the name.

"Cooper=USA94, Hessler=ADAMY, Jacklin=JACKY, Palmer=KELLY, Tausney=BINGO."

Nothing happened, so he tried it again, nothing happened and again, and again.

"You must have one of the codes wrong," Charlie said.

"I don't think so, I got the correct codes off each person individually," he said "I even got them to repeat them and tell me why they picked that code."

"Go through them," Charlie asked.

"James Cooper loved football, especially Brazil. He went to America to watch them when they won the World Cup in 1994, so he choose USA94."

"Okay that sounds right, next."

"Ray's two kids were called Adam and Amy, so he choose a password with both names in ADAMY."

"That sounds right."

"Fiona's nickname as a child was Jacky, after her favourite magazine JACKY."

"The magazine was *Jackie* not Jacky, carry on we will come back to that one if we have to."

"John Palmer's first dog was called KELLY after his nan."

"Okay and the last one."

"Louise Tausney was a bingo fanatic so she chose BINGO."

"That sounds right, so it must be JACKY, try JACKI instead,"

It worked, the box clicked open.

"Well done Hercule Poirot," Archie said. "Let's look and see what's inside the magic box."

There were five sheets of paper with the "W5" emblem on the bottom of each page. They had the name and signature of each member of the five.

Written above the signature was the instruction to be signed that they agreed for the property to be sold after the death of the first member, and the money from the sale to be split into seven portions.

The date on the signed sheets was the 2nd of September 2014, well after the property had been purchased in 2012. The deeds and paperwork were gone, so they presumed the castle had been sold after Louise Tausney died in October 2015.

What happened to the money from the sale, and why was it being split seven ways?

"Bloody hell," Archie said. "What the hell is going on?"

"I don't know, but I'm sure you will find out."

"It looks like another visit to see Mr Palmer," Archie said thoughtfully. "Are you coming?"

"No Archie, nobody knows that I know about this."

"This scam would never have gone through so easily without the head of the department knowing about it," he said. "They surely weren't that stupid?"

"That's what I thought," Charlie said. "They should know all the monthly stats are scrutinised and have to get approved by me, and these additions stood out like a sore thumb."

"At least if they were found out you could have pleaded ignorance, and the bullet could be pointed at the five musketeers?"

"Exactly, that's why you told me in the first place."

"It was, I sussed it out from Ray Hessler early on, it was going smoothly for a couple of months but he was getting too greedy and would have been caught."

"Yep and that's where I came in and covered everything up like a proper little hero."

"We should have told them before, but we didn't want to be in the frame if they were caught."

"Exactly, and now it's almost payday the money's disappeared."

"Let me talk to John, I'm sure there's a perfectly good explanation."

"Then why didn't he tell you when he gave you the code?"

"He's a bit of a joker is Mr Palmer, he will be laughing his socks off at the moment."

"If he doesn't tell you he will be laughing on the other side of his face."

"Easy tiger, it will be fine."

***

Detective Inspector Darren Ashcroft was at his desk in the main Carlisle Police Head Quarters. He had paperwork everywhere across his desk and was trying to sort it out. He got a call from Lee Monk earlier and was waiting to call him back.

He was out with Detective Inspector Glenn Thomas in Scotby when he called.

Sergeant Beckett in Glasgow told Daz about Lee's visit to HQ with one of the SID officers and wanted an update on his thoughts.

"Hello can I speak to Lee Monk please?" Daz said. "Tell him it's Darren Ashcroft from Carlisle HQ."

After being kept on hold for what seemed like ages, his call was finally put through.

"Hello Lee Monk speaking, can I help you?"

Daz went through the normal preliminaries and told Lee he had been assigned to the cases of Ray Hessler and Fiona Jacklin from the DWP.

Lee was devastated at the news of these deaths and specifically surprised at the fact that they were murdered.

"I would like to know what was found in the cases of James Cooper and Louise Tausney," Daz asked him, "and what your opinions were on both cases."

Heather Mooney had told Daz about Lee Monk's attitude with the SID agents, and his reluctance to see any flaws in the investigations from before.

"To be honest I couldn't see any problems with the results of the investigations before, especially in the case involving James Cooper," Lee said. "I felt that the agent was looking for a scapegoat and wanted to blame the police enquiry."

"So you would say that James Cooper was definitely killed by accident?"

"Erm, nobody seen him being pushed and witness statements backed that up," he said, "so I would say yes, it was an accident."

"Did you know that the cases have been re-opened?"

"No I didn't, but I should think they will come back with the same results."

"We will see, I look forward to seeing the new report from the investigation."

"I didn't see anyone from the Louise Tausney case, the two officers that visited Keswick didn't even ask the victim's friend about the death as she was in hospital having private treatment done."

"We've heard about that thank you, we will be in touch Sergeant Monk, thanks for your time."

Daz wasn't impressed by his attitude either and could see why Heather had made a complaint.

He wouldn't be asking for his assistance again and made a note to contact his superiors about replacing him working alongside the DWP.

Daz had finally sorted through his paperwork and put it in some sort of order.

Firstly he would visit the working men's club Ray Hessler visited on the night of his death, then contact all the garages in the area to see if anyone had booked a vehicle in for repair.

He asked the local policeman if he knew of any sites or houses in the area where Ray's body was found that had CCTV installed.

He came back with two companies and a private address that could be contacted.

Daz asked the policeman's superiors if he could use him to assist in his enquiries, and was given the go ahead, welcome Jason Keay to the squad.

Jason had worked in the area for the last three years and was known to the local businesses and members of the public alike, he was a friendly, caring copper with a big heart.

"He would be good at contacting the locals to get some background about the Hesslers," Daz thought.

So he got him door knocking.

"Hello I'm Detective Inspector Darren Ashcroft," Daz introduced himself. "Can I talk to the club steward please?"

"You're talking to him," said George Forsyth. "How can I help you?"

"It's about the accident concerning one of your customers the other night."

"You mean Ray," he said. "Ray Hessler, nice fella he was always talkative and a friendly type."

"Was he drinking with anyone?"

"No, he liked to drink by himself," George told him, "chatted up the bar staff more than anything. We had a birthday function on with '70s and '80s music that he seemed to enjoy."

"So he was by himself?"

"Yes, he normally has two or three pints then goes home, but he stayed longer that evening and probably had seven or eight."

"Did he seem depressed or miserable?"

"No, totally the opposite, he was singing and dancing like a teenager, the music got him going I think."

"Do you know if anyone driving a car left after him?"

"Probably a few," George said. "The women were doing the driving and the men the drinking, bust most of the regulars had gone before Ray. A group of party revellers were last to leave about 10 minutes after him."

"Do you know them?"

"No, but they were guests of the birthday girl, it was her 60th so they weren't youngsters."

"Have you got the name and contact number of the birthday girl please?"

"Of course," George said tracking down his diary and writing the information on a piece of paper.

"Thank you," Daz said walking outside.

Daz phoned the woman whose details were written down on the paper and introduced himself.

He found out the last people to leave the club were her two brothers and their wives, they left in the same car and were going in the same direction as Ray.

He got the details of the driver and called him, his name was Nigel Brown. He introduced himself again and made an appointment to see him in 15 minutes' time.

When he got there Nigel opened the door.

"Hello Mr Brown, sorry to bother you, it's just that the gentleman that died on the road on Monday night looks to be the victim of a hit and run driver," he told him, "we just wondered if you saw anything or if any other car was on the road when you left the club?"

"Our car was the last one on the car park as far as I can remember," Nigel said, "but a car did go past us when I stopped to fasten my seat belt. The wife always has a go at me about it even if it's only just over a mile to get home."

"Did you see the car?"

"It was going too fast, I know it was either black or a dark colour as they didn't have their lights on."

"Did you report this afterwards?"

"Well no, I didn't give it a thought really."

"Did you see anything when you drove up the country lane stretch of the road?"

"No I didn't, but I ran over something that felt like glass on the road."

"Where's your car?"

"In the garage, why?"

"Have you used it since Monday evening?"

"Only once to go shopping, why?"

"I need to check the tyres."

Nigel fetched his keys out of the kitchen and reversed his car out of the garage. "No damage to the car, so it wasn't this one," Daz thought.

There were some pieces of glass in the front and rear passenger side tyres.

"Have you got a bank coin bag or something I can collect these in?" Daz asked with a lump of glass in his hand.

Nigel disappeared indoors and came back with a couple of change bags from the bank, perfect.

He took all the glass he could find from the tyres after getting Nigel to reverse stage by stage to make sure he didn't miss any.

"What time did you leave the club?" Daz asked.

"11:45 exactly," he confirmed, "as the wife wanted to watch a film that started at midnight, so she was clock watching."

That gave Daz an almost exact time of the accident for when he found someone that had CCTV footage.

Jason the local bobby started his door to door enquiries to dig up some information on the Hesslers, but their neighbours were full of praise for them.

One of the neighbours that lived at the back of the Hesslers' home was a bit confused, she knew who they were but not by name.

She didn't know them to talk to, but her back fence almost joined onto theirs.

When Jason had described them she wasn't aware that the woman was in a wheelchair.

The two back fences were lined with conifer trees, so it gave a better defence for privacy.

The woman's house was raised about 10 ft. above the Hesslers' place as it was at the top end of the hill, so you could see into their garden, especially on a windy day.

She told Jason that on more than one occasion she saw her hanging out her washing onto a clothes line, and it wasn't from a wheelchair.

"She could have a walking frame at the back to help her," Jason said.

"I don't think so, I actually saw her running to get her washing in when it started raining."

The woman was a bit of a gossip and other neighbours tended to avoid her. She used to stay up at night, and sleep

168

during the day apparently, so Jason took what she said with a pinch of salt.

He found out they had two cars, Ray used to drive both as his wife couldn't drive after her accident.

She wasn't confident even going out on her own, and her husband always went with her.

They had two children that only visited at Christmas or on special occasions, and kept themselves to themselves.

Daz contacted all the local and surrounding garages to see if anyone had booked a car in for repair, but there was nothing registered for a dark coloured car needing new headlights and potentially a new windscreen.

His next stop was the car hire company located on the main road between the club and the Hessler house.

The CCTV mostly covered their car park and the front and back entrances, but one of the cameras caught the main road on its angled lenses.

He contacted the owner and asked permission to view the one camera at around the time of the accident. He was now in the manager's office logged onto the computer watching the screen.

He saw something fly past the camera range, but it was dark and just like Nigel Brown had said, it didn't have its lights on so it was impossible to see what car it was.

He also saw what looked like Nigel Brown's car go past a few minutes later.

He tried playing it back and slowing it down but nothing he tried made the image any clearer, or the vehicle recognisable.

The other business address that Jason informed him that had CCTV. The system was out of action so nothing would be registered from Monday night.

That left the private address which was located past where Ray's body was found away from the club.

Daz drove up to the address, the house was massive with electric gates at the entrance which were opened when he arrived.

He had phoned the Patels before coming to make sure they were in. Mr Patel was a neurosurgeon working at Carlisle's main hospital. His shifts varied so it was lucky he caught him in.

The CCTV covered both sides of the entrance gates, so you could see most of the roads from North and South.

Their property was approximately 1000 yards past where Ray's body was found. It was in between the club and Ray's house so each camera should pick it up and identify the car.

He played the tape from the North facing camera first, it picked up the car coming towards it, but to Daz's surprise the driver had blocked out the registration plate.

He then checked out the south facing camera and the rear plate had also been blocked out.

Both cameras had infra-red detection, so you could see the car clearly. It was a black Vauxhall Insignia and looked fairly new, you could see the damage to the front passenger side headlight and the windscreen was cracked from one side to the other.

You couldn't see the driver as they sat well back away from the front of the car and it looked dark inside.

Daz asked Mr Patel for a copy of the tape, and thanked him for his time and hospitality.

Jason Keay arrived back in the office in Wetheral, approximately 5.1 miles from Carlisle, the same village that Ray and Jenny Hessler lived in. the phone was ringing as he walked through the door.

"Hello Wetheral police station Jason Keay speaking, how can I help you?"

"Crikey you're almost out of breath before you finish your sentence," Daz said laughing.

"It's this new customer service bollocks, the way to answer a phone call."

"Anyway Jason, meet me in Monkhill in half an hour, I've got a task for you."

"I'm on my way."

Jason didn't have to ask where he had to meet in Monkhill, it was big news in the area now, especially with two members of the management team in Carlisle DWP being killed.

It was splattered all over the newspapers in every village around Carlisle for miles, with pictures of the victims and their spouses.

When he arrived Darren Ashcroft was already there.

"Jason, my man," Daz said. "Mission, I've got a mission for you."

"Crikey, that sounds ominous," he said smiling. "Go on then what is it?"

"Since you did such an excellent job finding me locations with CCTV in the last little exercise I gave you," Daz said, "I want you to cover around here on a two mile radius and find me more CCTV sites that cover the roads. It's rural so you won't find many."

"That sounds easy enough," Jason said cockily.

"If you find any, I want the details including full address and contact details of who can authorise access to the footage," Daz told him, "then set up an appointment on my behalf for tomorrow."

"Okay but I will be lucky to find one, this place is so remote," Jason said shaking his head.

"Bye Constable Keay," Daz said ushering him back to his vehicle.

Daz nodded to Henry Jacklin and they disappeared into the house.

Chapter Sixteen

Tony gave John a man hug then went to find Lucy and her mother in the hospital canteen.

"Hello girls," Tony said sitting down beside them. "Did you enjoy your hot drink?"

"It was lovely," Angela confirmed, "I will leave you two love birds to it and go and see my husband."

Angela set off in the direction of the lifts and disappeared inside when one became available.

"Did you two have a nice gossip," asked Tony sarcastically.

"We were talking about Dad actually. Just hoping he lasts a bit longer than we thought two days ago."

"He seems to have perked up a bit, he's joking and laughing like his old self."

"Good, Mum's got a list of instructions as long as your arm from the doctors to keep him pain-free and a bit more energetic."

"Excellent he should be home tomorrow and you can see him as much as you want without being in this environment, I'm sure it doesn't help," Tony said.

"No it doesn't, there's nothing more depressing than being in a ward with patients that are dying with the same illness that your dad's got," Lucy said sadly.

"Anyway, changing the subject Lucy," Tony said looking in her direction. "How do you fancy a trip to Keswick?"

"What for?"

"I'm curious about something and I just want to put my mind at rest."

"You're not on the case anymore Tony."

"I know sweetheart, it's just bugging me."

"What's bugging you?"

"Why Louise Tausney's son would come all the way back from New Zealand without coming to see any of his mother's work colleagues. He knew how close his mum was to everyone, so why didn't he just pop his head round the door and say hello?"

"Maybe he didn't want reminding of the past, it's been almost two years since his mum died."

"Yeah maybe, it just seems unusual to me."

"Have you got a number or address you can contact him on?" Lucy asked.

"No, but I know someone who will have," he told her with a smile. "Agnes Newey."

"So that's where she lives then, Keswick?"

"Yes, why?"

"So she's having treatment at home?"

"Bloody hell Lucy, I'm so glad you're here," Tony said embarrassed. "She's in the Manor hospital here in Carlisle."

"Well that saved sometime and petrol fumes," Lucy said almost patting herself on the back.

It was only a couple of miles away so Tony suggested that they leave the cars there and walk.

Lucy agreed it would be nice to get some fresh air, and spend extra time with Tony of course.

It was a nice walk through town, stopping now and again to look in shop windows at clothes, holidays, furniture, they even had a sneak preview in a jewellers shop window as well.

Tony was thinking he was being slightly pushed, but he didn't mind this time.

He should have married Lucy years ago, the subject just never came up and they were happy as they were, so they thought.

They got to the Manor around 3 o'clock and the girl on reception recognised him from before.

"Agnes?" she asked.

"That's the one," Tony replied, "and no she's not expecting us."

The girl smiled and disappeared through the door towards Agnes's room. When she got back she asked them to take a seat on reception, as Agnes had someone with her.

"A doctor?" Tony asked.

"No, a young friend," she answered. "A young male friend."

"Do you know how long she's going to be?" asked Tony. "We've got to pick our daughter up from school in less than an hour."

They had both forgot about that as they dawdled round town without a care in the world.

They had to get back to the cars and drive to the school before four o'clock.

"I'll go," Lucy said, "I'll see you back in Scotby if that's okay?"

"If you don't mind," Tony answered, "I shouldn't be too long here anyway."

"It's not worth the risk," Lucy said. "The school won't be happy if nobody turns up for our daughter," she gave him a quick kiss then left.

Ten minutes later a young man came walking out of the door that the receptionist had entered earlier. "I know that face," Tony thought.

"Jake," he shouted, "Jake Tausney, is that you?"

"It is, and you are?" Jake said confused.

"Tony Lodge, I met you a couple of times at DWP functions when you came with your mum."

"That was years ago," Jake said with a strong Kiwi accent.

"Your face hasn't changed Jake, you still look exactly the same as when I last saw you."

"Thanks for the compliment," he said. "Did you say Tony?"

"Yes, Tony Lodge."

"I don't think my mother mentioned you in the past."

"I'm John Palmer's daughter's partner," Tony told him. "Do you remember John?"

"John. Of course I do. My mum idolised John Palmer and another three colleagues she worked closely with."

"Can we go somewhere so we can have a talk?" Tony asked him in a serious voice.

"I've got business appointments today and this evening, but I'm free tomorrow if that's okay."

"Perfect," Tony said. "Are you driving?"

"Yes, Why?"

"I've got to get back and pick my car up from the main hospital two miles away," he said, " I was just trying to cadge a lift."

"Yes, of course, I'm in the car park," Jake said walking towards the lift that led to the car park.

"Hello," the receptionist said calling towards Tony, "Agnes will see you now."

"No time," Tony said jumping in the lift with Jake.

He was parked on the ground floor car park and paid for his ticket on the way down.

"It's a hire car," Jake said opening the black Vauxhall insignia. "Jump in."

Tony thanked him as he dropped him off at the car park where his car was parked.

"See you in the morning," Tony said, "I will text you the postcode if you give me your number."

Jake rang him so they both had each other's numbers on their phones.

It was twenty past three so Tony still had time to pick Mellissa up from school, so he phoned Lucy to let her know she could stay at the hospital with her dad.

Lucy insisted that they dropped Mellissa off together, so they would pick her up together.

They reached the school at almost the same time, only five minutes before the bell rang to let the children loose.

They picked their daughter up and had a hand each and swung her up and down all the way to the cars.

"Your choice angel," Tony said. "Pick which car you want to go in"

"Is that an invite back to yours again?"

"It could be," Tony smiled. "I need to sort things out with Becky, I will call her later."

"Will she be okay?" Lucy asked. "I feel terrible."

"It's not your fault we still love each other Lucy, it just happens and I'm glad it's happened now before you met someone else."

"Okay we go back to your place, have something to eat, then you call Becky," Lucy suggested.

"It's a deal," Tony agreed.

Mellissa chose to go in her mum's car as she hadn't seen her as much as her dad recently. It looked like Tony won the race home, he pulled around the corner and to his surprise Becky's car was parked outside.

"Shit," he thought. He tried to call Lucy but there was no reply. Mellissa was probably on a game on her mum's phone, so it would be on silent and Mellissa wouldn't notice his call.

Becky saw his car as she came out to the door clutching her night shirt.

Tony could guess what was going to happen next, but he had to divert Becky's anger away from Lucy, especially when his daughter was with her.

He parked the car quickly and jumped out, he ran towards the house and pulled Becky inside.

"What the hell are you doing?" Becky shouted.

"Let's get inside, we don't want to cause a scene outside," he said. "Lucy is almost here with Mellissa, she's not 5 years old yet, she wouldn't appreciate a row."

"You should have thought of that before," Becky said still grasping her night shirt. "Since when did you start wearing my clothes Mr Lodge? I didn't take you to be a cross dresser."

"Lucy stayed, she was tired and didn't want to risk driving home so late."

"Hold on, if I remember correctly you told me your daughter was asleep and Lucy was on her way home."

"If I told you, you would have gone berserk, I was only trying to do what was right for my daughter."

"Robert Cowie!" Becky shouted. "Do you remember Robert Cowie?"

"Of course I do, what's he got to do with this?"

"He abused me physically and mentally, but he never lied to me or had an affair with another woman."

"But I…" Becky stopped him short.

"Don't say anything please, you will only make it worse," she said holding up a used condom she had found in the kitchen bin.

"You should dispose of the evidence a bit better than putting it in the food bin," she said with tears running down her face.

Lucy had seen Becky and Tony's cars parked on the road outside the apartment, so she diverted the car and went home.

Mellissa was still playing on her phone and was oblivious to what was going on.

"Tony will call me later," she thought smiling like a Cheshire cat.

"I'm sorry," Tony said starting to get emotional. "The last thing I wanted to do was upset you."

"You've got a funny way of showing it," Becky was crying uncontrollably. She had just found out her soul mate, the only love in her life was having an affair with his ex-girlfriend.

"What happens now?" Becky asked "Will you go back to her?"

"To be honest Becky the answer is yes," he told her, "I know it's difficult but I didn't realise how much I still felt for her until the last couple of days."

"So our relationship was a farce?" Becky asked him.

"No Becky our relationship was all about passion, getting things out physically and emotionally," he explained. "You needed someone to get over the abuse of Rob Cowie and I needed someone to enjoy sexually as it was lacking in my relationship with Lucy."

"So you used me as a sex toy?"

"We used each other Becky, we were both at the right place at the wrong time," Tony said. "You wanted security and stability and I wanted a woman to want me, and you did."

"I don't know Tony I'm still in shock," Becky said. "One thing is clear in my mind, I want you out of here with all your stuff by five o'clock tomorrow."

"Becky, don't be like that, I will need at least a week to move everything," he pleaded.

"Five o'clock tomorrow night or I call the police and get them to remove you," Becky said as she slammed the front door on her way out.

Tony sat feeling numb inside for at least half an hour before he called Lucy.

"Have you got space for one more?" he said bursting into tears.

All the guilt and frustration had got to him, he had to sort himself out.

"Daddy's coming home," Lucy shouted to Mellissa. "We're going to be a family again."

They arranged with a removal company to move all of Tony's things at three o'clock the next day. Was he going to spend the last night at the apartment in Scotby, or go to start his new life from tonight?

He left Scotby and headed home to Lucy and his daughter. He rang Lucy to let her know he was on his way.

***

Archie arrived at the hospital at ten past six, he went straight to John's ward and opened the door to his private room. He threw the five signed documents on the bed.

"What's all this about?" he asked.

"Exactly as it says on the tin," he said quoting an old advert.

"You've lost me."

"It was never easy to lose you Archie, it's about time."

"You know what I mean."

"We sold the castle in October 2015 for £88m, it looked a nice round number," John told him with a smile.

"So where's the money gone?"

"Split seven ways like it says with the exception of expenses for the people who organised it for us."

"Why seven?" Archie asked. "There were only five of you."

"We had several meetings between the day we bought the castle and the date on the agreement signed by all five of the Wicked Five," John confirmed.

"And?"

178

"And we decided to split the money seven ways," he explained, "none of us were greedy and we realised how much we were each going to make from the sale."

"Who are the seven?" Archie asked.

"James Cooper – one, Raymond Hessler – two, Fiona Jacklin – three, John Palmer – four, Louise Tausney – five," John hesitated.

"Come on mate, who's number six and seven?" Archie asked impatiently.

"Archie McPhee – six," John stopped.

"And seven?" Archie asked.

"The most important member of the team," John kept him waiting.

"Who?" Archie was going bright red.

"Charlie Grant – seven," John laughed. "Me and Ray had you two sussed out, I don't even know what you were after but we knew it would have been impossible to get away with it without you and Charlie's involvement," he said. "So what were you two after apart from money?"

"To see if it could be done without taking the risk ourselves. I picked up on it with conversations with Ray and I planted the seeds one at a time. Ray was an easy target, especially when I made it look as though he would get one over on my good friend Charlie," Archie laughed.

"So you knew each other?"

"Of course we did, it was me who recommended him for the job."

"At one stage I thought it could have been you two that were killing off the gang," John said, "but you were too close to all of us to even think about doing something like that."

"It wasn't Charlie either," Archie told him. "He could never have got to the money even if he did want it."

"I bet he will be surprised to get his share of £88m," John asked.

"He will probably give it to charity or something, he was left mega millions a few years ago from a rich family member," Archie told him, "so money doesn't interest him, it's the buzz that floats his boat."

"The police ain't 100% sure about James and Louise, but they reckon Ray and Fiona were definitely murdered," John said.

"Who the hell would want to kill them?" Archie asked.

"I don't know for sure, but I have my suspicions."

"Who's that then?"

"I won't say in case I'm wrong, we will see."

John told Archie what was happening with the money and when.

***

Jason Keay had scoured for two miles in either direction of the Jacklins' property but couldn't find any sites either private or commercial that had CCTV that covered the road side area.

The only site he found with CCTV but didn't cover the road was the local petrol station.

He asked the manager to get permission to view the CCTV on the date Fiona Jacklin was killed. Thursday 20th July 2017 he had written in his notebook, between 6-11pm was the time of death according to the coroner.

The manager was out so his assistant managed to get the authorisation he needed.

Jason decided to check the cameras himself, it was a quiet petrol station so not many vehicles would use it on a Thursday night.

It was quiet now so the assistant helped him to scroll through the time window he programmed in and they sat and watched. A total of two vehicles used the station during the times, a white van that fuelled up with fuel and a silver Mercedes being driven by a disabled woman using a wheelchair. "No black car," Jason thought.

He phoned Daz to report what he had found and was told to head back to Wetheral and await further instructions.

Daz was still having a lengthy conversation with Fiona Jacklin's husband about the week before she was killed.

So far he was told that she always went to work as normal, didn't mind her husband going out to his lodge meetings and loved watching soaps.

The night before her death she invited two of her work colleagues to join her for dinner.

"Was this a regular occurrence?" Daz asked him.

"No, it was completely out of the blue," Henry said thinking back. "She said she had run into Ray Hessler in a supermarket and they had arranged it then."

"Didn't they work in the same office?" Daz asked.

"Yes in DWP Carlisle."

"I wonder why they didn't organise it there instead of meeting in a supermarket," Daz implied.

"They didn't arrange to meet in the supermarket, Ray's wife went for an appointment at the hospital and he was filling in time until she finished," Henry was getting annoyed.

"Why didn't he stay with his wife at the hospital?"

"Look I don't know what your implying but I suggest you ask his wife these questions," Henry said, "I've got things to do so I suggest you leave."

"Just one more question Mr Jacklin," Daz continued, "is it possible your wife could have been having a relationship with Ray Hessler?"

"OUT NOW, I've had enough of you," Henry opened the door and almost threw Daz out.

"What's got his back up?" Daz thought as he opened the car door.

Chapter Seventeen

Becky woke up in her old room at her mother's house, the last time she slept there it was only until Tony came back from Gretna on duty with the fraud squad.

Now it looked as though it was indefinitely.

Her mother persuaded her the night before to sell the apartment in Scotby.

She knew it would be the right thing to do, so she would start to put things in motion.

She also made her mind up to move out of the property in Edinburgh and go back to her parents permanently.

She was hurt emotionally this time and didn't know whether that was even worse than the physical and mental abuse she experienced in the relationship with Robert Cowie.

Her mum told her it was all part of growing up and she would eventually find the right guy, obviously Tony's feelings were elsewhere.

"Thanks Mum" she said, "I love you too."

Tony and Lucy woke up in the bed they had slept in on many occasions in the past, her parents' house used to be like a home from home.

Mellissa was over the moon that Mummy and Daddy were together again, but she said she would miss Becky as she was her friend.

They couldn't tell her it would be almost impossible for her to see Becky again, so they told her she had moved away.

"I'm going to have to contact Heather today," Tony said.

"What for?" Lucy asked.

"To get back to work of course, I obviously won't discuss our personal life but your dad comes home today. So there would be no reason for me to have Mellissa during the day."

"Can't you have another week off? I like spending time with you."

"No way, I have to get back to work, I've only just started remember?" he said kissing her on the lips. "I've got an appointment with Jake Tausney at ten, do you want me to take Mellissa to school and you can have a lie in?"

"That sounds good to me," Lucy said turning over and closing her eyes.

She was a happy lady now that she had her Tony back and didn't intend to let him go.

Tony dragged himself out of bed and had a quick shower, he woke Mellissa up and prepared some breakfast before he phoned the office.

"Hello Heather?" he said.

"Yes Tony it's Heather, how are things going?"

"On the mend for now. John comes back home today," he told her, "he's a million times better than he was and he's been given the thumbs up to go home."

"That's brilliant news, how's the family bearing up?"

"Fantastic and relieved," he laughed. "So I'm back in work on Monday raring to go."

"The case on the fraud has been dropped due to major police involvement in the deaths of Fiona Jacklin and Ray Hessler," she said. "So we will find something else to occupy you when you get here."

"Okay, I look forward to it."

"Be here at 8 o'clock sharp, I will see you then."

Tony said goodbye and hung up the phone. He then got his daughter ready and dropped her off at school.

He arranged to meet Jake at Cumbria's Museum of Military Life in Carlisle Castle. It was normally quiet until lunchtime so it would give them the time to have a chat.

"McDonalds for breakfast," Tony thought, "I haven't been there for ages."

After breakfast Tony met Jake at the entrance to the castle.

"Good morning Jake," Tony greeted him with a handshake. "Have you been here before?"

"I can't say I have," Jake replied, "I kept meaning to come but never got around to it unfortunately."

"It's full of military history of the Cumbrian forces," Tony explained, "but still, that's not what we are here for."

"What are we here for?" Jake asked.

Tony told him about the demise of the other three managers that worked with his mum and the special bond that they had together.

"I know all that," Jake said, "my mum always talked about the Wicked Five as she called them, but didn't go into much detail. I was surprised when the letter came from Dominic O'Sullivan to be honest."

"What letter?" Tony asked surprised. "Wasn't he the property developer that knew Ray Hessler?"

"Yes, I think so," Jake said. "He wrote to me not long after my mother died."

"What for?"

"To tell me about the inheritance my mother had left me and to give me the details of an account in my name."

"An inheritance?"

"Yes, for £12m," Jake told him, "it was transferred into an account in my name on 31st October 2015, three weeks after my mum's death."

"Wow!" Tony gasped. "And when were you able to draw funds from the account?"

"Immediately," he said, "but under the proviso that I didn't discuss it with anyone."

"You're discussing it with me," Tony smiled.

"I found out where it came from Tony and I'm sure you already know, so I don't mind."

"What did you do with the money then?"

"Invested it in property in New Zealand, and also in the UK," he said. "That's why I'm here."

"So if you were paid your share after your mum died, what about Sonia Cooper? She was James Cooper's next of kin."

"Funny enough, she actually contacted me at the end of January 2016," Jake told him, "she was very cagey to start with, trying to see if had received the same as her when my mum died."

"So she had £12m as well?"

"Yes, exactly the same as me," he said. "A letter from Dominic and the details of an account in her name."

"Why did she call you?"

"She thought it was someone having a joke, she heard about my mum passing away and was curious I suppose."

"I bet she was well impressed?"

"Just a bit, I haven't heard from her since so I don't know what happened after."

"So if the trend is followed both Fiona Jacklin and Ray Hessler's next of kin will be £12m better off shortly?"

"Yes, I believe so."

"And you haven't told anyone about this?"

"Only Sonia Cooper and now yourself Tony, nobody else."

"I can't believe you're only driving a Vauxhall Insignia with all that money," Tony laughed.

"It's only a hire car like I said, I'm going home at the weekend," Jake said. "Everything is going well here and I just employed a management company to look after the properties."

"Excellent I'm pleased you invested it wisely."

"I always did have a business brain, just like my mother," Jake smiled. "She would be proud of me."

"It's been a pleasure meeting you Jake," Tony said holding out his hand.

"You too Tony," he said shaking it. "Let's hope we meet again."

Tony jumped back in his car and went back towards his new home.

When he got to the Palmer house Angela and Lucy were helping John inside.

"Crikey they've let you out early," Tony said, "did they want your bed for someone else?"

"They must have," John said with obvious relief, "I'm so glad to see this place again."

"Me too," Tony winked. "Have you heard I've moved back in? Temporarily of course."

"It's been the best news we've had for years," Angela cheered. "A proper little family again."

"I've got to collect my things later," Tony reminded them, "is it okay if I put them in the garage until we get sorted?"

"Of course it is," John said taking control. "You can stay as long as you want."

"Thank you, can I have a chat when you're settled in please John?"

"Yeah sure, give me half an hour or so then I will be with you."

Angela and Lucy gave Tony a funny look, "What's that all about?" they were thinking.

Without being asked, Angela prepared the tea and coffee and put it in the study after half an hour was up.

"Drinks are served gentlemen, make yourselves comfortable."

"Thank you wife, see you in bit."

Both men sat down after closing the study door for a bit of privacy. "I'm sure the women would love to know what was going on," John thought, "and so would I."

"What can I do for you Tony?" he asked.

"First things first John," Tony replied. "I would like your permission to ask your daughter to be my wife Mr Palmer."

John's face was a picture, tears started streaming down his face.

"I never thought I would see this day Mr Lodge, it would be a privilege and an honour to have you as part of our family."

"She hasn't said yes yet," Tony laughed.

"She will be the happiest girl alive when you ask her," John said rubbing away the tears. "Ask her now."

"Not yet," Tony said. "Just one thing, I met Jake Tausney today."

"Oh yes," John looked surprised. "Where?"

"He was visiting his mother's friend Agnes Newey in the manor hospital in Carlisle yesterday," he explained. "So I arranged to meet him today and he told me he's paying for her treatment from the £12m he inherited from his mum."

"Oh that Jake Tausney," John smirked.

"Yes and apparently a certain person called Sonia Cooper also came into some money," Tony smiled.

"Oh well it was bound to come out in the wash eventually," John told him, "only a matter of time."

"I presume Fiona's and Ray's spouses will be the next to see a windfall?" Tony asked.

"Hell no," John said. "Neither of them were listed as next of kin. Ray's will go to Adam and Amy, his children."

"And Fiona Jacklin?"

"She wants her money to go to cancer research, she didn't want her husband to get a penny."

"Any reason why?"

"She didn't really say in too much detail, she only changed her mind recently."

"Do they know about the fraud?"

"No, neither of them knows," John said thoughtfully, "they didn't want them to know. It was different for me, I loved my wife and when I got cancer the first time around I told her everything, but they wouldn't tell their partners."

"So I take it you won't get your cut until you've gone?"

"It's being released on the 1st August, next Tuesday. It's lucky we agreed all this before Ray and Fiona were killed."

"What will you do with your fortune?"

"Look after my kids of course," John said, "and my beautiful wife."

"It's amazing how things change," Tony said, "a couple of years ago you were supposed to be the first one to go when you got cancer. Now you're the last."

"Tell me about it."

"I'm even more confused now why someone would want to kill the Wicked Five," Tony said.

"Maybe you're looking at it from the wrong angle," John suggested. "We were all happy in each other's company and would do anything for each other, so none of us would even think about hurting one another."

"I'm back to work on Monday," Tony told him, "it will be good to be able to concentrate on something else for a change, and not feel under pressure that you could drop your future in-laws in the lurch."

"Okay Tony," John said standing up. "Go and put a huge smile on my daughter's face."

The screams of joy could be heard ten miles away when Tony asked Lucy to marry him.

Her mum couldn't stop crying and must have phoned everyone on the planet to tell them.

Even Lance was happy for his sister, but totally surprised.

Tony just hoped that he wouldn't be labelled as a gold digger as he knew his intended was about to come into a lot of money.

At that moment in time nobody had even given that idea a thought.

"What shall we do to celebrate?" Angela asked them.

"Shall we throw a big party and invite all of our friends and family?" John suggested.

"Can I let it sink in first please, I'm still in shock as it is," Lucy told them.

"I will do whatever the majority decide," Tony said sitting on the fence as usual.

"We've got a few days to sort it out," Lucy said. "Will you come and help me choose a dress Mum?"

"Of course I will sweetheart, and a bridesmaid's dress for my granddaughter."

"What colour do you think Tony?" asked Angela.

"Lucy always liked turquoise, so I think it's a turquoise wedding for the bridesmaids."

"I'm not sure now to be honest," Lucy mumbled still excited after her proposal. "We can have a look around and choose then."

"Is it top hat and tails for the men Tony?" John asked.

"I would rather just wear a smart suit," Tony replied screwing up his face, "I'm not a top hat and tails person."

"Suits it is then son," John said with a gleaming smile.

Last week Lucy was planning the revenge of a rapist, and this week she was planning her wedding.

She felt on top of the world, her dad was back to his old self at the moment and the love of her life had just asked her to marry him. "Life couldn't get any better," she thought.

***

Jason Keay sat at his desk at the police station in Wetheral and was looking at all the actions he had taken over the past two days.

He was focusing on the interview he had with the neighbour of the Hesslers and looked at the footage of the CCTV from the petrol station in Monkhill.

Something was bothering him but he didn't know what, he wanted to impress Detective Inspector Ashcroft so he was looking at everything he could to find a clue or a lead.

Three years he had been stuck in the local station that didn't have more than a traffic offence or a breach of the peace from a local that had one too many.

This was the break he needed to try and move up the ladder to a busier precinct, even Carlisle would be progress.

***

Lance and Geoffrey had just eaten a late dinner and were in their lounge watching TV.

"What's happened there then?" Lance asked.

"What's happened where?"

"With my sister, do you think Tony felt sorry for her after the rape?"

"I don't think so, don't forget they did see each other at least once a fortnight when he had Mellissa."

"Yes, but he looked happy with Becky, so why the sudden change?"

"Maybe it made him realise how much he still cared for Lucy after the rape incident."

"Yeah, I suppose so," Lance agreed unconvinced, "I'm still really surprised."

"Let them get on with it dear, it's really none of our business."

"Getting back together I can just about accept, but to announce their getting married seems a bit soon."

"Think about it Lance," Geoffrey said, "your father is almost on deaths door, maybe they are doing it for him. Haven't you thought about that?"

"Oh shit, of course," Lance nodded his head, "that makes sense, you're probably right darling."

"I'm always right Mr Palmer, remember that," he laughed.

"Asshole," Lance commented walking towards the kitchen. "Would you like a Horlicks?"

"Yes please. Hurry up the soaps are starting in ten minutes."

***

Tony had been to Scotby and packed all of his things and loaded then into the van that had turned up spot on three o'clock as arranged.

Becky had spent what must have been most of the morning transporting his things from their house in Edinburgh to Scotby to avoid him going there.

She had also not wasted any time on making decisions about her future. When Tony arrived there was a "For Sale" sign outside on the pavement. Becky was obviously moving on, "Good for her," Tony thought.

He would miss her, but not as much as he had missed Lucy when they parted. The situation was a mess, but hopefully in time it would sort itself out for the good of all parties.

When everything was packed in the van, and Tony had double checked nothing was left behind, he left Becky a note wishing her well, then put the key as instructed through the letterbox.

When the key hit the floor Tony knew this was the end of another chapter in his life.

"Now let's move on," he thought to himself.

Chapter Eighteen

Lucy woke up early still excited from the day before, she was going to be Mrs Lucy Jane Lodge and she couldn't wait.

She had an appointment at 11am that morning at Springkell, a beautiful Palladian mansion, six miles from Gretna Green where they hope to get married.

She asked Tony to go with her, but he said it was better if her mother went with her instead, he trusted their choices.

It would be very expensive but her father had agreed to pay for everything. "It's traditional for the bride's father to pay," he told her.

She would discuss the honeymoon with Tony when they had finalised the date of the wedding, the Caribbean always appealed to her.

***

Darren Ashcroft was meeting Jenny Hessler at 10am at her house, he had a couple of questions he needed to clarify, he told her.

When he arrived she was standing at the front door holding onto an aluminium walking frame with wheels. She invited him in and slowly made her way into the lounge.

"I thought you were wheelchair-bound," Daz asked.

"I was, but recent therapy has had an amazing impact on my back," she said, "and a new drug from the States."

"Excellent, how long have you been on that medication?"

"Just over a week, and as you can see its working."

"I'll take your word for that," he said, "I didn't see you before so I can't compare."

"You can take my word for it, it's had a fantastic impact on me already."

"That's good news," he said brushing it aside, "a couple of questions regarding your husband's death."

"Go ahead," she said curiously.

"On my notes it says the night he went out you had a couple of sleeping tablets and went to bed?"

"That's right I did, what's that got to do with things?"

"Do you normally take sleeping tablets?"

"No, only if I can't sleep, and I hadn't slept very well for a couple of nights before."

"Can I see the bottle please?"

"I haven't got it," she said, "I finished the bottle and threw it away."

"Was it prescription tablets?"

"Of course it was, I can't take any other medication that hasn't been approved by my GP."

"Okay that's fine," he made a note in his pocket book. "It says you didn't wake up until around 9, is that correct?"

"I would have probably slept for longer if the telephone hadn't woken me up," she told him, "it was his personal secretary from work."

"Yeah we know all that. So you didn't know he hadn't come home until you checked after the phone call?"

"I checked while she was on the phone actually."

"But you didn't know until then?"

"No I didn't, why would I?" she replied. "I was asleep."

"You didn't report him missing until 4pm in the afternoon, can I ask why?"

"I thought he might have had a few drinks and stayed at a friend's or something."

"Does he often stay out at a friend's, or something?"

"No, not for a few years."

"So why would you think he would have stopped out on Monday night when he was working in the morning?"

"I don't know, I couldn't think of any other reason why he wouldn't have come home."

"Well obviously the reason he hadn't come home was because he was run over and killed at the side of the road on the way."

Jenny couldn't hold back her annoyance anymore.

"What the hell are you trying to say?"

"I'm not trying to say anything, I'm just curious."

"You think that if I had reported it earlier someone could have found him alive?"

"Not unless you reported it before midnight, he was probably dead by then."

Jenny then blew a fuse, she jumped up and ran towards Daz in a rage. He moved out of the way and put his arms around her waist.

"Crikey," he said, "I think you were right, those new drugs are amazing."

"You bastard," she screamed. "You led me into that. How did you know?"

"My nan uses a walking aid similar to yours and I watch her use it to assist her balance," he told her, "you were only leaning on it slightly without putting any weight on the frame, so it was obvious."

"I've been putting this charade on for over 12 months and Ray didn't notice," she said, "and within minutes you caught me out."

"That's why I'm a Detective Inspector and not a manager at DWP," Daz joked, "so why the pretence with your husband?"

"Have you got a couple of hours?" she smiled.

"I've got as long as it takes."

"Do you like tea?" she asked him.

"Yes, please."

"Okay let me make a pot of tea," she said leaning towards the walking frame, then she laughed and walked straight past it into the kitchen.

She came back with a large pot of tea and two cups on a tray, she also brought some chocolate biscuits and cake.

"I take it it's going to be a long story?" Daz said pointing to the tray. "Looks like my cholesterol is going to be sky high."

Jenny then started her story.

"As far as I'm aware it all started soon after my husband started his new job in Carlisle in November 2006," she said, "the offices were brand new and they recruited from within to fill the management positions. Ray applied for the Finance Manager's job as he was working as Assistant Manager in Glasgow. He had worked in Glasgow from when he started in 1993 working his way up through the ranks. The only downside was that we had to move closer to Carlisle if he got the job, which he did."

"Was that a problem?" Daz asked.

"For Raymond it wasn't, but all my family live in Glasgow and the kids were at the age they didn't want to uproot because of their friends. It was difficult to start with but we eventually worked it out, well I thought we had."

"Go on," Daz said pouring the tea. "Milk and Sugar?"

"Two sugars, and milk please," she continued, "after a couple of months Ray started spending weekends away with the other managers. I hadn't met any of them at that time, but it seemed okay as they were forming a bond between themselves, and with it being a new office it seemed a good idea."

"Did he say where they were going for the weekend?"

"Not to start with, but on the fourth or fifth occasion he told me it was somewhere in Brampton, Cumbria. There was a three-month period in between when they didn't go, Ray said it was because the old chief had retired and a new bloke started. He was a bit stricter than the previous boss, so they had to cool it down a bit he told me."

"I'm with you so far, carry on," Daz said munching on some cake, "my wife will kill me."

"This happened over a four or five-year period and each time he came back from his weekends away, he would get colder towards me and push me away when I tried to get close."

"Did you confront him about it?"

"After I found out two of the other managers were female I asked the question, but he denied that anything was going on."

"Did you believe him?"

"I did at first, but when he was getting further and further away sexually I thought I would go and see for myself."

"When was that?"

"It was 2012, March 8th," she said stirring her tea, "I remember that day as though it was yesterday."

"What happened?" Daz asked pushing the plate away from in front of him with the biscuits and cakes.

"They went off for their weekend away as usual, and Ray took the Silver Mercedes with him as he normally does. They went on Saturday morning and I left it until late afternoon and jumped into the Ford Mondeo and headed for Brampton."

"What happened then?" Daz asked sitting back on his chair.

"I presumed Brampton wasn't going to be a massive place and I would be able to find my husband's Mercedes in one of the hotel car parks. I found it in the Country Hotel, parked at the front so he wasn't trying to hide. I went to a local restaurant and got myself something to eat, to give them time to settle down in their rooms. I was sure they would be getting up to something late on."

"And did they?"

"Oh yes, they certainly did," she said going red in the face. "I found out what room my husband was in and pretended he was expecting me and had gone out. The girl on reception gave me a key and I opened the room door, I was horrified."

"What did you see?" he asked.

"I can only describe it as an orgy. All five of them were in Ray's room naked, I couldn't look anymore and just threw the key towards my husband and stormed out."

"Did he see you?"

"Yes, he saw me alright but before he could get dressed and come downstairs I had gone. The tears were streaming out of my eyes, I was furious. When I got home his stuff would be packed and he would be out on his ear."

"And did you?"

"I didn't get home, I woke up in hospital after being in a coma for two weeks to find out I couldn't walk. The crash had damaged my spine and I was lucky to be alive."

"Did you remember what happened with your husband?"

"Not straight away but eventually I got my memory back. He told me the weekends had stopped and he would never do anything like that again, he would be there for me and never

195

leave my side. I put it down to guilt, not love just 100% guilt, he didn't want me to tell the children."

"Did you tell them?"

"No, I didn't, I would never upset my kids."

"That's commendable, and you've stuck with him all this time?"

"Well we had a hiccup a couple of years ago that almost tore us apart."

"What was that?"

"Louise Tausney contacted Ray about something and they met up. He told me all about it when he got back, she asked him to go to New Zealand with her to see his son. She kept pestering him for weeks, I think she even bought him a ticket to go, but he refused. She was infatuated with him and wanted him to leave me and go with her."

"What happened after that?"

"She committed suicide, Ray was devastated, he blamed himself."

"Was he still seeing her after your accident?"

"He said he wasn't but I think he just said that to keep me happy. He said he wouldn't leave me after I was paralysed and he never did."

"And even when you could walk again, you never told him?"

"No, I didn't, the hospital knew I could walk but he hated hospitals and never stayed when he dropped me off, he always went somewhere else then came back for me. I told the hospital that I was tired after the tests so I could borrow a wheelchair, to make it look good."

"I must admit you were good, but you couldn't fool me. Did you know he saw Fiona Jacklin the other day?"

"Yes I did, and I wasn't happy. I thought here we go again, he told me he was pulled in by the two SID officers when he was supposed to pick me up from the hospital, and it turns out he was with her. If he told me the truth I wouldn't have minded, it was just the fact that he had lied to me."

"How did you find out?"

"One of my friends saw them in a café chatting, laughing drinking coffee. When I confronted him he admitted it and said he met her in a supermarket."

"Did he meet her in a supermarket?"

"Yes he did, I believed Fiona when she told me."

"When did you speak to Fiona?"

"I went to see her at her house, I think it must have been the same night she had her accident."

"What accident?"

"I heard she had an accident and fell and bumped her head."

"That's what we thought until we got the post mortem results back," Daz told her.

"So now you think my husband and Fiona were murdered?"

"It definitely looks that way."

"Holy moly," she said, "she was alive when I spoke to her."

"What time was that?"

"About 8 o'clock I think, Ray went to the club for a drink."

"Was her husband in when you got there?"

"No it was just Fiona, she told me about John Palmer and his cancer and the fact that she had invited both my husband and John to dinner the day after they met. She laughed when I suggested they were having an affair. Fiona had problems with her womb area when she went through the change, and couldn't let anyone near that area for years. She told me her husband was having an affair with the secretary at his club, it was common knowledge but she didn't tell him she knew."

"It's amazing what you can find out when you ask the right questions," Daz told her.

"It certainly is, I was only there for about half an hour, I think EastEnders was just finishing, she turned the volume on the TV down, but I could hear the silly music they play at the end."

"Great thanks for that," Daz said thinking that it narrowed the time of death to after half past eight and before half past eleven, only three hours.

"So you think Louise Tausney's death was definitely suicide?"

"Yes, she was after my husband leaving me and going to New Zealand with her, but he wasn't going anywhere and she wasn't pleased."

"Interesting," Daz said. "They're opening the case back up along with the death of James Cooper."

"I don't know James Cooper, but apparently he was gay or bi-sexual."

"Yes, he was"

"Each to their own I say, you can't help the genes you were born with I suppose."

"He was supposed to be having sexual activity with the other four members of the group," Daz said.

"It's not something Ray would have told me if it was true, but it wouldn't surprise me the way they were. Didn't he get pushed in front of a train?"

"Accidentally as far as witnesses informed the police at the time."

"Alcohol is a drug, you can either handle it, or you can't. When Ray had too many he used to get the giggles, he was never a violent man."

"How long have you been able to walk?"

"About 12 months or so, why?"

"I just wondered."

"Just to let you know, I didn't kill anyone. Don't get me wrong if I thought I could get away with it there would be a list as long as your arm," Jenny laughed.

"Thanks for the tea and goodies," Daz said, "you can stop pretending now and get some proper exercise in your legs, Mrs Hessler."

"Well thank you very much Mr Ashcroft."

"Detective Inspector Ashcroft actually," he laughed. "By the way do your kids know you can walk?"

"No, they would have told their father, but they will tonight," she winked.

"It's been a pleasure talking to you, I wonder where the conversation would have gone if I didn't notice you weren't disabled," he commented.

"Nowhere Detective Inspector, I'm glad you did it's such a relief."

Just as Daz was leaving the Hessler household he got a call from Constable Jason Keay.

"Hiya boss, I need to see you urgently I think I've found something you might be interested in."

"What's that Jason?"

"A few things about Jenny Hessler and something I've found on the Patel's tape."

"That's interesting, let's discuss it when I get back into the office," Daz said with a smile.

**

Charlie Grant came out of his house in Cecil Street, Carlisle.

He was now on his second wife and had sold both their properties from before and bought a luxurious house in the centre of Carlisle.

His wife was in charge of the maternity ward at North Cumbria University Hospital on Newtown Road.

She was scheduled to work every other weekend and this was one of them, so Charlie was on his own.

He followed his normal habits for a Saturday when his wife was working, on his way for a couple at his local and a visit to the bookies to put the horses on.

He picked his Gigi's after reading the form and looking at tipsters' selections in the Sporting Times on a Saturday morning.

It was very rare for him to win but it gave him something to watch in the afternoon while she was at work.

After consuming two pints of his favourite lager and placing his bet, he walked back home to the comfort of his two seater leather sofa.

He didn't set the alarm as he was only going to be out for an hour at the most.

He unlocked the door, walked into the kitchen and opened the fridge, he was reaching for his four pack of cold beers when he was struck from behind.

Charlie Grant was dead within seconds, the strike had caved his skull in at the back of his head and he fell to the floor.

The intruder avoided the blood spurting in their direction and casually opened the front door and disappeared into the city centre.

They walked up to the second floor of the civic centre car park and got into the black Vauxhall Insignia that was taking up two parking spaces.

"I've got to get that light fixed," they thought, "and a new windscreen."

The car was drivable but if the police saw them they would be pulled over.

Chapter Nineteen

"Hiya darling," Lucy said when Tony answered the phone. "It's booked for the 5th of August."

"Crikey, you don't waste much time Lucy."

"Strike while the iron's hot as they say, I don't want you changing your mind."

"That won't happen sweetheart, but it doesn't give you much time to choose your dress and get the bridesmaids dresses sorted out."

"There's only one bridesmaid Tony, and that's our daughter," she said excitedly. "Who's your best man?"

"Crikey I haven't thought about that yet, I better be quick," Tony chuckled.

Angela had tried to get Lucy to have the next available date after that one which was 26th August, but she was too hyped up.

She didn't realise that she only had just over a week to get invitations done, dresses picked and altered, a guest list of 80 people selected, menus done, shoes and anything else her mum hadn't thought of yet.

They were going to be busy.

Angela told Tony to organise his and the best man's suits and cars. She would sort out the flowers including the button holes.

Tony could feel the tension, but it felt fantastic, he was getting excited himself.

He decided to phone Heather at home, and ended up chatting to her for over half an hour.

She was surprised but happy for the family, especially John and his daughter.

She gave him the following week off with compliments of DWP, she said it was an extension of his privilege time to look after his daughter.

When he told Lucy she jumped up and down with joy.

"An extra pair of hands to prepare the wedding of the century," she shouted.

It was just after three when Charlie's body was found by his screaming wife, and it was the main story on the 6 o'clock news.

John Palmer called Tony to come and watch.

John started to shake, he hadn't drunk alcohol for a few months but he wanted a large whisky now.

"I just can't believe it," John said. "It's definitely not who I thought it was, I'm concerned for our safety now."

"Who did you think it was?"

"Jenny Hessler," John told him. "She found out about the weekends away and turned up one night."

"That's not enough to kill somebody surely?"

"It almost cost her her life," John explained. "She was in a coma for over two weeks and blamed the five of us."

"Why didn't you mention this before?"

"I didn't want everyone to lose out on the money if it came out in the open."

"I thought you said she didn't know about the money?"

"As far as I'm aware, she doesn't."

"She's in a wheelchair for Christ sake, how could she get around to kill anybody?"

"She can walk Tony, Ray caught her a couple of times when she didn't see him, but he just let her have her fun, it was his secret."

"How long did he know?"

"About six months or so, he told me and Fiona but nobody else, not even his kids. He said they would tell his wife."

"Who could it be then John?" Tony asked. "If you're concerned then so am I, it has to be about the money now."

"I agree, but who?" John said racking his brain.

"Who knew apart from you five, Charlie and Archie?" Tony asked.

"BOLLOCKS!" John shouted. "It has to be him."

"Who?"

"Dominic O'Sullivan," he said. "Think about it, we only brought the date forward to 1st August recently."

"Yes, meaning?"

"Ray contacted him to get the funds ready to be released," John explained, "so if there was a problem with the money then he would have to do something about it, right?"

"But we don't know that do we?"

"It's only been since Ray called him that people have started being killed," John said, "it's got to be him, it makes sense."

"Jake Tausney and Sonia Cooper were paid," Tony told him.

"Of course that was when the castle was first sold and there was plenty of money in the account," John said. "Don't forget there was £88m in there."

"Why did you give one person the responsibility for so much money?"

"Ray knew him, he trusted him," John said. "He had contacts in the banking fraternity to set up the accounts that couldn't be found, which I believe he did."

"Whose names were they set up under?"

"The Wicked Five, Archie and Charlie," John continued. "When James Cooper and Louise Tausney died he just changed the name on the accounts to the next of kin and sent them instructions on how to access the account."

"Yes, Jake told me that, he said it was so easy and the funds were available immediately," Tony told him. "So what are you thinking?"

"Those two were paid with no problem, so there was no reason to think the others wouldn't be paid when they were due to be released."

"And when you brought the date forward?" Tony said. "Hey presto."

"And the sad thing about it is that he knows we can't say anything without dropping ourselves in it," John pointed out. "So we need to get the bastard before he gets us. Phone Archie urgently."

"Shall we get a hold of Lance and Geoffrey too," Tony suggested. "The more the merrier."

"Good idea," John said. "We need a plan."

They decided to use the study at John's house as a meeting room.

Archie, Lance and Geoffrey were on their way.

When Archie arrived he was absolutely petrified.

"I can't believe it," he said. "Why did I get Charlie involved in this? I feel so bad, his wife will never forgive me."

"He knew what he was doing Archie," John said. "It was always a risk, to all of us not just Charlie."

"Yes, maybe to get caught, but not to get killed," Archie said with a sad look on his face.

They told Lance and Geoffrey the whole story when they arrived and you could see the look of horror on their faces.

"Crikey Dad, who is this guy?" Lance asked. "Who knows him?"

"Unfortunately Ray was the one that put him in place," John informed them. "He knew him from the past and recommended him highly."

"Has anyone else at least spoken to him?" Lance asked.

"I did once early doors," John told them. "Just after Louise Tausney died. Ray was on holiday and he wanted to make sure it was okay to release the money to her son."

"At that time we had £88m to play with, so £12m was a drop in the ocean."

"I got his mobile number from Ray when I contacted him before he died," Tony said "Shall we call him and see if he answers?"

"And say what?"

"Just act as though we don't know anything, ask if everything is ready for Tuesday 1st August," Tony suggested. "Don't raise suspicion and see if one of us can meet him and organise things."

"Which one of us?" Lance asked.

"Well there's only two left that are entitled to a cut," Tony said. "Either Archie or John."

"I'm not going" Archie said without hesitation.

"I don't mind going," John replied, "I've got nothing to lose, I might kill the bastard there and then."

"Just arrange a meet and we will do the rest," Geoffrey added. "It would be my pleasure."

John dialled the number from his mobile as the others sat silent in the study. The phone rang for what seemed like an eternity before somebody answered it.

"Hello Dominic?" John asked. "Is that you?"

"Hi," the voice said on the other end of the phone "Yes it's Dominic O'Sullivan speaking, who's this?"

"Hi Dominic it's John Palmer, do you remember me?"

"Hello John, of course I remember you. What's wrong?"

"Hopefully nothing, I was just phoning to check everything was set up for Tuesday," John asked him.

"As far as I'm aware the accounts will be triggered at midnight on Monday night," he said. "You will receive confirmation in the post by recorded delivery on Monday morning of the account details. Why do you ask?"

"Obviously with Ray not being with us I was making sure everything was in place," John said with a stern voice. "Can we meet to go through the procedure you have in place?"

"There's no need John everything's sorted," he assured him.

"I would like to meet you anyway to thank you for your help with setting everything up."

"I got £4m that's a good enough thank you to be honest," he said laughing.

"Where can I get hold of you if I need financial assistance in the future?" John said fishing.

"I'm retiring after this little venture," he told him, "starting a new life in sunnier climates."

"Are all the accounts set up?" John asked.

"Yes," he told them. "The Hessler kids have £6m each, Archie McPhee £12m, Charlie Grant £12m, a banker's cheque for Cancer Relief from Fiona Jacklin for £12m and £12m for your good self," he confirmed.

"That's the right people and amounts, but how can I be sure they've been set up like you say?"

"Ray trusted me, so why don't you?"

"It's a lot of money to trust someone with, and I don't know you."

"I don't know you either Mr Palmer, but I trust you"

"Maybe, but I don't have £64m of your money in my possession, or maybe you wouldn't trust me either," John said, "can I check the address you've got listed for me? I've moved."

"Oh," Dominic said. "What's your new address?"

"My wife and daughter have gone on holiday today for three days with my granddaughter," John told him. "So I'm on my own, can you make sure it's sent by recorded delivery so I can hear the postman when he knocks?"

"Yeah sure, what's your address?" he asked again.

Tony scribbled an address on a piece of paper and stuck it in front of John.

"26 Low Road, Keswick, CA12 5DQ," John told him.

"Okay got it," he said, "I will send the account details to you there."

"Thanks Dominic, it was a pleasure doing business with you," John said sarcastically.

"Bye for now," Dominic said.

John put the phone down and looked straight at Tony Lodge.

"What the hell are you playing at?" he asked.

"Bait Mr Palmer, you're the bait," Tony told him.

"If he is the killer," Lance confirmed, "he's just had his next victim handed to him on a plate."

"Whose address is this?" John asked.

"Agnes Newey," Tony said. "Louise Tausney's best friend, she's in hospital in Carlisle at the moment. So the address is currently sitting empty."

***

Tony set off to the hospital to see Agnes Newey while the others sat tight waiting for a phone call.

Tony walked into the hospital and the receptionist recognised him as he arrived.

"Agnes?" she said smiling. "Are you going to stay this time?"

"Sorry about the last time, I was called away," Tony said apologetically.

"I will see if she's available."

"Thanks," Tony said sitting down.

The girl disappeared then reappeared through the same door as before and called Tony through.

"Hello Agnes," Tony said smiling in her direction.

"Bloody hell, I've seen you more recently than I've seen my family in the past two years," she said.

"I need a favour Agnes," he told her.

"What favour can I do for you? I'm in my 60s don't forget," she said smiling back at him.

"Behave young lady," Tony grinned, "I need to borrow your house for a couple of days."

"What for?" she asked.

"To do it up."

"It doesn't need doing up."

"Sorry it was Jake Tausney's idea, he told me he wants it finished before you get out of hospital."

"Oh, he never mentioned that the last time he was here."

"It was supposed to be a surprise, but he forgot we need the keys to get in," Tony said hopefully.

"That's really nice of him," Agnes said.

"All new things including carpets and curtains," he said to tempt her.

"Go on then I've had them for almost twenty years, my sister Edna's got the keys, she works in the corner shop."

"Thanks Agnes, you won't be disappointed."

"Don't you dare break anything," she said pointing her finger. "My ornaments are worth a few quid."

"We will be careful don't worry," Tony said as he walked back out into reception.

"Bye," he said waving to the girl.

"See you soon," she said winking at him.

"You never know my dear, you never know."

***

Tony phoned Lance and told him to make his way to Low Road with Geoffrey. He asked him to make sure Archie stopped with John and didn't move until this was over.

He also spoke to Lucy and told her to stay alert after explaining the situation to her.

"Tell your mother," Tony said. "Just keep everything locked up and if you hear anything call the police first, then call me urgently."

"Now you've got me worried," Lucy told him. "I won't be able to sleep until you're back home."

"Just stay alert and listen Lucy and you will be fine."

"Crikey I hope so," she said calling to her mum.

The women decided to sleep in one room with Mellissa while John and Archie stayed in the study with a bottle of 20 year-old Malt.

***

Tony got the key from Edna Newey at the corner shop and let himself in.

The house was like something from the Stone Age. Even though it was a detached house in a modern style, it was decorated in a very old-fashioned style downstairs.

There were ornaments everywhere.

Any space where you could fit an ornament, there was an ornament.

On top of the fire in the front room, there were ornaments, on top of the television, ornaments, the dressing table, the window ledge there were ornaments.

He was dreading going upstairs in case he fell over anything, but amazingly enough it was totally different.

A new shower unit in the bathroom was fitted where there was once an old bath, the sinks and toilet were modern.

She had four bedrooms upstairs and they were all fitted with wall to wall wardrobes and had double beds in all of them. Even the décor looked modern, Agnes obviously catered for visitors rather than herself as she lived downstairs.

Lance and Geoffrey arrived just after 9pm and Tony let them in, they had parked their car out of view in a road adjacent to Low Road so it wasn't outside Agnes's door.

"Shall we go upstairs or downstairs to wait?" Lance asked.

"Upstairs of course," Tony replied. "It's like being in a museum downstairs."

"If he comes he will obviously get in down here somewhere," Geoffrey commented.

"Of course, that's why I'm leaving the back door open," Tony told him.

"Won't that be obvious?" Lance asked.

"Not in a small town like this," Tony said.

"Won't it be better to stay down here?" Lance asked. "Catch him when he comes in."

"No," Tony disagreed, "let him feel comfortable inside and when he comes upstairs, we pounce."

"Don't you think he will be suspicious when he sees the house?" Geoffrey asked. "It's not exactly where John would live, now is it?"

"I'm sure he will be curious, it won't stop him from coming to find out," Tony predicted.

"Let's hope so, we need to nail this bastard as soon as we can," Geoffrey said getting impatient.

Tony took up position in the room facing the front of the house, and the two lads were watching from the back.

"It's going to be a long night," Tony thought. "Come to Tony you asshole."

***

Lucy and her mum decided to sleep in Lucy's room with Mellissa at the bottom of her bed. They jumped every time they heard a noise, even when Mellissa started to snore.

John and Archie had a good old chat about the old days in between swigs of Malt, at least it calmed their nerves.

"Did you actually sleep together on your weekends away?" Archie asked.

"Between you and me Archie, yes we did," John confessed.

"Even with James Cooper?"

"Yep, even with James."

"Well I never," Archie gasped.

"What was it Louise used to say? Don't knock it until you've tried it," John laughed.

"Not for me thanks," Archie cringed.

"Me neither, it was just the once for me, but Louise and Fiona were good," he winked.

"I bet they were."

The more they had to drink the deeper John went into the weekends away in more detail. Archie was wishing he had gone with them by the end of the conversation.

"What was that noise?" Archie asked.

"What noise?" John replied. "I never heard anything."

"I'm sure I heard something falling over."

"You're hearing things," John told him. "Too much whisky I think."

The girls heard something too.

"What was that?" Angela asked her daughter.

"Probably the guys," Lucy answered "I know they were having a drink."

"Let me go and find out what they're up to," Angela said heading towards the bedroom door.

"Be careful Mum, just in case it's not them."

"Don't worry I will."

Normally when they went to bed the last one upstairs set the alarm for the ground floor, but with the two guys stopping in the study the alarm wasn't set.

As Angela got to the bottom of the stairs she was grabbed from behind and a gloved hand was placed over her mouth.

"I was told you had moved Mrs Palmer," the voice said, "and I was also told you had gone away for the weekend."

She couldn't speak or scream as the hand was tight over her mouth, almost stopping her from breathing.

"Where's your husband?" the voice said. "Point to where he is."

Angela pointed towards the kitchen, she had a personal attack button under the work surface, maybe she would be able to press it if she got close enough.

Mellissa was fast asleep and Lucy had gone to follow her mum downstairs when she saw the figure grabbing her from behind. Instinctively she almost screamed, but instead she backed up into the bedroom and called Tony.

"He's here," she whispered, "he's got my mum."

"Put the phone down and lock the bedroom door Lucy," Tony advised her. "We are on our way."

It would take 30 minutes to get back to the Palmers' house.

"Why was I so stupid?" Tony thought. "I hope the girls will be okay."

Angela was led into the kitchen, almost carried.

"I didn't think so," the voice said, "where is he?"

Angela pointed to the writing pad on the kitchen table, she wanted to write something down. He took her next to the table and Angela reached for the pad and the pen that was beside it.

"Keswick," she wrote. "At his sister's, he's left me."

Dominic thought for a few seconds then he dismissed her comments.

"Bullshit," he said. "You've got ten seconds to tell me then you're dead," he took the biggest kitchen knife out of the rack and held it in front of her face.

"If you shout or scream I will cut your throat," he said releasing his hand from around her mouth.

He didn't see the baseball bat coming as it struck him on the back of the head, he was unconscious immediately.

Lucy dropped the bat to the floor and put her arms around her mother.

"Where did you get that from?" Angela asked her.

"Tony always told me to keep something to protect myself under my bed in case we ever had intruders and he wasn't there."

"What a good idea," her mum said trembling. "What do we do with him?"

"Let's get Dad," Lucy said. "If he's sober."

The two men came out of the study when Angela shouted.

"What's wrong?" John said. "Have we got a fire?"

"No Dad," Lucy answered. "An intruder. Is this the famous Dominic O'Sullivan?"

"I've never met him," John told them.

"Neither have I," Archie said.

"Do we call the police?" Angela asked.

"We can't, we've got to find out what's happened to the money," John reminded them.

"Tony's on his way back, he will know what to do," Lucy said proudly.

"Have you got the old set of handcuffs your dad gave us?" John asked his wife.

"How can you think of that at a time like this," Angela replied, and they all started laughing. "Yes, in the garage."

"Let's get him tied and cuffed before he wakes up," John said.

Chapter Twenty

When Dominic woke up he was strapped onto a chair in John Palmer's cellar. He was tied and handcuffed to the chair which was then bolted onto the wall, he wasn't going anywhere.

They gagged him and covered his eyes so he couldn't see.

John was in the cellar with Tony, Lance and Geoffrey.

Archie was upstairs with the girls.

"Hello asshole," Tony said tearing away the tape from around his eyes. "You've met your match this time."

"This is what's going to happen," Lance told him. "You're going to tell us where the money is, then we get it transferred to the accounts as originally planned."

"And if we don't like what you tell us, you're history," Geoffrey said.

Tony then removed the gag from his mouth and he started choking. John picked up a bottle of vodka and gave him a drink.

"Water please," Dominic said.

"No, Mr O'Sullivan vodka," John said pouring some more into his mouth. "Water comes when we get what we want."

"Please, I need some water," he pleaded.

John poured some more vodka into his mouth.

"You originally had £88m," Tony said, "£24m was paid out which leaves £64m."

"Where is it?" asked Lance.

"In the bank of course," he told them.

"Which bank is that?" Geoffrey asked.

"The Thai bank in Singapore," he answered.

"All £64m?" Tony asked.

"Minus my £4m, there's £60m in there."

"Show us," John said signalling to Geoffrey to set up the laptop which was on the table 10 feet away.

"I need my hands," he said.

"No Dominic, you need your mouth to tell Geoffrey what he needs to do to access the account," Tony told him.

Dominic hesitated and was silent for 30 seconds.

John poured some more vodka into his mouth.

"There's another five bottles of this stuff over there," John told him pointing to the corner of the cellar. "That will kill you without any problem."

"Have you set up accounts for everyone?" John asked.

"Yes, except for Fiona Jacklin, she wanted a banker's cheque instead," he answered.

"Let's see the £60m," Lance said.

Dominic gave Geoffrey the relevant details and passwords so he could access the account in Singapore.

It wouldn't allow him to see the savings part of the account, it was saying there were "Inaccessible codes input".

"At the moment I'm financially comfortable and so are my family," John told him, "Archie is an old man and has more than enough to see him through for the rest of his days. So if we kill you now and the money rots in a foreign account, I personally wouldn't give a shit."

This time John wouldn't stop pouring vodka down his throat until Tony pulled the bottle away.

"Proper codes and passwords you bastard or we leave you with John to finish you off," Geoffrey shouted.

This time he gave him the correct access codes to open up the account.

They found that on three occasions over the last twelve months £10m had been transferred into a different account.

It also showed two payments for £12m and a payment for £4m had gone out of the account earlier, they knew what these were for.

"You bastard," John said, "you killed five of our friends so you could get away with our money?"

"Three actually, I only killed three," he told them.

"Which three were those then?" John asked.

214

"The last three," he said. "When you brought the date forward to transfer the funds I wouldn't have had enough time to try and get it back."

"Where did the money go that you transferred out?" Lance asked.

"I put my £4m on a bet that I thought was guaranteed on the Asian betting market," he told them.

"And?" John asked.

"It went pear-shaped rather quickly and I lost the lot," he told them.

"So you decided to dip into ours?" John asked.

"Yes, after I lost the first £10m, they convinced me the second £10m would earn enough to pay the first one back, and when that went bump the third £10m was supposed to cover them both," he said putting his head down, "I found out after that it was all a scam and I had been ripped off."

"You mean we were ripped off," John said. "Did these people know about the DWP scam?"

"No, I didn't even know there was a scam," he assured them, "Ray didn't tell me where the money came from, he just said it was some friends with money to invest."

"Why the hell didn't you tell Ray when you lost your money?" John asked. "You never know he might have helped you."

"I was just so annoyed with myself," he said, "and I was so jealous seeing the amount of profit you lot made from a £15m investment."

"We didn't do it for the money," John said. "We just wanted to hide the money somewhere so it wouldn't be found, and we got lucky thanks to you."

"I've really screwed up this time, haven't I?" he said.

"Just a bit," Lance told him. "So you would have bumped the rest off and gambled away the other £30m?"

"No, I was going to disappear and live like a king abroad," he laughed. "What happens now?"

"Give us two minutes," John said calling Tony outside. They went upstairs and had a chat with Archie then came back down.

"Transfer the remaining £30m into the account for Archie McPhee," John said. "And do it now."

He talked Geoffrey through the procedures on transferring accounts and within ten minutes the £30m was sitting in the account of Archibald James McPhee.

Geoffrey then changed all the security codes and passwords on the other accounts that were set up by Dominic, and cancelled the original one.

He triggered the account set up in Archie's name to send the information to his home address.

Archie could then have access with immediate effect on receipt of the details.

He also changed Archie's passwords and security profile originally set up by Dominic, this account was now secure.

Geoffrey packed up the laptop and disappeared upstairs with Lance. Tony followed soon after just leaving John Palmer.

"Why did you have to kill them?" John asked.

"Just like you Mr Palmer, I didn't want to be caught," he said.

"It's a shame you didn't know the money had come from a fraud. Then you could have blackmailed us instead of bumping us off."

"That's true, but killing them was a lot easier than I thought it was going to be."

"What do you mean?"

"With Fiona Jacklin I watched her house for a couple of weeks and got to know her and her husband's routines. When she was doing the garden I sneaked round and took the back door key from the lock," he told him. "Then I went to the village and got a copy cut, then went back while she was still doing the weeding and replaced the key."

"Cunning," John said.

"When her husband went out to his club I intended to get it over with as quick as possible," he said smirking, "but Ray's wife turned up just as I was about to go in, it was lucky she didn't see my car."

"So you left it?"

"No, I waited until she had gone, then opened the backdoor. I had to make a noise to attract her attention as she was watching TV, and when she walked into the kitchen I struck."

"With what?"

"I carried an old police truncheon in my car for protection, I took it in with me and hit her on the back of the head twice."

"What about Ray?"

"He was even easier," he said, "it was becoming a habit for him to go to the club a couple of miles from his house and walk home. I watched him for just over three weeks. He always went on a Monday night for some reason, so I parked outside the club and waited for him to turn up."

"What happened then?"

"He normally only stayed for an hour or so, but that night I had to wait for what seemed like an eternity," he said, "I had already covered my registration plates as I knew there was a private house not far from the club that had video surveillance outside, and I had to go past there on the way home."

"Clever."

"I let him start walking for at least ten minutes then I switched my lights off and headed in his direction," he said thinking back, "I thought I was going to miss him as he was staggering along the side of the road, but he ended up almost throwing himself at the car. He hit his head on the windscreen and blood splattered all over, and the front left hand side of the car clipped a branch and smashed my headlight. His body went flying over the field so I sped off quickly in case anyone else came."

John could see he was enjoying telling him about his exploits, re-living the deaths.

"What about Charlie Grant?"

"Charlie was a bit of a betting man. But I don't think he had a bet on me being in his house when he got back," he smirked.

John was getting more and more annoyed as Dominic was telling him the stories.

"He was just getting a can out of the fridge when I whacked him on the back of the head with my beloved truncheon. The back of his skull cracked like an egg and I had to be careful I didn't get any blood on my clothes," he said enjoying every moment.

"Did it feel nice to kill an old man almost ready for his pension?" John asked.

"I wasn't thinking about his age, all I thought about was getting caught taking the money."

John was at boiling point by this time.

"Give me a few minutes," he said as he went upstairs and collected one of the guns from his collection.

He put three bullets into the barrel and went back downstairs.

The first shot was aimed between his legs "That's from Fiona," he said as Dominic yelled in pain.

The second was to his chest. "That's from Ray," he said looking into his eyes.

He then held the gun to his head and pulled the trigger.

"That's from Charlie you bastard."

John never dreamt that he would kill a man in his lifetime, but he didn't class this asshole as being a man.

Lance, Tony and Geoffrey came running downstairs when they heard the shots.

"What have you done dad?" Lance screamed.

"It was me getting revenge just like you did for Lucy," John said. "That was for my colleagues in the Wicked Five."

Geoffrey asked if they remembered the accident that happened about 18 months before in the lake about one and a half miles away from the house.

A joy rider took his father's car, and if it wasn't for the fact that he had smashed through a crash barrier on the corner of the road nobody would ever have found him.

The lake was murky and it took the emergency services two days to find the car and fish it out.

They mended the barrier afterwards and Geoffrey remembered exactly where it was as it was the only shiny silver panel on the road.

"That's where Mr O'Sullivan and his car are going," Geoffrey said. "They will never find him in that lake."

John drove his car while Tony followed him in the damaged Vauxhall Insignia to the corner of the lake.

Lance and Geoffrey grabbed John's tool box along with his socket sets and off they went.

You could see other vehicles coming in either direction due to their headlights in the distance, so now and again they would have to stop unbolting the barrier and stay out of sight.

When they eventually undid all the bolts and removed the length of barrier, they rolled Dominic's car with his body on the back seat and the gun in the glove compartment into the lake.

They all watched it submerge until the last bubble had risen to the surface.

Lance and Geoffrey then put the barrier back in place and they all headed back to John's house.

When they arrived back and went downstairs to the cellar, they found it was absolutely spotless.

Even forensics wouldn't find anything.

"Now what?" John asked Tony.

"We get some sleep and sort out the financial side tomorrow."

"Good idea," Lance said, "I'm shattered."

***

Darren Ashcroft met Jason Keay in Wetheral police station at 8am.

Jason sounded so convincing the day before that Daz didn't mind meeting him on a Sunday morning.

"Come on then Sherlock Holmes, what have you got?" Daz joked.

Jason switched on the tape and pressed play.

Getting out of a Silver Mercedes and wheeling herself into the petrol station was a middle aged woman.

"I think this might be Jenny Hessler," Jason told him.

"I think you're right," he said smiling.

"I also found out from one of her neighbours that she can probably walk."

"Once again Jason you're 100% correct."

"Are you just agreeing with everything I say?" Jason asked.

"If it wasn't for the fact that I found both of these things out yesterday, this would have been invaluable," Daz told him.

"I contacted Mr Patel and he told me they always kept one week's memory on the tape for the two cameras," Jason said looking in his boss's direction.

"And?"

"So I asked if I could have a look at them," he smiled. "They very kindly let me watch them in their house for four hours and it was worth it."

He swapped over the tapes in the player and again pressed play.

After a few cars had driven towards the camera, Jason pressed pause.

"Watch this," he advised him.

Driving towards the camera was a black Vauxhall Insignia, registration number EN17 DOM.

"After watching the tapes from different days over the past week," Jason said, "this car was seen going in both directions on several occasions."

"Do you think this is the car that hit Ray Hessler?"

"I would bet my life on it," Jason told him. "The times the car is seen passing coincides with the days and times Ray Hessler went to the club. So why would a car looking identical to the suspect vehicle go on the same journey several times?"

"What do you think?" Daz asked him.

"I think we just found the car," he told Daz. "It's registered to a company called Elite Properties Nationwide Ltd that are based in Edinburgh."

"Anything else?"

"The company has only got one person registered against them and he is a guy called Dominic O'Sullivan who lives 60 miles away in South Shields."

"Interesting. Shall we go and find out what he was doing here?"

They both jumped into Darren's car and set out for the address in South Shields.

Daz was starting to think that he'd found himself an excellent copper who didn't mind taking risks just like him.

He could possibly have another assignment for him when they get back from South Shields.

***

Tony drove past the point where they had ditched the car the night before and couldn't see anything unusual, so did Lance and Geoffrey.

"So far so good," they thought.

Good thinking Geoffrey Cropper.

Archie picked up the phone and called John Palmer.

"Hi John, how are you feeling today?"

"I'm fine thanks Archie, it's not every day you blow somebody away," he said feeling remorse.

"He did actually deserve it I think. He was too cocky for his own good."

"Maybe he was but I only did it for my friends, I'm sure they would have done the same thing."

"I've been thinking about this all night John," Archie said, "I would rather not tell Charlie's wife about his cut, she doesn't know anything about it and I think she would probably let the cat out of the bag."

"What do you want to do then?"

"Split it between Tony and Lance," he suggested, "£3m each."

"Are you sure Archie?"

"Yes, I'm positive. They've done a lot for us over the past few days, I think they may have earned it."

"As long as you're sure."

"I'm sure, we just need to organise splitting it out of my bank without raising awareness."

"I think Geoffrey is planning to use the accounts Dominic has already set up and rename them accordingly," John told him. "They are all off-shore accounts that can't be traced apparently."

"Okay I will let you know when I get the details through in the post," Archie said hanging up.

***

Daz and Jason reached South Shields in good time. The traffic was quiet due to it being a Sunday.

"Number three High Street, South Shields. That's what you said wasn't it Jason?"

"Yep, that's the one. They look like flats above the shops."

They parked the car and had a look for number three.

The door entrance was in between an off licence and a pizza takeaway.

The door was closed and there were buzzers for each flat at the side of the door.

They pressed number three a few times but were still left standing outside several minutes later.

An intercom was on display above the numbers so they pressed a couple of the other numbers to see if they got a response.

"Hello who's this?" a voice said over the intercom.

"Hi, we are after Dominic in flat number three," Jason said.

"Dom hasn't been back to his flat for at least 5 weeks," the voice told them.

"Hello this is Detective Inspector Darren Ashcroft," Daz said taking over. "Is it possible you can let us in please?"

The door released and Jason pushed it open.

When they entered a rather burly male came to meet them at the door.

"His flat is all locked up mate," he said. "So you won't be going anywhere unless you've got a warrant."

Daz explained he didn't want to get in but just wanted to find out where he was and what car he was driving.

"He drives a Vauxhall I think it is with his name on the number plate," the guy said. "He's a bit of a loner to be honest. He doesn't really talk to anybody and only turns up here now and again."

"Hasn't he got his own company?" Jason asked.

"As far as I'm aware that went bump ages ago," he said. "He keeps getting guys that look like bailiffs coming to the door, that's who I thought you were."

"Can you give us a call when he comes back please, it's pretty important," Jason said writing his number down on fuel receipt he found in his wallet.

"Will do lads, but don't hold your breath," he said as he ushered them outside.

"Weird," Daz said, "very weird."

Daz dropped Jason off at Wetheral police station and headed home for his Sunday lunch.

"Tomorrow is another day," he said to Jason as he left.

He contacted Sergeant Beckett in Glasgow and told him he was sending his top constable to assist with the enquiry into the deaths of James and Louise.

Joseph Beckett was surprised, but was happy to have some assistance.

He then contacted Jason and told him to make his way to Glasgow HQ in the morning and report to Sergeant Joseph Beckett.

***

Archie met everyone at John Palmer's house at 7 o'clock on Monday evening and they made their way to the study.

This time there was no Malt.

"The account details arrived this morning," Archie told them, "and I followed the instructions and have now got £30m in my account. See you guys later."

Archie pretended to walk away and the guys started laughing.

"Okay, let's see how we are going to do this," John said looking at Geoffrey. "Can you still access the other accounts?"

"Yes," he said, "I checked them out last night."

"Okay, if we can send £12m to the account in my name," John told him. "Then I will issue a cheque to Cancer Research from Fiona Jacklin."

"That doesn't sound right John," Archie said. "You're dying of cancer and you're sending a cheque for £6m to cancer relief."

"Well hopefully it will help someone else after I've gone," he said smiling. "We can send £3m each to the accounts set up for Adam and Amy Hessler."

Geoffrey was beavering away transferring funds from account to account and Archie was watching his balance going down lower and lower.

"That only leaves one free account," John told them. "The account for Charlie Grant."

"You will have to put £6m into that account and Tony and Lance will have to share it," Archie said.

"If you put the £3m for Lance into my account," John told them, "we can sort that out as and when in the future and keeps it separate from Tony."

"So we need to change Charlie's account into Tony's name?" Geoffrey asked.

"Yep, then that's all done, it should leave £6m for Archie."

"All done," Geoffrey said after transferring the last two amounts. "Thank goodness for that."

"I will get in touch with the Hessler kids and let them know what's happening," John said. "Can you print the details off so I can give it to them?"

"You don't have to," Geoffrey said. "It will send them automatically along with their card and account information just like it did for Archie."

"I will have to let them know," John said. "Or they will wonder what the hell has just landed in their post."

***

Jason Keay had a pretty quiet day in Glasgow.

He got himself settled in and organised his accommodation as his boss told him to take an overnight bag.

He looked through all the investigation files including interviews and statements to familiarise himself with the two cases.

His big day was the next day, but he planned to have a look around the gay scene that night to see what he could find.

Chapter Twenty One

Jason went for a stroll and sussed out where the four bars were that James Cooper attended.

They were all very close to each other so he got himself a couple of slices of pizza and sat on a bench watching the world go by.

It was still daylight so he had plenty of time to absorb the early evening rush before it got dark.

"This is definitely the gay part of Govan," he thought, "you can tell by the way they're dressed."

Skin tight jeans, little shorts worn just below the arse cheeks, t-shirts clinging to macho chests, other t-shirts with weird artwork on the front, pointed shoes and even high heels on male feet.

He then spotted someone wearing a cream coloured trilby with blue motifs.

"Hold on," he said to himself as he took out his pad with notes on it, "cream trilby with blue motifs, now there's a coincidence."

The youngish male who was wearing the trilby had just gone into a tobacconist's shop, so Jason got himself ready for when he came out.

"Hiya mate, have you got a light?" Jason asked taking a cigarette from his packet.

"Yeah sure," the guy in the trilby replied digging into his pocket and producing a lighter. "You're not from around here with that accent?"

"No, I'm from just outside Carlisle," Jason replied, "I was bored in the hotel so I thought I would come out and see what the nightlife was like."

"It's always quiet on a Monday night, I'm Wayne by the way," he said holding out his hand.

"I'm Jason," he said shaking his hand.

"Do you fancy a drink if you haven't got anything planned?"

"Go on then just the one I've got a busy day tomorrow," he replied feeling a bit awkward.

They popped into one of the bars that Jason didn't recognise on his list.

They had a good chat about anything and everything.

Jason found out that Wayne lived in the student flats in the city centre and was studying architecture at Glasgow University.

He also found out that it was study day on a Tuesday and Wayne used to spend it in the library for most of the day.

"Where are the best drinking places around here?" Jason asked him.

"There's a few to be fair it depends what you're after."

"What do you mean?"

"Whether you are after some company, or just a quiet drink."

"So I presume you mean there's company available if you want it?"

"Of course there is," he said. "If you let me know what you want I'm sure I can organise it for you."

"So, I see you're the local pimp," he said smiling.

"Some people would say that, yes."

"Not tonight thanks Wayne, maybe another time," Jason said standing up. "Thanks for the drink, I owe you one."

"Any time," he said. "You know where I am if you need me."

Jason couldn't believe his luck and neither would Darren Ashcroft when he eventually told him.

He had a bit more to find out before he could tell his boss.

***

John Palmer contacted Adam Hessler and arranged to meet him on Tuesday morning. He found out that he was home on leave from the forces for a few days.

They met in Wetherspoons in Carlisle centre as John told him he would treat him to a breakfast.

"Good morning John," Adam said giving him a big hug, "I'm sorry to hear about your cancer coming back."

"What will be will be Adam, I was devastated when I heard about your dad."

"Me too it came as a bit of a shock, especially as the police are treating it as murder according to my mum."

"Can I tell you something in the strictest of confidence Adam?" John asked him. "You might not like what you hear but you need to know."

"That sounds serious," Adam said. "Try me."

John started by telling him about the Wicked Five and the fraud in DWP.

He then told him about Dominic O'Sullivan and his demise, before telling him the reason why he had brought him there today.

"Does my mum know all this?" he asked.

"No, she doesn't and I don't think your father wanted her to know."

"Why not?"

John then told him about the weekends away with the five managers and their antics. He also told him about his mum catching them in the hotel room and then having the accident on the way home.

"It's funny you say that, she called me the other day and told me she could walk again. Some magical cure or something she said."

"She's been walking for quite some time to be honest," John told him. "Your dad caught her six months ago or more, but didn't let on as he thought she was happy letting him feel guilty."

"Why didn't he leave the money to my mum?"

"I'm not sure if he thought she would tell the authorities. Your mum hated everyone in the Wicked Five. She blamed us for her having the accident which you can understand."

"I see," Adam said. "£3m is a lot of money and it's not something I can hide."

"Don't forget it's in an off-shore account, so you only need to touch it when you have to and it's not detectable from anyone unless you tell them yourself."

"Okay that's a relief."

"Exactly, I would like you to do me a favour," John asked him.

"What's that?"

"I wanted you to explain everything to your sister," John told him, "I'm sure it would sound better coming from you."

"Crikey, pressure or what?" he laughed. "Not only do I have to let this sink in for myself, but I also need to look after my sister's feelings."

"You've got thick skin Adam Hessler, you will be fine," John said. "You will need to tell Amy as soon as you can otherwise she will wonder what the hell has just popped through her letterbox."

"Leave it with me."

***

Sergeant Beckett and Jason Keay arrived at Carlisle library at 10am and found Wayne in the study room reading a book.

"Can we have a word please?" the Sergeant asked him.

"Hello Jason, what's this all about?"

Jason showed him his Police ID and introduced Sergeant Beckett.

"Would you like to come down the station Wayne? We need to have a talk with you please."

Wayne went with them without a fuss, they used one of the interview rooms behind the reception area.

"We are just following up on some outstanding enquiries," Jason said. "Can you remember about 2 years ago when somebody died after falling in front of a train in Govan Underground Station?"

"Of course I can, it was on Christmas Eve wasn't it?"

"It was," Jason confirmed. "Were you out that afternoon?"

"I think everybody was out that afternoon, everywhere was packed," Wayne replied.

"Can you remember seeing a guy with a bright yellow shirt on?" Beckett asked him.

"Yes, he asked me to get him a date actually," Wayne told them. "One of my punters gave him my number and he rang me in the afternoon asking me to fix him up."

"And did you?" Jason asked curiously.

"I thought I did," Wayne said. "But my man let me down and never showed up. This guy wouldn't stop hassling me afterwards and I ended up having to go and have a drink with him myself."

"So why didn't you come forward when we were asking for witnesses when it happened?" Sergeant Beckett asked him.

"I didn't want the hassle," he said. "The guy was pissed out of his brains and I ended up dumping him by the station and going home."

"You should have come forward when you found out he had been killed," Jason said. "It would have made a difference to the enquiry and saved us a lot of time."

"One of the guys that lived on the Campus saw him fall," Wayne said, "and I didn't want to get dragged into it, it was me that bought him a few drinks to stop him from having a go because his date hadn't turned up."

"What guy at the campus?" Jason asked.

"John Ellis," he told Jason. "He gave a statement to the police."

"Yes he did," Beckett confirmed.

"It wasn't my fault he fell so I wasn't getting involved, sorry."

"You shouldn't have let him drink so much," Jason told him. "He was already drunk when he went in to AXM, so a few more would have tipped him over the edge."

"I found out the reason my man that had the date with him was too embarrassed to turn up – when he saw him wearing that stupid shirt," Wayne told them, "he walked into the bar and then came straight back out."

"Okay you can go," Sergeant Beckett told him.

"How did you know it was me?" he asked Jason.

"I didn't, I just remembered the description of the trilby."

"It must have been your lucky day," he said, "I only wore that trilby yesterday because I left my new one at a friend's, I haven't worn it for nearly two years."

They all got up from the desk together and walked towards the door.

"Hope to see you again soon," Wayne said to Jason blowing him a kiss.

"I don't think so mate, I'm straight as a die."

"That's a shame."

Wayne disappeared into the sunset and Jason and Beckett headed for the police canteen for a coffee.

"Well that's pretty much that I would say in this investigation," Jason said.

"I agree, the only doubt we had in the case was tracking down the guy in the trilby to see if he was involved. Now you've managed to solve that one in a day, after we've been looking for 2 years," Beckett told him. "You must have the Midas touch."

"In the right place at the right time," Jason said smirking.

"Let's try and put the other case to bed," Beckett said. "Keswick here we come."

Jason read through the notes on Louise Tausney's case on the way there. He had also been given some information from his boss he received from Jenny Hessler.

It took them just over an hour to get there as the roads were pretty quiet.

The door at 26 Low Road was answered straight away, by Agnes Newey herself.

"I got your message," she said. "I just got back from the shops and listened to my answering machine."

"Nice one Agnes," Jason said taking over again, "I hear you were in hospital?"

"Yes, I got out this morning," she told them, "I feel like a new woman."

"I was led to believe you were bed-ridden," Jason said.

"I was, but with treatment and the help of a psychologist it seems to have worked wonders," she said almost dancing.

"Can I ask you a few questions about your old friend Louise?" Jason asked.

"Of course, fire away."

Agnes wasn't expecting to be grilled, but Jason Keay let her have it from all angles.

He didn't pull any punches and in the end she told them that in actual fact she was almost 100% sure that her friend had taken her own life.

"Thank you Agnes," Jason said as they were leaving. "We won't be bothering you again."

"If I thought you were going to wrap both my cases up so quickly we could have brought your car as well then you could have gone straight home," Beckett said.

It turned out that Agnes Newey had known all about her friend's affair and obsession with Ray Hessler and was hiding it from both her husband and her son.

When Ray refused to go with her to New Zealand with the possibility of moving over there, Louise fell apart.

She plucked up the courage to throw her husband out thinking Ray would come running, but it never happened.

She started to drink more than usual and take one or two of her father's depression tablets.

Agnes didn't dream that she would kill herself, "But when you look back on it," she said, "she probably did."

Sergeant Joseph Beckett contacted Detective Inspector Darren Ashcroft.

"I know you said this lad was one of your top constables," he said. "But he is unbelievable, he has closed out both cases in a matter of a day and a half. He needs to be highly commended."

"Thank you for the praise Joseph. I think this lad might be going places in a short period of time," Daz said making a couple of notes.

While Jason had been assisting Sergeant Beckett in Glasgow Daz made another couple of visits to South Shields trying to track down Dominic O'Sullivan.

There was no sign of him anywhere.

He had spoken to another couple of neighbours and they only confirmed what they learnt before. He only came back every so often and always kept himself to himself.

He didn't really speak to anyone, apart from to say hello, being courteous.

He then tried Jenny Hessler. Maybe she knew her husband's killer.

"Hi Jenny it's your favourite Detective Inspector," he chuckled.

"Hello Detective Inspector Darren Ashcroft," she said laughing. "What can I do for you?"

"Just to let you know that Dominic O'Sullivan is in the area, have you seen him?"

"Who?"

"Dominic O'Sullivan," he repeated.

"Who's Dominic O'Sullivan?"

"Sorry Jenny I must have the wrong person I do apologise," he said hanging up.

"It was worth a try," he thought.

He then put a bulletin around the police network in all counties to look out for Dominic O'Sullivan along with his car.

He couldn't think of anything else.

***

It had been hard work and non-stop preparation but the wedding plans were on schedule.

Invitations had been sent, and some responses had already came back.

They took a chance on the menu and picked what they were told were the most popular in all six courses, they wouldn't have time for individual choices.

Lucy's dress was chosen and almost altered for her final fitting and the bridesmaid dress for Mellissa was a beautiful shade of light pink, and the design was picked by Mellissa herself.

Tony's best man was going to be his brother Billy who he hadn't seen for over 15 years.

He had organised the suits from Souster & Hicks. Green label, hand-craft, bespoke tailored suits, top of the range.

He had also organised the cars.

One for him, and his brother. One for Angela, and Mellissa. One for Lance, and Geoffrey.

One for the bride, and her father.

Angela had organised the Flowers and the button holes.

She had also organised and paid for the suits for her son and his boyfriend avoiding Souster & Hicks so they didn't clash with the groom.

Everything was set, they just needed the big day to arrive.

***

When Jason Keay walked into the police station in Wetheral, Darren Ashcroft was waiting for him.

He had all the paperwork laid on the desk from the three murders of Fiona Jacklin, Ray Hessler and Charlie Grant.

There was also all the information that had been collated from the fraud department after the accusation aimed at Raymond Hessler before he died.

"Solve this little mystery Sherlock and you will have my job."

THE END